THE *Old River Road*

Long Lake Legacy Book 1

To the Rapelje family —

Love you all! I hope you will enjoy
this! ☺

Ivy Rose

Ivy Rose

Lakeside Publications

Hailey Dudenhe

The Old River Road
Long Lake Legacy—Book 1
Copyright © Ivy Rose, 2016

Published by Lakeside Publications
www.LakesidePublications.com

Cover by Perry Elisabeth Design |
perryelisabethdesign.com

All Scriptures taken from the King James Bible, public domain.

ISBN-13: 978-0-9976548-0-6 (Pbk)

ISBN-13: 978-0-9976548-1-3 (Epub)

Back cover photos: (Left) Clara Boutwell, (right) William McDonald, est. abt. 1880.

To Mom and Dad, who didn't let me give up even when I wanted to

&

To Toby, Ethan, Annie, Max, Levi, and Abel.

I love you all.

Contents:

Chapter 1

Clara couldn't contain a scream when she felt herself suddenly thrown off balance. Unable to catch herself before falling, she hurled her armload of books far away. Cold, muddy water splashed into her face as she broke the fall with her hands. Grime squished under her fingers and coldness seeped through her skin.

"Oh my word—I am so sorry! Are you all right? Can I help you?"

The words tumbled out of an unseen stranger's mouth almost before Clara realized she was on her hands and knees, up to her stomach in mucky water. She attempted to stand up, but her many skirts and petticoats were already soaked and heavy.

Strong hands grasped Clara's upper arms and plucked her out of the puddle as easily as if she were a pesky weed in the garden. Her knees wobbled when her feet were set on firm ground.

"Are you hurt?" the voice asked again.

Clara looked up—far up—to meet the face of a young man. His striking blue eyes were laced with embarrassment and concern.

"Ah...no." Clara shuddered as rivers of water trickled down her front and spiraled around her legs. "I'm all right."

"I am terribly sorry," the man said, though it occurred to Clara that he couldn't be much more than a boy. "I wasn't watching where I was going."

Clara raised her arm and put it to her face to wipe gritty water from her cheeks. But she stopped her hand midair, realizing that the sleeve was even wetter than her face was. She let it fall to her side. How was she going to make it home in this condition?

"Use this, please," the man begged. He offered a bleached muslin handkerchief, but Clara shook her head.

"I don't want to ruin it."

The soft cloth swiped over her face anyway, his hand behind her head. "There." The man stepped back and offered a half-smile, folding the handkerchief and replacing it in his pocket.

"My...books," Clara spluttered, pointing a soggy arm to where her precious study books lay sprawled on the damp ground.

He sprang to where the books were and, picking each one up, wiped the covers on his coat before offering them to Clara. Clara reached out to take the books, but then pulled her hands back. They were covered in mud.

"Oh." The man looked Clara up and down. "Can I walk you home? It's the least I can do after—"

Despite the goose pimples rising on her skin from the cold, Clara managed a small smile and nodded. She didn't want to ruin her books any more than necessary.

"Where do you live?"

"Ahh—" Clara's mind was still foggy from the shock of the cold water. "West side of town, near the new church." Two miles through Chicago in a soaking wet, muddy dress. *Wonderful.*

"Oh yes, I know where that is. My name is William, by the way. William McDonald."

Clara nodded slightly toward him. A curtsy would be more proper, but her stiff, dripping skirts clung to her legs, inhibiting the movement a curtsy would demand. "I'm Clara Boutwell."

William smiled. "I'm happy to meet you, Miss Boutwell. Though I wish it would have been in a slightly more comfortable way."

Despite the heat burning in her cheeks, Clara couldn't help but smile. William looked even more embarrassed than she felt.

More people, Clara's coworkers, streamed out of the Singer building. Clara averted her eyes from their stares and carefully stepped out of the way of other ladies' skirts. What business was it of theirs that she had taken a mud bath?

"You work for the Singer company, too?" William asked as they began walking.

"Yes." Clara looked up to meet her escort's eyes. His face was clean-shaven and long, with a distinct chin and thin, decisive lips. He wasn't the least bit homely. "I work in the design department."

William flashed a smile. "I work in engineering. But these books—" He looked down to the stack he carried. "These don't seem necessary for designing Singer sewing machines."

Clara chuckled. "I try to do some studying during the lunch hour; I'm preparing to take the teacher's exam."

"Are you?" William appeared surprised. "You hardly look much more than a schoolgirl yourself."

Clara tipped up her chin and straightened to her full four foot seven inches. "I'm nearly seventeen. I finished school two years ago."

"Seventeen! I aged you at thirteen or fourteen, if that."

Clara watched his face grow red.

"I mean...you're so...small. But it's not—" William fumbled with his words and his face turned even redder.

Clara couldn't contain a laugh, though she hardly thought her mother would approve of her chortling with a stranger in the middle of a busy Chicago street. Then again, her mother would probably die if she saw her walking down the street looking like a drowned rat.

"I am small," she said, any awkwardness between them suddenly gone. "And yes, I am nearly seventeen."

"How long have you been working for Singer?"

"Two years," Clara said as they stepped off the boardwalk, her shoes squelching in the muddy streets.

"I began four years ago. It's surprising our paths haven't met before now."

She nodded, shivering as a cold blast of October air blew through her wet clothing. She crossed her arms tightly over her chest in an attempt to hold the heat in, but it did little good. She was soaked to the skin.

"Here." William handed the books to her, and, before she could protest, he had taken off his coat and put it snugly around her shoulders. He took the books back and tucked them under his arm.

"You don't have to give up your coat." Even as she said it, though, she pulled the already-warm fabric tighter over her body.

"I don't mind." William smiled down at her. How nicely his blue eyes complimented his blonde hair. "Besides, I'm the one who knocked you into that puddle."

Clara smiled and laughed a little. "My mother is going to be horrified when she sees me."

"I'll explain that it was entirely my fault. Will she be hard on you?"

"Mother? Oh no. She's all bark and no bite. And besides, I'm the youngest in my family, so they're used to the messes I get myself in." Clara glanced down at her muddy dress and chuckled. *Though this will be a first.*

"You're the youngest?"

Clara nodded. "I have three older sisters. I've always wanted a brother, but I've had to settle for brothers-in-law."

"Brothers are fun," William said. "I have one, though he's many years younger than me. We have a good time together." A cloud settled over his face, and his Adam's apple bobbed inside his skinny neck. He took a shaky breath. "I had an older brother. But he was killed last year, in an accident in New York."

Clara said nothing, not knowing exactly what to say. What would it be like if one of her sisters suddenly died?

"I miss him, but it's not all bad to be the oldest brother." The little spark re-appeared in William's eyes, but Clara saw through it. His brother's death must have been very hard for him.

Clara was unable to keep from shivering by the time they reached the Boutwell family home. Even wrapped in William's large coat, which nearly fell to her knees, waves of cold swept over her.

Not bothering to knock, she turned the brass doorknob and stepped inside, welcoming the warm air from the hearth fire in the parlor.

"Clara!" a shrill voice gasped. "Whatever happened to you?"

Clara tried to answer her sister, but William spoke before she had a chance.

"Miss Boutwell had an encounter with a mud puddle, which was entirely my fault."

Clara vainly stifled a giggle as Esther looked up to William's handsome face, her cheeks flushing rosy and eyes widening.

"Your fault?" Esther asked, her gaze fixed on William.

"He bumped me and I fell into a puddle," Clara said quickly. She shrugged William's coat off her back and handed it to him. "I'm very sorry to ruin your coat."

William smiled and took the garment, handing Clara's books to Esther. "No problem. Dirt and water will wash out. Again, I apologize for my carelessness."

"No need to apologize. It's been quite a long while since I went for a swim in a puddle." Clara smiled, memories of the last time she swam in a puddle flashing before her eyes. That time, though, it had been purposeful.

William laughed as Esther opened the door for him. "Good afternoon."

Esther let out an exaggerated sigh when the knob clicked shut. "Ohhhh, Clara, he's so handsome!" She bounced on her toes. "Who is he? Where did you meet him?"

Clara groaned. "I'll tell you later. Please Esther, stop being dramatic and help me out of these clothes. I'm freezing."

"All right, all right." Esther dropped her playful teasing and helped Clara up the stairs.

Esther was twenty years old; three whole years older than Clara. Though she wasn't a biological sister, she bore such resemblance to all four Boutwell women that no one ever guessed she had been adopted.

"Clara?" a sweet voice called from the top of the staircase. "Is that you?"

"Yes, Mother." A part of her hoped that her mother would stay where she couldn't see her, shivering and filthy as she was.

"My goodness, Child, what happened to you?" Mrs. Boutwell asked as Clara reached the top of the stairs.

Too late! "I fell into a puddle on my way home." An attack of chills overcame her as she spoke, making her words tremble.

"Oh, Clara, you're so unromantic," Esther chided. "No, Mama, an *extremely* handsome young man bumped Clara into the puddle. He walked her home and even made her wear his coat."

Mrs. Boutwell's hand flew to her mouth.

"It was an accident, Mother." Clara firmly resisted the urge to roll her eyes at Esther. "He didn't mean to bump me. Neither one of us was watching where we were going. Mr. McDonald was kind enough to make sure I made it home without freezing."

Mrs. Boutwell sighed and shook her head, but Clara thought she saw a hint of a smile playing at her mother's lips. "Let's get you out of those clothes and into a hot tub. Esther, put some water on the fire."

"Yes, Mother." Esther turned back down the staircase and Mrs. Boutwell led Clara into the master bedroom.

The Boutwells certainly weren't considered wealthy, but they lived a comfortable life in the city. Clara's father, a veteran of the Civil War, was the pastor of a local Presbyterian church, as well as a successful real estate agent. He also earned a good living being in the Illinois Volunteer Militia, where he had risen to the rank of General.

Mrs. Boutwell helped Clara strip off her still-dripping dress and petticoats, and Clara stiffly eased into the claw-footed tub. She thought she saw a smile breach her mother's lips as she turned on the tap.

"Oh, Clara," Mrs. Boutwell said, placing her hands on her hips and gazing at her. "Will you ever learn to keep yourself out of scrapes?"

"I didn't do it on purpose, Mother, it was an accident. Mr. McDonald bumped into me, and I couldn't catch myself." Clara grinned sheepishly. "I saved my books."

Mrs. Boutwell looked wistfully at the ceiling, but she too smiled. "Sometimes I cannot believe that you are nearly seventeen. But then again, you've always been more concerned about books than your clothes."

Esther knocked on the door before entering with a pot of boiling water. She slowly dumped it in the tub, and Clara closed her eyes as the hot water mixed with the lukewarm water from the tap. It made her feet and legs tingle as they thawed.

"One more pot should be perfect," Clara said, leaning against the cool porcelain of the bathtub and trying to ignore her stinging toes.

Mrs. Boutwell helped Clara wash the dirt out of her long, curly hair. Clara's hair was annoying and frustrating, but she wouldn't get it cut for anything. The tight, curly locks fell to her waist, shimmering like her mother's best brown silk dress. Clara was the only one of her sisters to inherit her father's curly, Scottish hair. She couldn't decide if it was a blessing or a curse. Though complicated to care for, the curls were strikingly beautiful.

Clara chuckled a bit as her mother gently worked soap into her curls and rinsed them repeatedly to remove the dirt and gunk that had attached itself after her fall. Her mother had been trying in vain for years to convince Clara to wear her hair up, as most young ladies her age did.

But Clara liked wearing her hair long. She loved the feeling of the curls bumping against her back and shoulders. And besides that, wearing her hair up on top of her head was the surest way to get a dreadful headache. It was true, though—had she worn her hair up today, it wouldn't be in such a dreadful mess now.

Clara lingered in the warm water as long as she dared. Supper must be prepared, and her father would be home soon. Mrs. Boutwell left Esther to help Clara dress her hair while she began making supper.

"What was the young fellow's name?" Esther asked, carefully squeezing the water out of Clara's curls while she sat at the vanity in a fresh, dry dress.

"William McDonald."

"How old was he?"

"I don't know! I don't ask questions like that."

Esther giggled, then gasped. "Did you say his name was William McDonald?"

"Yes, that's what he said." *What's so important about his name?*

"Do you know what that means?"

Clara turned and looked at her sister's vibrant face. "That his parents gave him a nice name?" She cocked her head. "I have no idea."

"Sir John McDonald? The prime minister of Canada?"

"What does he have to do with Mr. McDonald?"

"Father was telling me about him. William McDonald must be the nephew of Sir John McDonald! Don't you remember Father talking about it?"

Clara shook her head.

"Ohhhh!" Esther faked a swoon. "The nephew of the one and only Sir John McDonald, prime minister of Canada, is sparking our little Clara!"

"What?" Clara spun about and faced her sister. *What a preposterous idea!* "He is not! Why would he be interested in me?"

"Why wouldn't he?"

Clara thought back to her exchange with William. Could he truly be the nephew of Sir John McDonald? He *had* been better dressed than most young men in the city. If he was indeed the nephew of such a predominant societal figure, he would no doubt be quite wealthy. Far too wealthy to be wasting his time with a poor little mouse like her.

"He's not sparking me!" Clara protested, her brows knitting. "He bumped me into a puddle, helped me out, and walked me home. What is so 'sparking' about that?"

Esther laughed as she brushed out Clara's long curls. "You came in the house wearing his coat. He was holding your books. What else would he be thinking?"

Clara groaned. "I was wearing his coat because he didn't give me a choice. And he was holding my books because I didn't want to ruin them any more than they already were ruined. I think you're taking this too far."

"Katie, Emma, and I know that you're far prettier than the three of us put together. Young fellows have been eyeing you for years now—you just haven't noticed it. Now, they're making themselves more obvious."

"I've never seen Mr. McDonald before in my life!" Clara burst. "It's not as if he were 'eying me', as you say. He was simply being a gentleman. Do stop teasing now, Esther."

Esther said nothing, but Clara's heart still pounded uncomfortably. Why must Esther tease her so? As if William had any motive other than to help her home. He felt awful about the accident, quite obviously, and simply wanted to amend his mistake. There was nothing romantic about that.

Esther finished dressing Clara's hair and put a shawl around her shoulders, pulling the still-wet curls out over the thickly knit material.

"There. That will keep your dress dry until the curls stop dripping. I'm going to help Mother with supper."

"I'll be down in a few minutes." Clara stood and fingered her damp hair, gazing at herself in the mirror. Her mind flitted back to what William said about her age. It was true. Because of her childish size, she did look much younger than she actually was, and the fact that she wore her hair down didn't help at all.

But she wasn't about to give herself perpetual headache just so people, even handsome young men, would think she was older.

Ivy Rose

Chapter 2

"Good afternoon, Miss Boutwell."

Clara recognized the voice, and, looking up, she saw William standing behind her, grinning. "Good afternoon, Mr. McDonald."

"I hope you are recovered from your—" he paused and pressed a fist to his mouth, "—little swim."

Clara smiled into the laughing blue eyes. It had been three days since her unfortunate experience with the puddle. "Completely, thank you. How did your coat fare?"

William's lips turned up in a lopsided grin. "My mum asked me what happened when I gave her the coat to wash, and I couldn't escape telling the entire story."

Clara's face flamed. What must the woman think?

"I didn't mention names, but Mum is eager to meet this girl who wasn't angry even after my clumsiness gave her a rather unfortunate mud bath."

Giggling, Clara followed William outside the building. "I'd love to meet your mother someday. She sounds like a kind lady."

"That she is." William stared at the ground for a moment, then raised his eyes to Clara's. "Do you mind if I walk home with you?"

Dryness settled on Clara's tongue. He wanted to walk her home? Could Esther be right?

Ridiculous. Likely he lived beyond her house and was simply looking for someone to talk to on the long walk. That, and it was getting dark.

"Not at all." Clara smiled, hugging her books to her chest. Thankfully, they had been only slightly damaged in her puddle accident.

"Allow me." William took the books out of Clara's hands before she had a chance to accept his offer.

"Ah...thank you," Clara managed.

She nearly stopped short as Esther's words came tumbling to the forefront of her mind. *"The nephew of Sir John McDonald, Prime Minister of Canada."* If William truly was Sir John's nephew, wouldn't he have a horse, if not a carriage, to fetch him home?

"—a cold?"

Clara shook her head to clear her thoughts. "Pardon me?"

"You didn't take a cold?" William asked.

"No. No, I'm fine."

William smiled down at her. "You are a tough one for being so small."

Clara raised her shoulders and let them fall. "A little water never hurts anybody. That's what my mother says."

"Your mother wasn't upset?"

"No." Clara grinned. "She teased me a little, but she wasn't mad."

William exhaled. "I was hoping that you wouldn't get in trouble for something that was entirely my fault." He paused for a moment, then chuckled. "My mum was more horrified that I knocked a young lady into a puddle than I had been."

Clara smiled, again catching that William called his mother *Mum*. Not many people in Chicago did that. "Why do you call your mother Mum?"

"My mother is Irish, and my birth father was Scottish. 'Mum' is what both the Irish and the Scotch people call their mothers." William shook his head, smiling. "However, I was born in Canada."

Canada? He was born in Canada? Esther's words darted through Clara's head again. *"Sir John McDonald, Prime Minister of Canada."* Could it be true? Was William really the nephew of Sir John?

"Are you perhaps related to Sir John McDonald?" Clara questioned. Curiosity—nosiness—was rude, she well knew. But she didn't care. Her knowing the answer wouldn't harm William in any way.

William nodded slowly. "He is my uncle."

Clara said nothing; her mind reeling. Why, if his uncle was such a distinguished man, was William working for a sewing machine company? And furthermore, why was he walking the streets of Chicago as if he was nothing more than a common civilian?

"Why do you wish to be a schoolteacher?"

Smooth. He was steering the conversation away from himself. Fair enough—she could satisfy Esther's curiosity with the small bit of information he had given. "I've wanted to go out west for as long as I can remember. Though it's hardly proper for a girl to go by herself, I keep hoping that I can join a family from my father's congregation on their journey west. Schools are scarce out there, and I believe that all children should have the chance at proper education."

William stared straight ahead, his mouth set in a firm line. His hands tightened around the books he held. "Have you…" His Adam's apple bobbed. "Have you found a family to go with?"

"No." Clara sighed, fingering the bottom of her coat. "None of them have gone west since last year." After a moment's pause, her lips pulled up. "In all honesty, I doubt that Mother and Father will ever let me go west. It's more of a dream; I doubt that it will actually happen."

A long, near-silent sigh escaped him.

Arriving at the end of the pathway, William stopped and handed her books back. "Do you mind if I walk you home tomorrow?"

Clara wasn't sure if the red tinge on his cheeks was from the nippy November air or something else. Or perhaps she was mistaken. It *was* almost dark.

"I'd enjoy that."

William grinned. "See you tomorrow, then."

Clara watched him walk down the street for a long moment. Should she have refused his offer? She was a grown woman—well, almost grown—and perfectly capable of walking herself home. Sighing and shaking her head, Clara turned and made her way to the house.

"Is that you, Clara?" Mrs. Boutwell's sugary voice called from the parlor.

"Yes, Mother," Clara called back, shutting the front door to a cold blast of early November wind. She removed her wraps and laid her books on the bureau near the door.

"How was your day, Darling?" Mrs. Boutwell asked, appearing in the doorway between the sitting room and corridor.

"Just wonderful." Clara returned her mother's smile.

Though Mrs. Boutwell's face was no longer youthful, the crinkles in her skin and deepness in her eyes told something of the difficult life she had lived. The deaths of two children; the long years of the Civil War…Clara was almost surprised her mother wasn't any grayer than she was.

"Who was that walking with you?"

Clara hung her coat on a hook mounted to the wall. "William McDonald. He's the man who bumped me into the puddle. He works at Singer, too."

"Does he live near here?" Mrs. Boutwell asked.

"I believe so. He offered to walk me home tomorrow. I—" Clara stopped. She had accepted

25

William's offer without gaining her parent's permission first. "I accepted, but didn't think to ask your permission first. If you'd rather I not, I can tell him tomorrow morning."

"Oh, no, you don't need to do that." Mrs. Boutwell ushered Clara into the kitchen and motioned for her to put an apron on. "You've proven yourself to be a good judge of character, so if you are comfortable with this young McDonald fellow, I trust you." Mrs. Boutwell grinned. "Only tomorrow, bring him inside so I can meet him."

Esther's fiancé, Lewis Cutler, was to be the Boutwell's dinner guest that evening. Esther and Lewis had been engaged for a short time and were excitedly planning their wedding, which was to be on New Year's Eve.

Clara was to be Esther's maid of honor. She had protested that Emma should be the maid of honor since they were closer in age and had spent more time growing up together. But Esther was persistent and, eventually, Clara yielded. Besides, Emma had just given birth to a baby girl, and it wasn't proper for an already-married woman to be a bridesmaid.

Studying, knitting, and sewing filled Clara's weekend. Why was it that her dresses seemed to get holes or tears in them so frequently? Neither Esther or Emma had such problems.

On Sunday, her family walked down the street a block to the Presbyterian church Clara's father pastored. Clara loved watching her father at the pulpit, passionately preaching about the God he so loved. She was glad that her father never yelled or became violent when preaching and, instead, said what he had to say in as few words as possible, as quietly as he could manage. Some people doubted the passion behind Mr. Boutwell's preaching, but Clara didn't. He spoke to his congregation just like he spoke to his girls—with a soft voice and gentle countenance.

That evening, as the family was gathered around the crackling fire in the parlor, Clara looked up from her knitting and glanced around the room with a contented sigh. Though the Boutwell's parlor wasn't large when compared to most Chicago homes, Clara loved the coziness their small parlor provided.

Emma's soft laughter bubbled across the room from the couch where she sat with her husband and tiny daughter. Clara smiled at their faces, flickering in the firelight. How amazing that such a little person could bring so much joy.

Emma and her husband, Wesley, had lived with the Boutwell's since their marriage two summers ago. Emma was twenty-three now, and had recently had her first child, whom she and Wesley named Maud.

Clara loved having the little Kopp family living with them. Emma was the calm, concise, relaxed sister of the bunch, always adding a feeling of security to Clara's adventurous spirit. Wesley was a quiet man, but he could be quite funny at times. And having baby Maud in the house was a dream come true for Clara; she loved children, but being the youngest of the family, she had never had much experience with babies.

"Clara?" Her father's low voice shattered the peaceful silence.

Clara turned her head toward where he sat with his Bible sprawled across his lap.

"With it getting dark so early, it isn't safe for you to walk home from Singer alone."

What? He had everyone's attention now.

"One of the men after service today told me that a young lady was recently assulted on her way home from work, near the area where you walk." Mr. Boutwell sighed. "I don't know exactly what to do. There isn't any way that I can fetch you at Singer myself, and it would hardly work for your Mother, Esther, or Emma to do it."

Clara's heart pounded. *Mugged?* She stopped her mind from visualizing horrid images of what city bums could do to unsuspecting women.

"I'd love to help, Mr. Boutwell," Wesley said. "I suppose I could leave work early and go get Clara."

"No need, Wesley, but thank you for offering. It would be too far out of your way to go by Singer."

Wesley did work on the opposite side of town. Who else might be available to walk her home every afternoon? Though riding the cable cars would get her home faster, they were hardly safer than walking. Such strange people rode the cars.

"What about that young man who walked you home on Friday?" Mrs. Boutwell suggested. "William McDonald?"

Mr. Boutwell's face formed a frown. "William?"

"The man who knocked me into the mud puddle last week. Remember? Esther told you all about him." She smiled to herself, heat spreading up her cheeks. Esther hadn't spared her personal thoughts about William's intentions during that conversation. "He works at Singer, too, and I believe he lives just beyond us. He's been very kind to me."

Her father rubbed the side of his head, as he always did while thinking. "Well, I don't see why that won't work, if he comes by here on his way home."

Mrs. Boutwell looked up from her knitting, her needles still clicking together rapidly. "I spoke with him for a few minutes the other day, and I must say that I was pleased. But perhaps we should all get to know this boy more before we trust him with Clara."

"True."

"Why don't we invite him over for supper? That way, all of us could get to know him."

"Wonderful idea." Mr. Boutwell nodded his approval. "Clara, can you invite Mr. McDonald to supper Tuesday evening?"

Clara nodded. "Certainly!"

A strange tingling feeling attacked Clara's innards, and her knitting needles clanked together uncontrolled. *What's the matter with me?*

William was just coming over for supper. What was there to be nervous about?

Chapter 3

"Thank you for your kind invitation," William said, shaking Mrs. Boutwell's hand. "Clara has told me about your amazing cheese biscuits. I've wanted to try them for myself ever since she mentioned them."

Mrs. Boutwell gave Clara a playful glare, followed by a smile. "They are on the menu tonight, so I hope you enjoy them." Gesturing towards the parlor, she said, "Please, make yourself comfortable."

William followed Mr. Boutwell into the parlor, where he was introduced to Emma and Wesley. Clara was about to sit down, but her mother stopped her by a gentle tap on the shoulder, reminding her that she was to assist in setting out supper.

"My, is he handsome," Mrs. Boutwell muttered as both she and Clara took serving dishes into the dining room.

"Mother!" Clara's eyes darted towards the parlor.

Mrs. Boutwell chuckled, her grey eyes sparkling.

First Esther teases me and now Mother. Clara sighed inwardly, grasping a dish to carry to the table. She was thankful that Esther was dining with her fiancé's family tonight. If she weren't, Clara knew that she would get an earful about William when they were supposed to be sleeping later that night.

With supper set out, Clara went into the parlor and announced that the meal was served. Then, leading the way into the dining room, she saw her father discreetly grant permission for William to seat her, while Mr. Boutwell seated his wife, and Wesley his.

"Shall we pray?" Mr. Boutwell folded his hands and bowed his head, and the others followed suit.

Clara listened intently as her father offered thanks for their food and for their company. He spoke to God with such passion and gentleness, his deep voice rattling her chest.

"Amen," Mr. Boutwell said, the voices around the table echoing the word.

Clara squeezed her wet, clammy hands together, then rubbed them on her skirt. Her stomach was all aflutter. *Stop it!*

"So, William," Mr. Boutwell began as he dished up his meat and passed the serving platter along, "you work in engineering at Singer?"

"Yes, sir."

"Do you do anything else?"

William swallowed before answering. "I am in the Illinois Volunteer Militia."

Clara saw her father brighten. Her fork halted midair, eyes watching William's face.

"Are you now?" Mr. Boutwell said, smiling. "Private?"

"No, sir." William hesitated, and Clara felt him tense. "Cavalry Captain."

Mr. Boutwell coughed behind his napkin. "Captain? You hardly look old enough to be accepted as a private!"

William chuckled and looked down at his plate. "I'm twenty-three, sir." He smiled modestly. "I truly think that my general promoted me to captain only because there was no one else willing to take the rather frustrating responsibility of so much paperwork."

It was quiet around the table for several moments. Mr. Boutwell appeared both surprised and pleased at this discovery about William.

"Father is a general," Emma said in a quiet voice. Clara and her sisters knew that her father was too modest to say anything about his high rank in the Militia.

"I am." Her father nodded slightly. "Now that I think about it, I'm sure I've heard your name mentioned before. Something along the lines of 'Youngest Captain in the history of the Illinois Militia'?"

William's smiling eyes fell to his plate. "Yes, sir, they do call me that on occasion."

The remainder of the meal was spent with William and Mr. Boutwell talking of their experiences in the

33

Militia. Clara and her mother smiled to each other, feeling that Mr. Boutwell had found a kindred spirit in William and vice versa. Surely, her father would be comfortable with William escorting her home from Singer.

"Lovely meal, Mrs. Boutwell," William said when they had finished. "Your biscuits were everything your daughter said and more."

Clara watched her mother's face flush with pleasure. "I'm glad you enjoyed the meal, but Clara did most of the cooking. It's her you should thank."

He smiled broadly and his blue eyes twinkled as he thanked her. A fluttering, nervous feeling came over Clara. She clasped her shaking hands behind her back and accepted William's thanks, then ran to help her mother take the dirty dishes into the kitchen.

Mrs. Boutwell and Clara served dessert in the parlor, joining the men around the warm fire. Clara herself had made the divine chocolate cake they ate. It was a rarity to have such lusciousness for dessert.

Mr. Boutwell didn't waste any time asking his question. "William, I'm sure you've heard about the young women being harmed on their way to and from work."

William nodded slowly, setting his coffee cup down. "Yes, sir, I have. It is most unfortunate and extremely concerning."

Mr. Boutwell nodded. "My wife and I are concerned for Clara's safety as she comes home now that the days are becoming shorter. No one in our family is available to accompany her home every evening, and, since you travel this direction to get to your home, we were wondering if you would be willing to walk with Clara regularly."

Clara carefully watched William's face. His jaw slackened, then his cheeks flushed, then his hands gripped each other. Retrieving his jaw, William managed, "I'd be most honored to walk with Miss Boutwell."

His eyes settled on Clara for a short moment, and his cheeks reddened further. He turned his gaze back to Mr. Boutwell, Adam's apple bobbing.

"You're sure it wouldn't be any trouble?" Mrs. Boutwell asked.

William swallowed again. "No ma'am. No trouble at all."

After William left and Esther had returned from the Cutler's home, Clara listened while Esther chattered on and on about Lewis.

"He's just so wonderful," she finished with a sigh, staring at herself in the vanity mirror.

Clara laughed quietly as she pulled on a second pair of stockings. The November nights made for chilly air in the girl's attic bedroom, necessitating the girls to wear woolen long johns under their flannel nightgowns. They even pushed their two beds together and slept under the same blanket in order to share each other's body heat.

Clara remembered the days when all three of her sisters and herself had slept in the same bedroom. When Clara was hardly more than an infant, she had slept in a large bed with Katie while Emma and Esther had their own smaller beds. She had been much warmer those winters, especially when Emma and Esther came and squeezed into the big bed.

Esther plucked at her tight bun. Clara watched as the shining braid, released from its prison of pins, dropped down almost to her knees. Esther's hair was a stunning golden blonde. Not light like William's hair, but the golden color of a summer sunset. And it was so long and silky, quite the opposite of Clara's own curly tresses.

Esther coiled the long braid around her hand, then stretched her flannel nightcap over it. She smiled as she walked toward her bed. "Good night, Little Sis."

"Sleep well."

Clara took her turn at the vanity. She loosely braided her hair, hoping that the curls would look better than cotton fluff in the morning. She stuck the braid into her cap and secured it on her head.

Crawling into bed beside Esther, Clara turned up the lamp on the table near her bed and pulled her Bible off the shelf above her. Since childhood, she had made a point to read her Bible every day. She yearned for her relationship with the Lord to be as deep as her father's.

Dear Lord, she prayed silently, flipping to where her mark lay. *Thank You for such a lovely day today. Thank You that William could come for supper and is willing to walk me home every afternoon. Please be with me as I continue to study for the teacher's exam and help me to pass if it would be Your will. In Your name, amen.*

"My little night owl," a deep voice said beside Clara.

Nearly dropping her Bible in surprise, Clara looked up to see her father standing near her bed. His eyes glowed in the lamplight, a soft smile on his face.

"I didn't have time to do my devotions this morning, Father." Clara spoke softly, for Esther's gentle breathing indicated that she was asleep. She glanced at the small clock and saw that it read almost midnight. She had read four chapters.

Mr. Boutwell sat on the edge of Clara's bed and laid a hand on her quilt-covered leg. "I'm very proud of you and your dedication to read the Bible."

Clara smiled. "I enjoy it very much. Only a few books are boring...most are interesting."

Mr. Boutwell chuckled. "That is true." He said nothing for a moment, then bent forward to kiss Clara. "Good night, Darling. Sleep well, and soon. It's getting late."

Clara smiled and yawned, setting her mark back in the Bible and replacing it on its shelf.

Mr. Boutwell went to the other side of the bed and softly kissed sleeping Esther's cheek, then exited the room. Clara blew out the lamp and snuggled under the covers. Unfortunately, morning would come earlier than she wished.

During the entire month of November, William consistently walked Clara home every evening. It was so bitterly cold that they were rarely able to talk because of the multiple layers of clothing around their bodies and faces. Even so, Clara enjoyed having someone to walk with, especially now that it was nearly pitch black when her day at Singer was over.

William was a frequent supper visitor. He ate with the family once a week, if not twice. Typically, he came on Saturdays, when Lewis also came. Though Esther occasionally teased Clara that William was courting her, Esther was too consumed with Lewis and their upcoming wedding to pay much attention to Clara.

Most evenings were spent sewing Esther's wedding gown. The three Boutwell women would sit around the fire in the parlor, stitching, stitching, stitching with thin silk thread that wanted to snap every time Clara touched it. Emma helped if she could, but little Maud had been colicky as of late and needed more cuddles. Lewis was a frequent visitor as well and was happy to sit quietly near his lady as she worked.

Clara's seventeenth birthday passed, but not without a little celebration. Much to her delight, she received three books; one from her parents; one from Emma, Wesley and Esther; and one from Katie and Frank—her oldest sister and her husband. The three books were novels she had wanted for many months, titled *The Lamplighter*, *The Wide, Wide World*, and *A Lost Pearle*. Clara couldn't contain a squeal as she pressed the books to her chest.

As December rolled around, Clara became increasingly anxious for the upcoming teacher's examination. Every moment not spent sewing Esther's dress was spent studying. It soon became apparent to Clara that she was the only one who thought she might not pass the exam. Everyone else in the family was confident that she could.

The day of the exam, William came to pick her up and accompany her to the library, where it was being held. Clara couldn't tell if she shivered because of the bitter air, or because of nervousness. William offered his arm to steady her on the icy ground.

"Why are you shaking?" he asked, casting a concerned smile on Clara.

Taking a deep breath of icy air, Clara managed, "I'm a little nervous." Did her voice sound as high and squeaky to him as it did to her?

"You're going to be just fine," William said, squeezing her gloved hand. "'Cast all your fears upon the Lord.'"

Clara exhaled, shuddering. She had been studying for months. There was no reason why she should not pass the exam. Unless God willed her not to.

Once at the library, William held her things while Clara stripped layer upon layer of winter clothing off. Finally baring the mossy green dress, Clara took her folder from William and tucked it under her arm. Her fingers picked at the soft paper. Just having something to fidget with was comforting.

Her sisters had insisted that Clara wear her hair up and, for once, she consented. She too was afraid that because of her size, the administrator would not believe her age and refuse to give her the exam. It felt strange to have all of her hair piled on the top of her head and swirling down to the nape of her neck. And Esther had used so many pins to tuck in stray curls that Clara felt as if her head were a pincushion.

Straightening her skirts and running a clammy hand over her hair to be sure it was in order, Clara glanced backwards at the stern librarian. She looked none too friendly. Would the examiner be more kind than this sour-faced woman?

"You're going to do wonderfully." William grinned. Clara's heart gave a nervous leap. "I have some things to get for Mum at the store, but I'll be back within two hours."

Clara nodded, trying to let her hands fall nonchalantly to her sides. Her mouth felt dry and rubbery, and her head swam.

William bent down to her ear and whispered, "I'm praying for you." He took her hand in his, gave it a comforting squeeze, then disappeared into the snowy streets.

Clara watched him for a long moment, then drew in a hitching breath and turned about. There were two other women sitting in the row of chairs along the wall. Were they also here to take the exam? They appeared much older than Clara.

Finally, the examiner came out from a door down the hallway and asked for Miss Boutwell. Clara stood on shaky legs and moved toward the older gentleman.

"Good afternoon, Miss Boutwell. My name is Easton Noel, and I'll be administering your exam today."

Clara nodded and shook the man's hand, desperately wishing her own would stop trembling.

"Follow me, please."

Dear Lord, please clear my mind and—if it is Your will—help me pass the exam.

Ivy Rose

Chapter 4

"William! Will-iam!" Clara waved her certificate high in the air.

William was only halfway inside the library before Clara threw her arms around his neck.

"I did it!" she breathed, her voice raspy with excitement. "I passed!"

Clara hung on as William spun around, bits of snow dropping from his britches onto the floor. "I knew you could do it!"

"Shh!" the librarian hissed from her desk.

Clara hardly heard. As William set her down, she held up the certificate, hiding her violently heating face behind it. Had she truly just *hugged* him?

"'Certificate of teaching,'" William read, oblivious to Clara's thoughts. "'Awarded to Miss Clara Hannah Boutwell, on this tenth day of December, 1885.'"

Clara scrunched her toes in her shoes and was half afraid that her lip would split from smiling. She had passed the exam! If it weren't for the heavy weight of her curls atop her head, she might have flown about the room.

"Congratulations!" William grinned broadly.

"I can't wait to show Mother and Father." Clara carefully placed the paper certificate inside her folder for safe keeping. "But oh, I'm so glad that's over."

William chuckled as he helped Clara into her coat. She carelessly wrapped her scarf around her head and neck and plopped her hat on top of the worn-up curls, far too excited and relieved to care much about what she looked like. Tossing on her mittens, she waved to the scowling librarian and stepped onto the snowy boardwalk.

"Oooh, I can't believe it!" Clara squealed once they were outside, clasping her mittened hands together and pressing them to her lips. She couldn't resist doing a little skip as they walked.

William laughed, reminding her that the boardwalks were icy and that she should be careful not to fall.

"Now what are you going to do with this fancy certificate?" he asked, smiling down to her.

Clara rubbed her hands together, a relieved jolt shaking through her body. "I don't know. I suppose I could go west now if I find a family to take me. In the spring."

"You really want to go west?"

The strange tone of disappointment in William's voice made Clara forget her excitement for a moment.

"I do want to go west, eventually, if that's what the Lord has for me." She paused, drawing a breath. "But for now, I'm happy staying here in Chicago. I *would* miss my family horribly if I left."

A bitter blast of wind forced Clara to shut her eyes for a moment, and when she opened them again, William's face had regained its color and his eyes were sparkling.

"Good."

The remainder of the short walk was spent in silence due to the painful blasts of wind that enveloped them once outside the protection of the covered boardwalks. William bent into the wind and Clara clung to his arm, closing her eyes to the icy shards of snow that cut her face.

They were barely inside the door of the Boutwell house before Esther attacked Clara with questions. Clara managed to stutter between chattering teeth that she had passed the exam. She was engulfed in arms; first Esther's, then Emma's, then Mrs. Boutwell's, and then her father picked her up and swung her about, exactly as William had done earlier.

Clara's cheeks hurt from smiling. When Mrs. Boutwell helped her remove her winter wraps, they all hurried into the warm parlor and everyone inspected her gold-stamped certificate. Her heart swelled. She had worked so hard for that little piece of paper.

"Oh, it's so lovely!" Esther said, rubbing her fingers gently against the shimmering seal.

Lewis was seated near Esther. He sat quietly, smiling along with the rest of them. Was he smiling about her certificate, or because he was so near his beloved Esther?

After removing his snow-speckled outerwear, William came and sat beside Clara. She was glad that he didn't say anything about her nervousness before they reached the library. Or her exuberant celebration when he walked in the door after the exam.

The memory of that brought warmth to her cheeks. Was he still thinking about her rude boldness? Or had he brushed it off like flakey snow?

Even in the midst of one of the coldest, snowiest Decembers on record, Clara found herself enjoying the daily talks with William. He was quite intelligent and funny, and Clara often begged him to stop making her laugh because the cold air burned her lungs. She wondered if he enjoyed her company as much as she enjoyed his. After all, he *was* twenty-three; almost seven years older than she was. She was practically a child in comparison to him!

They had almost reached the Boutwell's home one Friday afternoon, two weeks before Christmas, when William stopped Clara at the end of the walkway.

"Would you enjoy coming to my home for supper tomorrow night?" he asked in half-hesitating tones. "My mother is quite anxious to meet you."

Clara smiled, but then remembered that he couldn't see the grin under her scarf. "I must ask my parent's permission, but I don't see why they would have a problem with it. I feel like I already know your family, as much as you talk about them."

William chuckled, but it was a rather embarrassed chuckle. "Miss Boutwell, just so you are aware," he paused and drew a long, slow breath. "My father, the father I was born to, was killed in the War. I never knew him; he died when I was just three years old. The father I speak of is a most wonderful man whom my mother married two years after my father's death. He is the only father I've ever known, and I'm incredibly grateful for him."

A sharp pang went through Clara's heart. First, he had told her about his two deceased brothers, and now, his birth father had died, too. What else could go wrong in his family?

"Also, my father, mother, and brother have a different last name than I do. My mother took on her second husband's name, Mitchell, but she allowed me to keep my birth father's name, which is McDonald."

Clara nodded.

"I know; it's confusing. I just wanted you to be aware." William reddened cheeks told of his embarrassment about his mixed-up family.

"I think your family is wonderful." Clara smiled up at him. "How special that the Lord gave you two wonderful fathers."

"You think so?"

"Absolutely!"

A puff of breath escaped William's scarf.

"Thank you for saying that. Good afternoon, Miss Boutwell."

William walked away, leaving Clara shaking her head. She wished that he would stop calling her 'Miss Boutwell.' It was much too formal for friends.

Clara was dressed and ready by the time William came to get her on Saturday. Esther had begged and pleaded to put Clara's hair up, but Clara stubbornly refused. Even Emma had tried her hand at gentle persuasion.

"I don't *feel* like myself when I look like such a grand lady," Clara argued, seated at the vanity in her and Esther's room. "And if you don't let me go to Mother so she can fix my hair, I'll do it myself!"

Esther yielded at that threat. Clara and everyone else knew what happened when she styled her own hair, and no one wanted her to leave the house looking like a French poodle.

There was a knock on the door, and Clara flew to open it as she finished putting her coat on.

"Good afternoon, Miss Boutwell," William said, touching the brim of his hat. His blue eyes glittered in the lamplight.

"Good afternoon, Mr. McDonald. I'll be ready in just a moment." Clara hurried into the kitchen and wrapped the loaf of apple spice bread she had made in a towel and placed it in a basket. She kissed her father good-bye and hugged her mother.

"Bring her back before ten," Mr. Boutwell called after them as they walked down the path.

"I will, sir!" William replied, a smile in his voice.

"And don't let Clara eat all of the bread she made before you get there!"

"Esther!" Clara cried, glad that her scarf hid her burning cheeks.

William just laughed and patted the small, mittened hand resting on his arm. "She'll have to beat me to it!"

"Have a good time, Dear!" Mrs. Boutwell called.

They walked away from the softly lit house, Clara's heart beating in a funny pattern. She felt that strange, shivery feeling that had come upon her when William first ate supper at her house. She clenched her hands to keep them from shaking.

"Is something wrong, Miss Boutwell?" William asked.

Clara's face reddened under the scarf again when she realized how tightly she was gripping his arm.

"No, not at all." Thankfully, her voice was more confident than she felt. "Mr. McDonald, would you please call me Clara? It seems much more proper for friends to call one another by their first name."

William said nothing for a moment. Had he heard her? Perhaps she hadn't spoken loud enough and her words had been muddled by the scarf over her mouth.

"Certainly," he finally said. "But you must call me William."

Again, Clara felt that strange tremor in her insides. But this time, she was careful not to clench her hands. "All right."

The streets of Chicago were surprisingly busy for such a cold Saturday. Folks bustled hither and thither on the boardwalks, and in the middle of the snowy streets. Clara figured it had something to do with Christmas being so near.

Her eyes trailed upwards, where the setting sun cast stunning shades of pink, purple, and orange over the snow below. She gasped softly, wondering where such lovely colors came from. *Jesus painting.* That's what her father had always said.

"Isn't it beautiful?" William's voice was as soft as the fluffy snow.

"Mmm-hmm." Clara breathed in the cold air, closing her eyes momentarily. Even in the busy city, God's presence was so near.

After a few minutes of quiet walking, Clara realized that they were headed in the opposite direction of her home...back towards Singer.

"William, don't you...I mean I thought—" Clara wasn't exactly sure how to say it. "I thought you lived beyond my home."

"Did I say that?"

Clara thought back to their first conversations. "No, I suppose you didn't. I just assumed that you did, since you offered to walk home with me."

William chuckled a bit, and Clara turned her confused gaze to his forward-facing, grinning one.

"You don't have to go past my house to get to yours?"

"Well, that is one way to get to my house."

"What?" Clara was utterly confused.

"I can get to my house from yours, but it is faster going to the left outside of Singer, past the department store and around the Catholic church."

Clara thought carefully. The way William described it, his home was almost the complete *opposite* direction of hers!

"Then...then why didn't you say something before now?"

"Because I enjoy walking you home."

What? Clara's mind was reeling. What man would go out of his way just to walk her home? "My parents are going to feel terrible when they know. It was their idea to have you walk with me."

"Then don't tell them."

"I'm not going to lie to my parents!"

"I'm not saying you should. If you feel like you need to tell them, go ahead." He paused, then added under his breath, "It won't change what I do."

"I don't understand," Clara said, absently shifting the basket that pulled at her arm. "Why didn't you tell us before now? My folks could have come up with a different way for me to get home safely."

"Like I said, I enjoy walking with you. There aren't many girls who are fun to talk to."

Clara wasn't sure if she should be flattered or disgusted. She was feeling a little of both.

"To be perfectly honest, Clara, you're the nicest, most pleasant girl I've ever met."

What is that supposed to mean?

"I've been—sort of—courting you, I suppose."

Clara thought for sure that her heart had stopped pumping completely. Her mouth was as dry as Esther's biscuits, and there was no butter to help wash them down.

"Courting me!" she gasped, barely spitting the words out.

"I thought...you would have suspected it before now." William's tones mingled surprise and disbelief. "Why else do you think I made myself such a frequent visitor at your house?"

Clara's mind was spinning. "I thought we were only friends! And I thought you came over so much to talk with Father about the Militia and such."

William chuckled lightly, and Clara felt red stealing over her face. How could she be so naive? Of course he had been courting her. Silently dropping her head to her chest, Clara willed herself to calm down. Surely, being courted wasn't something to get upset over.

Ivy Rose

Chapter 5

"Here we are."

Clara pulled her eyes from the ground, fully expecting to see a towering, three-story mansion looming above her.

But it was not so.

The house before her was not unlike her own. It was a bit larger, had fancier trim, decorative gables, and snow-covered flower beds. Clara could only imagine what they would look like in the summertime, without the soft blanket of snow.

William unlatched the picket gate and ushered Clara inside. Then, reaching the door, he opened it for Clara and followed her in.

"Here we are, Mum!" William called. He began taking off scarves and coats, and Clara, setting down her basket, did the same.

The inside of the house was even prettier than the outside. It wasn't overly-decorated or exceedingly fine, but the tasteful way in which William's mum had arranged the decorations had a stunning effect.

A slender, elegant woman appeared in the hall. Her hair was darker than William's, though not by much, and she wore it up in a delicate crown of curls atop her head. Her eyes were deep-set like William's and a brilliant, dark blue, though her nose was narrower and longer. The rose-colored dress she wore suited her beautifully.

"Mum, this is Clara Boutwell."

Clara picked up on a hint of pride in William's voice, and his gaze made her spine tingle.

Mrs. Mitchell smiled at Clara and enveloped her in a warm, motherly hug. "I'm very glad to finally meet you, Miss Clara. William talks about you almost constantly."

A heated blush came to Clara's cheeks. What exactly did William say about her?

"I feel as if I already know you too, Ma'am," Clara said, forcing herself to recover quickly. She offered a smile. "And please, just call me Clara."

Mrs. Mitchell nodded. "Certainly, Clara. Please, come in and warm yourself near the fire."

Clara took a step to follow Mrs. Mitchell, but her foot struck her basket. "Oh, I nearly forgot." Clara bent down to snatch the bread. It was no longer warm...the frigid outdoor air had seen to that. "I made this as a thank you for your kind invitation. I hope you enjoy it." She placed the towel-wrapped loaf in Mrs. Mitchell's hands.

"It smells divine," Mrs. Mitchell said, peeling back one corner of the towel. "William has already spoken of your superior cooking skills. We will enjoy this for certain. Thank you."

Mrs. Mitchell disappeared into the kitchen, but not before ushering Clara and William into the warm parlor.

The Mitchell's parlor was slightly bigger than the Boutwell's and had the same level of finery. And, though rich, the furniture was quite old.

Two men rose when William and Clara entered. Well, one of them was a rather young man, likely not much older than she herself.

"Clara, this is my father and my brother, both named John Hamilton Mitchell."

Clara shook the elder Mr. Mitchell's hand as he said, "It's a pleasure to meet you, my dear."

The younger Mr. Mitchell, or Hamilton as William had told her he was usually called, also held out his hand. "Nice to meet you," he said in a voice that seemed far too deep for someone his size.

Despite William's surprising confession on their walk, Clara soon became quite at ease in the Mitchell's home. Mrs. Mitchell was very much like her own mother, and Mr. Mitchell was a dear, kind man with a ready smile and laugh. As for Hamilton…he kept quiet for most of the meal, but it was easy for Clara to see that he adored his brother and that William adored him.

The Mitchell's dining room table was quite small and cozy. Clara constantly bumped William with her elbow as they ate, and she found his in her face a few times. It didn't appear to bother him that they had to take turns cutting their meat, so Clara didn't let it irk her. And besides, the conversation was engaging enough that she could almost forget William's nearness. *Almost.*

In the middle of a rather complicated game of chess with Hamilton, as well as an animated discussion with Mr. Mitchell, William announced that it was getting late.

"I promised your father I'd have you back by ten," he said, grinning.

"Hmm," Mr. Mitchell murmured, stealing a glance at the grandfather clock near the wall. "Walk quickly, then."

Clara bid the family good night, with a great many 'thank yous' thrown in. Mrs. Mitchell invited her to come back again soon, and Clara said that she would very much like to.

During the walk back home, Clara's mind was too busy to speak. The sound of the cable cars and of her own feet crunching on snow was soothing to her rather frazzled thoughts. She could hear carolers singing *Silent Night* off in the distance, and she welcomed the homelike glow of Chicago's gas streetlamps on the snow. A near-silent sigh of relief escaped her.

"Did you…" A sudden thought came to Clara's mind. "Did you ask my father for permission to court me?"

William nodded. "I did, two Saturdays ago. He granted permission. I must apologize, Clara—" William faltered, and even in the dim light, she could see color rising in his face. "I apologize for assuming that you would know I was courting you. I should have asked *your* permission, as well as your father's. So," he cleared his throat, "would you be interested in entering a courtship with me?"

Clara's insides tingled and her smiling lips brushed against her scarf. What an unusual man William was!

"I accept your apology." She paused, licking her lips. "And yes; I'm interested in a courtship." Clara smiled up at William, and, though she couldn't see his eyes, she knew that they were sparkling.

William drew her hand into the crook of his elbow and squeezed it, sending yet another excited quiver down Clara's spine.

With Christmas and Lewis and Esther's New Year's Eve wedding rapidly approaching, Clara was busier than ever. The finishing touches of embroidery still had to be put on Esther's cream-colored wedding gown, and nearly every evening was consumed with tiny silk stitches.

Even when William came for supper the Saturday before Christmas, Clara, her mother, and Esther had to continue working on Esther's gown while the men sat talking.

Mrs. Boutwell had invited the Mitchell family over for Christmas dinner, much to Clara's excitement. Though the Boutwell and Mitchell parents were acquainted, both were happy for an opportunity to get to know each other better.

On Christmas morning, Clara awoke early, a smile already on her lips.

"Come on, Esther!" She flung herself out of bed, poking Esther's toes as she tugged on the blankets. "It's Christmas!"

Esther moaned and dove under the quilts. "You're worse than a five-year-old." Her voice was muffled and hoarse.

Clara laughed and yanked the warm quilts off her sister's back. She knew what Esther said was true, but she didn't care. And besides, Esther was just as excited as she was, but her excitement would come after nine o' clock.

Christmas had always been Clara's favorite holiday. Other than the outstanding food, her favorite part was when her father read the Christmas story aloud from the Gospel of Luke. She loved hearing his deep, expressive voice telling the old story that still gave Clara chills.

Clara hurried through dressing in her new gown, grabbed a handful of pins, and ran downstairs into the kitchen where her mother worked, busily preparing the luscious food for the day. Already, scents of savory meats, spices, and pies filled the house.

"Good morning, Mother," Clara greeted, giving her mother a hug and kiss on the cheek. "Merry Christmas."

"Merry Christmas, Darling. I'm nearly done with the rolls, and then I'll fix your hair. How do you want it done today?"

"The usual." Clara's eyes roved through the kitchen, seeing all of the delightful, half-made dishes strewn about.

When Mrs. Boutwell was ready, Clara took a seat on one of the kitchen stools and tried to sit still while her mother gently fixed the frizzy curls. Then, Mrs. Boutwell pulled back the sides of Clara's hair and pinned it behind her head, just as she liked it.

"There you are. Will you please put on an apron and help me for a few minutes? Are Esther and Emma awake yet?"

Clara grabbed an apron off the pegs behind the door and tied it over her dress. "Esther is awake, but not entirely so. I don't know about Emma."

Mrs. Boutwell chuckled. "I suppose we'll have to make do without them for a while."

As Clara and her mother worked side by side preparing various dishes for later on in the day, Clara couldn't help but think of her father's church.

The Presbyterian church always opened its doors to the public on Christmas day, providing a delicious meal and even little gifts to those who had no one to spend Christmas with. For the past several Christmases, the Boutwell's themselves had organized and run the event, leaving them little family time. But this year, one of the elders and his family volunteered to cook and welcome people.

Esther soon joined Clara and their mother in the kitchen. She looked lovely with her blonde hair atop her head, adorned with holly. The shimmering crimson dress made her blue eyes stand out like pearls among gems.

"You look beautiful, Esther." Clara smiled at her older sister.

Esther hugged their mother and grinned at Clara. "You look quite lovely yourself."

Clara looked down to her dark blue satin and smiled. It *was* a pretty dress. "I think Mother looks the loveliest."

Esther couldn't argue with that. Mrs. Boutwell looked stunning in her emerald green satin dress, accented with black trimmings. And her chestnut hair, wound in a flattering bun at the nape of her neck, was surrounded by a black lace snood. Her face was flushed slightly from working over the warm stove.

"I agree."

Clara turned to see her father standing in the doorway, grinning. He crossed the kitchen and stood beside his wife, eyes glinting mischievously.

"Watch this." With that, he grasped his wife about the waist and shoulders, dipped down, and planted a solid kiss on her lips.

Clara giggled and Esther's hands flew to her face, covering a gaping smile. Mr. Boutwell stood up again wearing an expression of triumph, while Mrs. Boutwell wore a half-horrified, half-amused look.

"Oh, James, really!" she gasped, straightening her dress.

Mr. Boutwell just smiled and kissed her again, although he allowed her to remain standing this time.

Esther and Mr. Boutwell set the table for breakfast while Clara and her mother finished the preparations and set the large turkey roasting for dinner.

When Clara sat down at her place, she saw that Wesley and Emma were already seated, and baby Maud was sleeping in her cradle in the corner. Emma, too, looked beautiful in her holiday gown. It was obvious that Wesley thought so.

Looking down at her plate, Clara found a paper-wrapped parcel lying on it. The parcel wasn't large, but it wasn't small either. Looking across the table, Clara saw that Esther and Emma each had one. Their parents gazed upon the girls with mysterious smiles.

"Can we open them?"

Mr. Boutwell nodded, and all three tore into the paper. Clara gasped when she saw what was inside.

It was a framed photo of her parents. In the photo, her father was sitting in a chair with her mother standing beside it. Both were smiling gently, even though it was rare that a photographer would allow his subjects to smile.

"Oh, it's beautiful," Esther breathed, voicing Clara's thoughts perfectly.

"We wanted you both to have something to take to your new homes with you, whenever that may be." Clara caught her father's wink, quite obviously aimed at her, and it sent blood to her cheeks. "We couldn't think of anything better than a photograph."

"It's perfect." Clara stared down at her photo once again. It was the first photograph her parents had ever posed for.

"Thank you," Emma said, gazing with tear-filled eyes at her parents. "It's the best gift you could have given us."

"We have a copy for Katie, as well," Mrs. Boutwell said. "She'll get it today."

Clara knew that her oldest sister would be just as excited about the photograph as she, Emma, and Esther were.

"Shall we pray?" Mr. Boutwell asked. The girls set their photos to the side, and the family joined hands.

The remainder of the morning flew by as meal preparations continued. It was after one o'clock when Katie, Frank, and their children arrived. Clara hugged her sister and brother-in-law and snatched her little namesake out of Katie's arms.

"How's my little girl? Did you miss your Auntie Clara?" She bounced young Clara May in her arms and pressed kisses into her soft, chubby cheeks. May, as the family had taken to calling her, was barely six months old. The baby grinned and giggled and reached for her downed hair.

Something smacked into Clara's legs, and she looked down to see Jimmy, hugging her through her skirts.

"Is Christmas, Auntie Clara! Is Christmas!" Two-year-old Jimmy gripped her legs harder and jumped at the same time. Clara ruffled his hair, laughing.

Frank had brought a small bag of parcels, which he deposited under the Christmas tree when his little son wasn't looking. Clara felt as excited as Jimmy was acting, but she kept herself in check.

There soon came another rap at the door, making Clara's heart leap into her throat. *The Mitchells!*

Ivy Rose

Chapter 6

Emma answered the door, with Mrs. Boutwell close behind. A slew of "Merry Christmas's" were thrown around, and Clara formally introduced everyone.

Mrs. Boutwell had to excuse herself to the kitchen. As she walked by, she bent to Clara's ear. "I know you'd rather be out here, but can you come help for a little while?"

Clara nodded.

"Allow me," Mrs. Mitchell's soft voice broke through the excited chatter.

"But you are a guest—" Clara's words didn't get far before Mrs. Mitchell raised her hand for silence and followed Clara's mother into the kitchen. Most everyone else was in the parlor, so, smiling to herself, Clara turned towards the kitchen. She may as well help;

the faster tasks were completed, the faster they could eat and enjoy Christmas.

She stopped when a gentle hand closed around her arm.

"Merry Christmas," William said with a wink, blue eyes sparkling. He looked quite handsome in his black suit.

Clara's face heated. She had been so busy introducing the Mitchells to her family, there hadn't been time to greet William. "Merry Christmas to you, as well."

"Are we having spiced apple bread tonight, or have you eaten it already?"

Clara laughed lightly. "I can't eat six loaves all by myself."

"Hmm...I'll help." William grinned mischievously. Then, with a quick squeeze of her hand, he turned and joined the others in the parlor, and Clara entered the kitchen, heart fluttering.

Since the turkey still was not completely cooked, the adults decided that it would be the perfect time to open presents. The women joined the men in the parlor, and Mrs. Boutwell stood and clapped for attention.

"Everyone find a seat, sit in it, and stay there!"

There was a giggle of astonishment that the even-tempered Mrs. Boutwell would raise her voice in such an unladylike manner, but Clara wasn't surprised in the least. She knew how much her mother loved Christmas.

William beckoned Clara to the empty seat next to him on the sofa, and Clara obliged, but not without a girlish blush. Would her face never settle on one shade of crimson?

Little Jimmy sat on his knees on the ground, trying his hardest to be still, but failing miserably. His papa gave him a parcel to open and, amidst his squeals of joy and laughter, Clara saw a wooden ship set that would keep him entertained for a long while.

Clara herself received a beautiful bolt of calico for a new dress, which she desperately needed. Her old work dress was in a sorry state. She also received, from Katie and Frank, a shell comb to put her hair up with. Esther gave her a pair of woolen stockings, saying, "Now you won't have to send your icy feet to my side of the bed!"

The Mitchell's had brought along their presents for each other. William received a flannel shirt and hat from his folks, as well as some books. Clara had set aside her gift to give him later.

When most of the gifts had been open and the turkey declared finished, everyone gathered around the extended dining room table and joined hands for prayer. Mr. Boutwell offered the blessing and thanked God for family and friends.

Clara couldn't remember a better Christmas. She soaked in the warm heat coming from the fire in the hearth, the sweet smell of Christmastime food, and the love of those surrounding her. This year was especially exciting. There were so many new family members...little May, baby Maud, and Lewis. What would next Christmas be like?

There wasn't a silent moment at the table. It seemed that everyone was talking at once, but Clara loved all the chattering, laughing, and jesting. Especially from Jimmy and the baby girls.

After dinner, Clara took little Maud into the parlor and seated herself on the settee. Maud was a tad fussy and wanted her mama, but since Emma desired to be included in the adult conversation, Clara thought she would try her hand at keeping the baby happy.

"Who's this little darling?" William asked, entering the parlor. "I'm having a difficult time keeping your family straight."

Clara slid over on the settee to make room for William. "This is Maud, Emma and Wesley's little girl. You've seen her lots of times before."

William grabbed one of the baby's soft hands and gently stroked it. Maud grasped his finger in both of her chubby hands and squiggled on Clara's lap.

"How old is she?"

"Just about three months."

"She's adorable."

Clara looked up into William's face and saw a wistful longing hiding in his eyes. "Do you want to hold her?"

William's face brightened. "Could I? Mrs. Kopp wouldn't mind?"

Clara shook her head and carefully put Maud in William's arms. For a moment, he held her awkwardly, and Clara was half afraid that Maud would topple out. But after a few minutes, the baby settled and started blinking long, slow blinks.

"She's going to fall asleep," Clara warned, smiling at William as he gazed at the little one in his arms.

"I don't mind," William said softly, rocking Maud gently from his seated position.

Clara was right. In moments, Maud's eyelids remained shut and she breathed peacefully.

"I don't remember when Hamilton was a baby." William tore his gaze from Maud's face and looked into Clara's. "I wish I did."

She smiled. "Well, I'm the youngest, so the only babies I've had to play with are Katie and Emma's."

"You like children?" It was more of a statement than a question.

"Of course!" Clara giggled softly. "The Bible says that they are a blessing. But besides that, they're fun to have around." She reached over and toyed with Maud's soft baby hand. What would it be like to have a little one of her own someday?

In a few minutes, Wesley came to fetch his baby. He smiled, seeing her so contentedly nestled in William's arms.

"Mrs. Mitchell wants to hold her," Wesley said.

"Ah well, I suppose I must share with my own mum." William reluctantly handed the baby girl over to her papa.

Clara watched as little Jimmy flew hither and thither, bouncing around like his new toy ball in excitement. He sang a baby-voice version of *Joy to the World* as he bounced. She leaned back into the soft cushions of the sofa and sighed contentedly, watching the quiet bustling of her family through the open doorway. Mother and Father, Katie and Frank, Emma and Wesley, Mr. and Mrs. Mitchell, and Hamilton sat in the dining room, talking and laughing in turn. Mrs. Mitchell crooned over Maud. Esther and Lewis sat near each other on the sofa across from Clara and William, holding tightly to the other's hands and speaking softly to one another.

William still sat at Clara's side. Though he said nothing, Clara felt that he was enjoying the day as much as she was.

"I have something for you," William said, reaching behind him to the shelf and drawing out a paper-wrapped object.

Taking the box, Clara carefully untied the string. She pulled back the paper to see a lovely, cream-colored rectangular case, embellished with hand-painted flowers.

"Oh, William," she breathed, carefully touching the top of the wooden box. "It's lovely."

"Open it," William urged, smiling broadly.

Clara flipped open the lid of the box and gasped. There, laying on a bed of pink silk, was an ivory comb. And above the comb, secured in the lid of the box, was a stunning ivory-set mirror. Both the comb and the mirror were painted with little flowers that matched the top of the box.

"The woman at the store told me that this was the right kind of comb for curly hair." William toyed with his hands. "And since I know nothing about hair, I took her word for it and hoped she knew what she was talking about."

Her lips stretched with a big smile as she touched the items. Ivory was expensive, and she had seen the monstrous price of a comb set just like this one several months ago. And the woman had been right: only wide-toothed combs worked with her hair.

"Thank you. They're absolutely beautiful." She looked up into William's shining eyes and broad grin. How thoughtful he was! "I'll be able to use these for a long time."

"What is that, Clara?" Esther asked from across the room.

Clara held up the box for Esther to see. "It's a comb and mirror set. Isn't it lovely?"

Esther gasped dramatically and came nearer. She carefully inspected the princely box and what it contained, and her open-mouthed stare told Clara just exactly what she thought of it.

"Couldn't you have warned me?" Lewis said in a whisper to William, but being sure the girls could hear him, too. "You're making me look bad...only giving Esther a vase."

The foursome enjoyed a good chuckle, and Esther convinced Lewis that her vase was as good as Clara's comb set. Better, even. Clara couldn't help giggling when she saw how Esther gazed at her affianced with love-filled eyes and how Lewis's mirrored her expression. Clara hoped she would never act so silly, even six days before *her* wedding.

Clara inspected every inch of her lovely gift over and over, hardly believing that the items belonged to her. William seemed about to burst with pride, giving Clara a slight idea of how much this gift had truly cost him.

Her cheeks flushed when she realized that her gift to William, a woolen scarf she had knit herself, was hardly dirt when compared to this lovely set. She decided that it would be better not to give it to him, but realized in another moment that she was being silly. Mother and Father always said that it was the thought behind the gift that was worth something.

"I have a gift for you, too," Clara said, gathering up the beautiful present in her lap. "I'm afraid it isn't as fine as this, but I hope—"

William placed his hand on Clara's arm to shush her. "I will love it, no matter what."

She found her heart racing and her hands began to tremble. Clutching the rectangular case to steady her hands, Clara rose hastily. "I'll fetch it."

She would have taken the stairs two at a time if it hadn't been for her long dress. Once inside her bedroom, Clara flung herself on the bed and breathed deeply.

What's the matter with me? She stared blankly at the oak ceiling, folding her hands in the small of her back to still them.

Shoving away the thoughts, she pushed herself up, leaving the comb set on her bed. She grabbed William's gift from her shelf, where it had been sitting for the past few weeks. Then, stealing a glance in the mirror as she walked past, Clara saw that her cheeks were still a deep pink. She almost didn't want to go back downstairs, but it couldn't be avoided.

Walking past Emma and Wesley's room, Clara heard a baby sobbing.

May.

Slowly pushing open the door, Clara saw baby May lying in her cousin Maud's cradle, fat alligator tears running down her red face.

"What's the matter, Little Girl?" Clara crooned to the baby, kneeling down and pulling her into her arms. "It's all right, Darling. Your mama can't hear you with your big brother being so noisy down there. Poor thing."

Clara stroked May's damp hair and patted her back, and the baby snuggled into her with a few whimpers.

Tucking William's gift under her arm, Clara scooped May and her blankets up and continued on her way downstairs. She carried little May into the dining room and over to Katie.

Katie's eyes grew wide. Rising from her chair, she met Clara near the door.

"I forgot to check on her. Is she all right?"

"She was crying pretty hard, but she doesn't seem any worse for wear." Clara handed little May over to her mama.

"Thank you, Clara." Katie's smile was grateful and relieved.

Clara nodded, left the dining room and took a deep breath before entering the parlor.

"Whose baby was that?"

A chuckle found its way to Clara's lips, all feelings of nervousness gone. It *was* amusing to see William struggling to understand which baby went with which parents.

"That was Katie and Frank's daughter, Clara May. We just call her May so that it doesn't get confusing with two Clara's. It's already hard with two Catherines."

"Which ones are they?"

"Mother and Katie. Mother goes by Kate and then, well, Katie has been Katie for as long as I can remember." Clara resumed her seat beside William and handed him the parcel. "It's nothing fancy, I assure you."

"I don't mind."

He gently unwrapped the paper and drew out the navy blue scarf.

"It's beautiful!" He held the scarf in his hands and inspected a few stitches. "I've been needing a new one so badly but I didn't want to bother Mum." He lowered his voice. "And no offense to my dear mum—it's not her fault that she never learned to knit properly—but

76

her knitting is quite chunky and lumpy and tends to unravel."

Clara smiled and giggled, feeling sorry for Mrs. Mitchell, yet thinking it was rather comical that even her son noticed her…unusual…way of knitting.

"Thank you so much."

Before Clara knew it, William had reached around her shoulders and pulled her into him. Instantly, the pounding in her heart returned, her hands trembled, and her stomach felt jittery, as if she had eaten too much for dinner.

"My—my pleasure," Clara managed to say. She smiled, though she knew her face was red to the tips of her ears. "I'm glad you are pleased with it."

Chapter 7

The remainder of the afternoon went by all too fast for Clara's liking. Mr. Boutwell gathered everyone in the parlor once again and read the Christmas story from Luke, his deep, powerful voice reverberating throughout the room.

Before she knew it, it was time for everyone to say good night and traipse through the snow to their homes. Not Katie and Frank, though. With their two little ones, they thought it best to hire a sleigh.

As Clara and Esther were preparing for bed, Esther mooned over Clara's new comb set. Clara even let her use the comb to brush her curls with.

"Oooh, Clara, that dashing William wants to marry you!"

Clara rolled her eyes. "Why else would he be courting me?"

Esther giggled. "He spent a lot of money on this set. He must be madly in love. Do you love him back?"

"Esther." Clara groaned.

"You *do* love him!"

"No! I mean…" Clara closed her eyes and sighed. Esther could be so aggravating at times. "I don't know yet. I enjoy spending time with him and I think he's a wonderful man, but I don't love him. Not yet, at least." Her voice sounded pained, even to her own ears. "Please stop teasing."

"Beg pardon, Clara."

Clara glanced in the mirror and saw the remorse in Esther's face. She even looked halfway sad.

"I never want to hurt you, I love you too much, but sometimes I don't know how much is too much teasing." Esther gently set the comb down, and began twisting Clara's hair into a lose braid.

Clara's heart throbbed. "I forgive you, Esther."

It was quiet for a few moments while Esther's nimble fingers tucked stray curls into Clara's nightcap.

"Do you have your new socks on?" she asked, her smile reappearing.

"Yes, they're very warm, thank you." Clara scrunched her toes up in the socks.

"I was afraid that they would be too small."

Clara looked down at her feet in the thick, chunky socks. "No, quite the contrary; my little feet are near swallowed up in them."

Crawling into bed, Clara shivered under the cold sheets. She closed her eyes and replayed her favorite moments of the day in her mind: father kissing mother in the kitchen, herself, Esther, and Emma receiving the photograph of their parents, caressing little May and Maud, Jimmy trying to bounce as high as his new ball, opening the comb set, William hugging her…

Clara's face grew warm against the cool sheets.

What was it that William saw in her? He was almost seven years older than her—practically a lifetime. She couldn't deny that she greatly enjoyed being with him, but was it really love that she felt, like Esther had said?

New Year's Eve came, along with Esther and Lewis's wedding. Though the day was cold and snowy, Clara thought it was the perfect day for a wedding. Or it would have been perfect, had her throat and head not ached so. Perhaps she was catching a cold. If Mother found out that she wasn't feeling well, she might make her stay home.

Clara was bound not to let that happen. She crept to the medicine cabinet and poured a spoonful of syrup that her mother always used to cure sore throats. Though bitter, it did dull the pain, and Clara went about her day with as much normalcy as she could muster.

The Boutwells hired a sleigh to take them to the church, because they had so many things to transport there. Clara held her dress, the maid of honor dress, in her lap as they flew down the snowy streets.

Once at the church, she immediately set to arrange the stage to accommodate the wedding party. Everyone else was busy, so Clara herself moved the heavy oaken pulpit.

I might be small, but nobody can argue that I'm a weakling.

Clara wished that there were flowers to decorate the sanctuary, but finding flowers for Esther's bouquet had been difficult enough, and it had cost a pretty penny. The church would have to go undecorated. A smile tugged at her lips. Lewis and Esther likely wouldn't notice the absence of flowers.

Before Clara put on her dress, she, Emma, and Katie helped Esther into her creamy gown. It took a bit of work to get all of the different petticoats positioned correctly, and Esther continually shivered and jumped around to keep warm.

"Esther!" Clara scowled as her sister hugged herself, arms bare.

"I'm sorry!" Esther's teeth chattered. "It's so cold."

"Cope with it," Emma chirped, re-adjusting the cockeyed corset. "You'll be warm in a few minutes."

Once Esther was dressed, Emma helped Clara into her dress, which took considerably less time than Esther's had. Clara loved the flowy feeling of the half-full skirt on her dress—the one she had worn on Christmas day. And the fabric, a shimmering deep blue, was durable yet beautiful and would serve her well for many years to come. She was proud to have made this dress entirely by herself. From cutting material to sewing, she had placed every stitch, every bit of lace, and every button. It was a truly beautiful dress.

Emma fixed Clara's hair and put it up at Esther's request. Then she placed one, precious, hothouse-grown, cream-colored rose in Clara's dark hair.

"You look lovely, Little Sister," Emma said with a smile. "And you can pull your hair down as soon as the ceremony is over."

Clara laughed. "I might do that."

The Mitchells had been invited to the wedding, but to their disappointment, weren't able to attend. William had said that he would try to be there, and Clara roved the guests for his face.

Esther had requested to keep the wedding party small, and Lewis had agreed with her. There weren't more than thirty guests all together. Clara thought it was the perfect size for a wedding.

The ceremony was about to start when Clara felt a hand on her shoulder. She spun around to find William standing behind her.

"I was wondering if you would be able to come," Clara said, bestowing a gentle smile upon the handsome fellow.

William grinned, his eyes quickly flitting over her outfit, then meeting her face. "You look absolutely lovely."

Clara's insides shook. "Thank you." She dropped her gaze to the floor.

Heather, the other bridesmaid, peeked her head out the door and motioned to Clara.

"I have to go now," Clara said, taking a step toward the room.

"I'll find someplace to sit. Come see me afterwards, all right?"

"I will."

Clara pushed open the door to where Esther and Heather stood. The three girls joined hands and Esther prayed quietly for her and Lewis to be blessed in their new life together. Clara hugged her sister one last time before Lewis's brother, also his best man, came to fetch her. They walked down the aisle to soft organ music, followed by Heather and the second groomsman. Clara was in her place as Esther and Lewis came down the aisle together.

Clara had never seen her sister's face beam so. And Lewis—he looked so proud as he walked with Esther on his arm. For a brief moment, Clara's breath caught. Esther was leaving...her last sister! But really, she wasn't going anywhere; she and Lewis had rented a home not far from the Boutwell's. And besides, Emma still lived at home with her little family. It wasn't as though Clara was to be left completely alone.

Even with such consoling thoughts, a lump rose in Clara's already-sore throat and she feared that she might cry. Prying her eyes away from Esther and Lewis, she surveyed the small crowd seated in the pews. Most of the faces she recognized from church. Her eyes descended on William, and he offered a smile and a wink.

Clara's heart pounded and her insides felt squiggly. It hadn't been a rude wink at all; it was as if he were trying to tell her something. Whatever his meaning, it distracted her from lonely thoughts.

"Dearly beloved," her father began, forcing Clara to pay attention to the ceremony. "We are gathered here today…"

Clara was thankful that her father made the ceremony short and sweet. Esther looked so beautiful standing there beside tall Lewis. When Mr. Boutwell at last announced them husband and wife, Lewis bent down and planted a firm kiss on Esther's lips. Clara couldn't help but smile at Esther's beaming face. She looked and acted so grown up whenever Lewis was around.

When the new couple had been sent off to their new home, Clara went to find William before she was bombarded with well-meaning church people.

"That was a perfect ceremony," William said, grinning. "It wasn't so painfully long, like a lot of others I've attended."

Clara couldn't help but laugh. Of course, it was just like a man to think of how short a wedding could be. "You wanted to see me?" A chilly draft blew from the door, penetrating her satin dress and soaking into her skin. What a shame that she couldn't wear her flannel petticoats under this dress!

"Yes; are you able to come to my house for supper on Monday?"

"I believe so. I need to ask Mother and Father."

"We could go straight there from work."

"I can ask them and give you an answer tomorrow."

William grinned half-embarrassed. "Well, actually, I was wondering if I could walk you home tonight."

"Oh!" Clara's head ached so badly, she was looking forward to the speedy ride home in the sleigh. But maybe a brisk walk in the cool air would cure her headache. After all, her house wasn't terribly far away. "Well, I need to stay for a while and get the church put back together. It might be an hour or so before I'm ready. Mother and Father are going out for supper tonight by themselves, so they won't miss me."

William chuckled. "Good for them. Is there anything I can help with to put the church back together?"

"Ask Peter over there. He'd know."

William set off to find Peter, and Clara went to put her comfortable, serviceable, calico dress back on. She was wearing so many layers of clothing it was hard to move normally, but at least she was protected from the drafty building.

The church was put in order in record time. William gained Mr. and Mrs. Boutwell's permission to walk Clara home, and after helping load items into the sleigh, they set off behind it at a comfortable walking pace. It was quite dark out, but the gas lamps of the streets helped ignite the icy road.

"What will it be like with Esther gone?" William asked after a few moments of small talk.

Clara sighed, a lump coming into her throat. "It will be strange, for sure. I'll miss her. Sleeping in that big room by myself is bound to be lonely."

She was quiet for a moment. "William, did I ever tell you that Esther isn't a biological sister?"

William shook his head. "No, you didn't."

Swallowing the lump, Clara spoke. "Esther's mother died in childbirth, and her papa was an older man when she was born. She was their only, much-awaited child. When she was eight, her papa got the typhoid and died. There was no known family, and it had been resolved to send her to an orphan asylum. My father didn't want to see that happen to Esther. He and Mother agreed to adopt her and treat her just as they treat Katie and Emma and I."

In the silence that followed, Clara realized with a pang the thought she'd been pushing away through all the bustling and excitement: she was losing one of her best friends.

Well, Esther wouldn't be lost, exactly, but lost in that she would no longer be living in the same household. Yes, she would be residing not even five blocks away, but it might as well be miles.

"How noble of your parents to do that!" William's words returned Clara to the present. "It would have been tragic for her to spend the rest of her growing-up years in one of those wretched asylums. How old were you when she was brought into the family?"

"Five," Clara said. "I don't remember much, but I do remember being so glad to have another older sister." Clara was surprised to hear a tremor in her voice.

William squeezed the little hand that rested in the crook of his arm. "You're really going to miss her, aren't you?"

The lump in Clara's throat grew larger until she was sure she would cry. She responded by nodding and kept quiet for several long minutes. Her mind was going to need a bit of time to recover.

Both Clara and William knew that the streets of Chicago were not the safest place to be late at night, but it was better to stay on the main streets than take the back way to Clara's house. However, the main streets forced them to pass by several taverns, and because it was New Year's Eve, the saloons were filled to more than normal capacity.

The roads were too icy and treacherous to walk on in the dark, so Clara and William took to the boardwalks. Clara held tightly to William's arm as he speedily walked, feet clomping on the frozen boards. She had to take two steps for each of his one.

"Hi, purty one," a drunken voice slurred, far too near to Clara for comfort. "Com'ere for a minute…I jus wan'oo talk."

Clara's heart pounded in her ears as they continued walking. Feeling a tug on her skirt, she thought that her dress had caught on a stray nail on a post, but looking back, she saw that one of the men seated near the door of the tavern had grasped a handful of the colorful fabric. Thankfully, the calico was sturdy, and Clara yanked it back without any seams ripping out.

There came a drunken shout of protest, and Clara heard feet clattering on the boardwalk. She turned her head to see if they were following her and William, but William's hand gently pushed her face to a forward-facing position, and his arm went around her shoulders.

"Don't look back," he whispered tersely. He coughed, as if the air was affecting his lungs. "And keep walking." He steered her as they half-ran down the boardwalk, away from the taverns.

Several times Clara nearly slipped as they flew down the boardwalks. Thank goodness William was sturdy enough to keep them both upright.

"You all right?" he asked once they were away from the tavern.

"I'm fine." Clara drew a shaky breath.

"This was a bad idea. I should have let you ride home with your parents. I forgot all about it being New Years and the taverns being busy."

Clara didn't answer him; her mouth was too dry. Her legs felt shaky and unstable, but William kept up a steady clip for a while longer.

When he finally slowed his walking to a more comfortable pace, Clara realized that his arm was still around her shoulders, holding her firmly against him. But her cheeks didn't heat, and she didn't pull away. It felt strangely right, being shielded and protected by him.

Chapter 8

It was a quiet walk to the Boutwell's. William took Clara all the way to the door, not just to the end of the path.

"You said your folks were eating out tonight. Is anyone else home?"

Clara glanced upward to the window above the door…Wesley and Emma's room. The light was glowing, which meant that they had decided to come home after the wedding instead of going out to supper. The knot in Clara's stomach eased just knowing that they were there.

"Emma and Wesley are."

"Good."

Clara's eyes wavered back in the direction they had come from. She swallowed. William had to pass the taverns again on his way home. "Will you be all right walking home by yourself? I could give you some money for the cable car—"

William chuckled. "No, no need for that. I'll be fine. Typically, men aren't bothered by those tavern bums. They might ask me to join them, but they won't hurt me."

"You're sure?" Clara wasn't sure at all. And she certainly didn't want William getting hurt.

Smiling softly, William nodded. "I'm sure. Don't forget to ask your folks about supper on Monday."

"I won't. Good night."

William made his way down the icy path, stepping carefully to avoid slipping. He coughed again. Clara's stomach tightened. *God, help him make it home safely!*

William turned and waved at her once more, and Clara waved back, then let herself in the house.

Emma was coming down the stairs with Maud in her arms, both already in their nightclothes. "Clara, what's the matter?" Emma covered the remaining stairs. "Your face is so white."

Clara didn't doubt her face was pale. She felt as if her whole body was pale.

"Is everything all right?" Emma stepped closer.

A thickness settled in Clara's throat. She nodded stiffly, tears burning in her eyes.

"Whatever is the matter?" Emma shifted Maud into one arm and embraced Clara with the other.

"Nothing, really," Clara managed between teary breaths. She wasn't sure why she was crying. It did feel good to release the pent-up feelings, though.

"Well, it must be something. You've never been one to cry for petty things." Emma released Clara with a gentle smile. "Let me get Maud's clean diapers from the kitchen, and I'll meet you up in your room. Wesley isn't feeling well and he's already in bed."

Clara nodded and rubbed her sleeve over her face. Leaden feet carried her up the stairs and into her and Esther's bedroom. Only, it was just her bedroom now. Esther wasn't coming back.

Another lump arose in Clara's throat when she saw their two beds, still pushed together so they could share each other's warmth. The bedspread was neatly pulled over both beds, just as it had been last night. Most of Esther's things had already been moved to her and Lewis's new home, but a few items remained. Walking forward, Clara lit the bedside lamp and eased herself onto the edge of the bed.

How could she sleep in a room all alone? Clara couldn't remember ever sleeping in a room without one of her sisters. Surely she would freeze without someone's body heat to share. Fond memories of the late-night 'sister talk' she, Esther, Emma, and Katie had often engaged in flooded her eyes.

Clara's breathing slowed and her chest felt heavy. Why did she have to be the youngest?

Flopping backwards across the two beds, she heard paper crackle underneath her head. Curiosity overtook emotions, and she sat up, revealing a folded page laying on the bedspread. The letters on the page spelled Clara, and she instantly recognized the handwriting as belonging to Esther.

Clara unfolded the note and began reading.

Dearest Clara,

If you are reading this, then you will have returned from the wedding and it will be rather late. I miss you already, and I hope you miss me just as much. You are the best little sister ever, and I'm so glad that I have been able to call you mine for the past twelve years. Yes, there were times when I would have rather disowned you, but as of late those moments have been few and far between. I am going to miss our midnight conversations and fixing your lovely hair for bed, but mostly, I will miss seeing you every single day. You must come see me very often, and I know that I'll be making frequent trips home.

Happy New Year, Little Sister. Sleep well, and I'll see you soon.

Much Love,
Esther

Clara couldn't stop her tears from flowing. She could hardly believe that Esther, spunky, teasing, goofy Esther, had written her such a sweet note. How had Esther known that she would be needing it?

Her tears continued to flow, but they were mingled tears of sadness for herself and happiness for Esther and Lewis. She quickly changed out of her dress and put her nightclothes on, along with the chunky stockings Esther had knit. She sat before the vanity, removing pins from her hair and crying at the same time.

When Emma finally came in carrying Maud, Clara was seated on the bed, re-reading Esther's note. Her tears were spent, and she felt far calmer.

"I'm sorry, Clara," Emma said, laying Maud on the bed and sitting next to her. "Wesley needed a medicine that I had a difficult time finding."

"Is he all right?" Concern for her brother-in-law prodded Clara's chest.

"He will be. He just picked up a nasty chest cold from being outside so much in this freezing air. Where's your comb? I'll braid your hair, if you'd like."

Clara pointed to the box on the vanity; the box William gave her. Emma carefully drew the ivory comb out of it and sat behind Clara on the bed.

"What were all those tears about when you came in?"

Her chest heaved. "Oh…several things."

"Such as?"

"I was missing Esther." That was part of it, at least.

"What were you missing?"

Clara sighed. "I was thinking of how cold I will get without her in bed with me."

"What else?"

"How she can't fix my hair at night anymore."

"What else?"

"I've never slept in a room by myself ever in my entire life."

Emma chuckled slightly. "That is true."

Maud gurgled and sucked on her fist. Clara pulled the baby into the pit of her crossed legs and stroked her downy-soft hair. She couldn't help but smile. Her fast-beating heart slowed considerably just by holding the baby. "I suppose I was feeling lonely."

"Mmm-hmm." Emma tied off the end of Clara's braid with a ribbon. "That's how I felt when Katie got married."

Clara turned on the bed with the baby in her arms and faced Emma. "But you had Esther and I! It wasn't as if you would be sleeping in a big, black, frightening room all by yourself."

Emma smiled in the dim lamplight. "True, but I still felt terribly lonesome. It seemed empty in here without Katie."

"I remember." Clara traced her finger around Maud's bright eyes and button nose. She had been just fourteen when Katie and Frank got married, and Katie had been twenty-three—far into old maid status. Though they were happy for Katie, losing their oldest sister had been difficult for all three girls.

"I'm thinking that missing Esther wasn't the only reason for your tears."

Clara glanced sharply upward, but her anger melted immediately when she saw the love and care in Emma's eyes. Emma wasn't going to tease her, as Esther did. Emma had always been the quiet, gentle one, ready with a listening ear and no reproof. She wanted to get to the root of the problem, not so that she could tease or punish, but to encourage and uplift.

"No, it wasn't." Clara let her eyes fall to the baby in her lap. "I was very much concerned about William."

"What about him?" Emma's voice was soft.

Clara didn't answer for a long moment, and her hands trembled as her mind replayed the few moments when they passed the taverns.

"On the way here, when we passed the taverns, one of the men on the boardwalk grabbed my dress." Clara squinted her eyes closed. A tear dripped out and splashed onto Maud's little nightdress. "I pulled it away easily, but I think they chased us for a little while. William wouldn't let me look back."

"But you're all right?"

Clara nodded. "A little frazzled, but unhurt. William has to go back that way. You know what intoxicated men can do to themselves and others. It frightens me that he's going that way alone."

Clara felt a tearful swell in her chest and more tears dripped onto Maud. "I don't even know why it bothers me so much. He's a man; he can take care of himself. But still, I'm worried."

Emma laid a gentle hand on Clara's folded knee and rubbed it with her thumb.

"You worry because it's a God-given trait to worry about the men we love."

"Love?" Clara stiffened.

"Certainly. I would be terribly frightened for Wesley if he had to go past those horrid taverns. Or

Father. I love them both so much, I'd rather be hurting than see them in any pain, whether it be an illness like what Wesley has now, or a fight injury."

Clara shook her head. "I don't think I love William."

"How do you know?"

"Well, for one thing, he's so much older than me. Imagine marrying someone nearly seven years older than yourself!"

Emma chuckled lightly. "So your difference in age is what's keeping you from loving him?"

"No…well, yes…but—" Clara sighed and dropped her head to her chest. That sounded ridiculous, even to her. "I don't know. I don't know what it feels like to love a man other than fathers and brothers-in-law. What if these silly feelings I get are just my mind playing tricks on me?"

"What silly feelings?"

Maud's eyes were beginning to close, and Clara kissed the baby's hand. "I get all jittery inside whenever I see him. And my hands start shaking. It's terribly embarrassing."

Emma laughed softly, and Clara, feeling quite puzzled, looked up into her sister's smiling face.

"Oh Clara, you don't even know what's hit you."

She straightened. "What do you mean?"

"I mean that you sound very much like you love William."

"But these silly jitters and my frazzled mind aren't at all like what I imagined being 'in love' to feel like."

"More often than you think, you will find that the ideas in your mind are quite different than what it is really like in life. Loving someone is a choice that you have to make. Love, especially with a man, is not all gushy lover-like feelings and thoughts."

Clara watched her sister's face. No teasing. No silly-little-sister look. Just honesty and affection.

Emma continued. "Take little Maud here, for instance. Yes, when she was first born she was sweet and innocent and easy to love, but as she's gotten older and has been so colicky and difficult, those gushy feelings of what I imagined motherhood to be like have vanished. But still, I choose to love her."

"You have to love her!" Clara protested. "You're her mother! You don't have a choice but to love her."

"No, that isn't true. I could quite easily send her off to an orphan asylum, or give her to another family to take care of. But what kind of mother would that make me?"

Clara gazed down at the sleeping baby in her lap. She couldn't imagine not loving such a pretty little baby, but Clara had heard Maud's frequent crying and had herself been upset by it. "A pretty wretched one, I suppose."

"Exactly. And it's the same thing for fellows. Sometimes, it's harder to love them when they're cranky or tired or sick, but that's where the commitment part of marriage comes in. I choose to keep loving Wesley when he's irritable and sick, like he is now. I guarantee there are no gushy feelings when he's coughing his lungs out."

Clara grinned.

"Mother chose to love Father when he enlisted during the Civil War, even though that was the last thing she wanted him to do. And you know what? Our two brothers died when Father was away. Mother had to take care of that entire situation all on her own. But she kept loving Father, even though she didn't agree with his decision."

A deep ache settled in Clara's chest. She fixed her eyes on little Maud's face and watched the baby's chest rise and fall with each little breath. "So, you're saying that I love William?"

Emma touched Clara's chin and forced her to look up. "Only you can answer that question." She paused for a moment, then smiled softly. "Do you love him?"

Clara pushed a stray curl back behind her ear and swallowed hard. "I don't know if I could call it love, but I greatly admire him."

"What specifically?"

"I like that he is such a strong believer in Christ; we've had many conversations about that. And that he loves children so much. And that he is so caring with his family. He's a hard worker, too. I like that Mother and Father respect him so much."

Emma smiled, and Clara realized, as she had many times before, how similar Emma was to their mother.

"You're a smart girl, Clara, and I know you can figure this out. Don't stop praying about it and asking

God for wisdom. I'm happy to talk to you about it more if you wish, and I know Mother would be, too."

Both their eyes fell to the baby in Clara's lap.

"I'd better get her to bed and check on my cranky husband," Emma's eyes flashed playfully and Clara smiled. She kissed Maud's cheek before handing the baby over to her mama.

"Sleep well, Clara. I'll leave the door open to let the heat in. And so you won't get too lonely."

Clara smiled at her sister's thoughtfulness. "Good night."

For a brief moment, Clara wondered if she should stay up and welcome the new year. Reaching for a novel on her shelf, she crawled under the quilts to begin the lengthy warming process. But before she read a sentence, her eyes closed and the book fell across her chest.

Ivy Rose

Chapter 9

Two mornings after Esther's wedding, on Monday, Clara awoke with her throat aching twice as much as it had been the night before. Her lungs were burning and it took a gigantic effort even to draw a breath. Her throat felt like sandpaper whenever she swallowed. The bedroom was miserably cold, even under the usual three layers of quilts.

She must get to work; she must! But after just pushing the covers back, a violent tremor started as what felt like icy water was poured on her. Clara barely refrained from crying as she pulled the covers back over her frigid body.

"Clara, Darling?"

It was her mother's voice.

A soft hand rested on her shoulder, but it sent arrows of pain shooting throughout her body, and she moaned.

"It's time to get up."

Clara moaned again. "I can't," she croaked, "My chest...hurts." She tried vainly to focus on the blurry face of her mother, but it was too hard.

"Oh dear."

Clara felt a hand placed on her forehead and cheek and it made her shiver.

"You must have caught what Wesley has," Mrs. Boutwell said.

"I have—to go to—work." Clara groaned, again attempting to push the covers back and sit up.

"No you don't, young lady."

Clara felt herself gently pushed back into the pillows and the quilts snugged around her neck.

"You can't even get out of bed, much less walk all the way to Singer. I'll send a wire and tell them you are ill and won't be coming. Go back to sleep if you can, and I'll bring up some medicine and tea in a bit."

Everything ached. Clara felt as if she were sleeping on a bed of rocks. It took far too much effort to move about and talk, so she stayed put and focused on breathing.

She didn't remember falling asleep, but was awakened when her mother entered the room with a tray of bottles and a mug of tea. Clara choked down some of the nasty liquid her mother fed her from a spoon, managed a swallow or two of tea, and tried not to shiver as her mother tucked a hot potato at the foot of her bed.

For the remainder of the day, Clara fell in and out of sleep. Her mother was always at the bedside when she woke, ready to stuff yet another spoonful of that wretched black syrup down Clara's throat. Though she would rather not admit it, the medicine *did* help get rid of the chills.

Clara lay in her bed, gazing out the window. Every few minutes, a coughing fit would overtake her, and she would curl her knees into her chest. It felt as if someone were cutting her lungs from the inside.

Turning back to the window, Clara looked out into the whiteness. She couldn't see much even from her high vantage point, as it was snowing very hard and had been all day. Everything was white and fluffy with the fresh snow.

Mrs. Boutwell had left Clara's side an hour earlier to prepare supper. Emma had taken baby Maud to stay with Katie and Frank until the sickness was gone from Wesley and Clara. If a little baby like Maud were to catch this illness, it could be fatal. Clara knew that Emma would have a difficult time leaving her little one in someone else's care—even that of her beloved sister—but Clara also knew that Emma wasn't foolish enough to risk her daughter's life.

There came a woody rapping from below Clara's room. The front doorknob clicked loudly, as it always did, and Clara heard her father's deep voice speaking to someone. She didn't think much of it and was able to

105

doze for a few minutes before her mother brought up a bowl of steaming soup.

Carefully, Clara pushed herself to a sitting position and leaned forward while Mrs. Boutwell stacked pillows up behind her. Clara made slow, deliberate movements to avoid another coughing fit.

"William was just here," Mrs. Boutwell said as she set the tray across Clara's lap.

"What for?" The deepness and crackling in her voice was shocking even to her.

"He was wondering where you were. Apparently, he waited for you at Singer for a while, but, when you didn't appear, he came here to make sure you were all right."

"Mr. Kagan didn't tell him I couldn't make it?"

"Evidently not. He was quite concerned when he got here." Mrs. Boutwell spread a napkin over Clara's front. "He wanted you to know that he will be praying for you."

Clara couldn't tell if her heart beat faster because a coughing fit was coming on or because of something else.

Much to her own disgust, the illness lasted the entire week, but Clara remembered little of it. She did remember waking up a handful of times to find her mother anxiously hovering over her, and she thought she remembered both of her parents kneeling beside her bed, hands folded and heads bowed. She occasionally heard murmurs of "scarlet fever" and "pneumonia," but Clara didn't understand what those meant. She thought she remembered a doctor visiting, but it was a faded, fuzzy memory.

William came to see how Clara was twice during the week, or so her mother told her, though he wasn't allowed in because of the high contagiousness of the fever.

On Saturday afternoon, Clara felt well enough to get out of bed and join the family in the parlor. Wesley had been out of bed for two days, but Clara thought he still looked rather ill.

Thankfully, no one other than Clara and Wesley had contracted the illness. Maud, who was still safe at Katie and Frank's, hadn't gotten the fever, and her parents praised God for that. With neither Clara or Wesley contagious, Emma would be bringing Maud back home after church tomorrow.

Mrs. Boutwell had told Clara that she would be allowed to attend church in the morning, but when she woke up, the sun was shining brightly in her room, golden rays spilling over the floor. She sat up and scrambled out of bed as quickly as she dared. Had her mother forgotten to wake her?

She went downstairs, still nightgown-clad. The house was empty and still; almost scarily so. She cautiously pushed open the door to the kitchen.

"Oh!" Clara exclaimed with relief, clinging to the door. "I was afraid I had been left alone."

Mrs. Boutwell chuckled softly and wiped her hands on her apron. "Goodness, Child, I would hope you'd know by now that you wouldn't be left alone on purpose."

Clara smiled.

"I let you sleep in a bit and I am going to make you rest all day today."

"But you said—"

"I know what I said," Mrs. Boutwell interrupted. "But after talking with your father and with Mrs. Mitchell, I changed my mind. You must go to work tomorrow, and though it's against my better judgment, it can't be helped. If you don't show, they will give your position to someone else."

Her stomach clenched. She couldn't lose her job at Singer...she needed that money! It wasn't much, but it did help her parents a little. And slowly, her 'going west' jar was filling up.

"Go back to bed, and I'll bring you some breakfast in a while."

Clara obeyed, glancing down at the ugly rash that lingered on her hands, arms, and chest. She hoped it would be gone by tomorrow. Though the rash looked hideous, it was completely harmless to everyone but her. And to her, it was rather painful.

Climbing back into bed, Clara shuddered under the quilts. The mere thought of going to Singer tomorrow made her tired.

Monday morning seemed particularly bitter as Clara trudged to Singer. Upon arrival, she plopped down in her chair and closed her eyes, wishing to be back home in bed. How could she make it through the day with her head pounding so? And her heart…it seemed to be beating double time.

Clara did make it through the day, but barely. She wanted nothing more than to go home and curl up in her bed for a good long sleep. But first, she had to get back home.

No one had told William she would be back at work today, and Clara hoped to catch him before he left. She had no desire to walk home by herself.

"William!" Clara let the door to the factory slam behind her and tried to run after his retreating form, but her legs refused her. "William! Please, wait!"

William turned, saw Clara, and strode towards her.

"Clara! I'm so glad to see you well again!" He grinned, and his eyes sparkled. "I've missed our walks."

Clara smiled and settled her hat more comfortably around her head. "So have I."

"Are you truly recovered? I hear that the lingering effects of the fever can be quite exhausting."

"No, I don't feel quite like myself yet. I'm extremely tired after today and will be glad to get home and sleep."

"Shall I call a hack? I don't want you overexerting yourself."

Clara was flattered. "No, thank you. It's far too much money to ride for such a short distance. I'll be fine."

William gazed at her through narrow eyes for a long moment, then pulled her arm into his as if to say, "in that case, this is the least I can do."

"What still lingers from your illness?" he asked.

"Mostly tiredness, but also this dreadful rash." Clara pulled off a mitten and showed him.

"It looks terrible! Does it bother you much?"

Clara replaced her glove. "Not much, but sometimes it will start tingling."

William was silent for a long moment, but Clara felt his eyes upon her multiple times. It was as if he were making sure it was really her beside him.

"I was terribly worried about you." William's words gave Clara warm tingles. He went on. "Your father told me when I came on Wednesday how terribly sick you were. I am so thankful that the Lord answered our prayers and spared your life."

Clara's heart pounded and her hands began trembling. Had she truly been sick enough that her parents and friends wondered if she would live?

"Th—thank you for praying. It means a lot."

William smiled, softly.

Wishing to divert their conversation away from herself, Clara asked, "Did you have any trouble going past the taverns the night of Esther's wedding?"

"The taverns? Oh no, none at all. Nobody seems to acknowledge that I exist. It's only when you are with me that I get any attention."

Clara's breath caught. William was unusually handsome—even her mother said so. His creamy blond hair and those striking eyes... He didn't seem to have caught the hint that she was trying to divert conversation elsewhere. "I doubt that," she answered in a teasing voice.

She was too tired to talk much, so their walk home was quiet, save the usual noisy bustling of Chicago. And William's dreadful cough. She wanted to ask him if he were getting sick, too, but it took an enormous amount of concentration just to keep her legs moving.

As they walked, it seemed that the road was forever stretching longer and longer, keeping her house out of reach. Never had two miles been so long.

"Are you all right?" William asked with concern, and Clara realized that she had inadvertently slowed her steps.

"A little tired."

"We're almost there."

William saw her in the door, and Clara bid him good night with a tired smile and wave.

Mrs. Boutwell sent Clara directly to bed, and Clara wasn't about to argue. She drank some tea for supper and curled deep into her quilts.

And I've got to do that all again tomorrow.

Clara walked carefully across the slippery boardwalks the following Monday. It was early, but Clara had given herself extra time to get to Singer so she wouldn't have to rush along the icy ground. She was feeling almost completely well again, but the previous week had been long and tiresome. Clara was glad that she didn't suffer from a weak constitution.

The taverns were usually empty in the morning, but even so, Clara was glad her route took her a completely different way. She didn't ever want to walk past any tavern alone.

As she passed the post office, a yellow poster in the window caught her eye. She stopped in the middle of the not-busy boardwalk to read it.

CHEAP LAND!
SETTL—

"Ouch!"

Someone bashed into her and knocked her off balance. Barely saving herself from toppling off the icy boardwalk and into the snowy street below, she frowned and straightened her skirts. Didn't the hooligans have other places to play? Clara glared at the quickly-fleeing form of a shabby boy and jumped out of the way as two other boys, apparently chasing him, flew by.

Returning her gaze to the poster, Clara read the heading again.

CHEAP LAND!
SETTLERS NEEDED
Come enjoy the wonder and beauty Washington territory has to offer!

Clara looked at the drawing on the poster. Tall evergreen trees, a gentle lake, a small creek, and two eagles soaring above the treetops. Smiling, she brushed the drawing with her mittened fingers.

Clara loved being out of doors. She loved the country, where birds flew free and deer visited regularly, where one didn't have to worry about being knocked into the street by rowdy boys.

In all the holiday festivities, she had almost forgotten her wish of going west. She stared at the peaceful drawing once again. Something about the quiet serenity of it tugged at her heart.

Sighing, she clutched her bundle of books to her chest and continued down the boardwalk towards Singer. What she had told William earlier was entirely true: her parents wouldn't allow her to go west for many years yet. As much as Clara wanted to hop on the next wagon train or locomotive going to Oregon or Washington, she knew as much as everyone else how foolish that would be. There was a large part of her that didn't want to leave her family, as well. She would get terribly homesick and lonely with all three sisters and both parents still in Chicago.

Once at Singer, Clara peeked through the window into the room that William worked in. She wanted to be sure that he had gotten to work safely, though she didn't understand why—he always did. Sure enough, there he sat. His back was to her, but Clara knew without a doubt that it was him. His blonde hair was quite unmistakable.

As usual, William was waiting outside the building for Clara at the end of the day. He greeted her kindly, and Clara was about to do the same when she noticed a purple bruise, the size of her palm, on his cheek. She could see it easily, even in the fading twilight.

Chapter 10

"Whatever happened?" She stood on her toes to get a better look, a jolt of mingled shock and fear shuddering through her. He must have gotten caught in a fight. "It looks absolutely terrible!"

"Nothing serious!" William said quickly, drawing Clara's hand into his elbow and beginning the trek to her home. "This was the result of my own stupidity."

"How?" Clara asked in a crackling voice, watching as William drew his scarf—the one she had made him—over his mouth and nose.

"I'm embarrassed to say," William confided.

"Why?"

"Because I was being such an idiot, I deserve every bit of this."

"Tell me, please!" Clara tugged on his arm and looked into his half-covered face. Was he embarrassed to say that she had been right about passing by the taverns?

William sighed. "I was running on the road in front of my house yesterday. My foot slipped on some ice, and I fell down…" He paused and cleared his throat. "…and my face hit a chunk of ice."

"Oh, William!" The tension in her chest eased. He *hadn't* been in a fight.

"I told you it was stupid."

"Are you all right, though? Nothing is broken?"

"Nothing's broken." William chuckled. "Thankfully, I was wearing this scarf you made me, and I think it was thick enough to protect my face from any further injury."

Clara wasn't sure whether to laugh or cry, so she did the former. It *was* rather ridiculous to think of William, sure-footed William, falling on the ice. She didn't think she wanted to know why he was *running* on icy streets.

"That bruise looks awful. Are you sure it will be all right?"

William nodded. "I'll be fine. I know it looks terrible…I wish I had a better story to go with it than simply falling down."

Clara laughed again. "I'm just glad it didn't give you a concussion or something."

"Me too. The Lord protected me…from myself."

They walked in silence for a few moments, Clara's mind churning. What unseen damage had his fall caused? And how long would it take to heal?

"I wish I could wear the scarf all day," William said, pulling Clara from her thoughts back to the snowy city. "Everyone who saw me asked what happened and, of course, I had to tell them, which was rather embarrassing."

Clara smiled grimly. "I'm sorry…I didn't help much with that."

William shook his head. "I was hoping that you might have some ideas on how I can hide the bruise. It will be awhile until it goes away, and my mum didn't have any ideas other than icing it."

"My mother has a salve that has worked well for me in the past," Clara said. "I always had bruises all over my arms and legs when I was little; I was a bit of a tomboy. The salve greatly cut down on the amount of time a bruise would last."

"Do you think she'd let me use some of it?" William asked, his voice full of hope.

"I don't know why not."

When they arrived at the Boutwell's home, Clara opened the door and let William in. She threw her wraps on the coat rack and strode into the kitchen, where her mother stood over the stove.

"Oh, hello, William." Mrs. Boutwell wiped her hands on her apron. "Good gracious, what happened to you?"

William grinned sheepishly. "I slipped on some ice and hit my face."

Mrs. Boutwell put a hand to her mouth and her shoulders shook. "I'm so sorry." Her tone exposed a hint of mirth. "It must hurt dreadfully."

"It is rather sore," William admitted.

"That's what the salve is for, Mother," Clara said, setting the jar on the butcher block and pulling up a stool for William. "I think it will help with the bruising, like it did for me so many times."

Mrs. Boutwell carefully inspected the large, purple bruise. "Yes, I think it should." She moved back to the stove to stir whatever was bubbling in the pot.

Clara took a large amount of the salve on her fingers and gently pressed it between her hands to warm it so it would spread easier. "Tip your chin up, close your eyes, and hold still."

She slathered the strange-smelling salve all over William's injured cheek, careful to keep it out of his eyes.

"Ouch," he mumbled through thin lips.

Clara chuckled. "Sorry. Just a little more."

Heat rose in Clara's cheeks when she realized how close she was standing to William and that her hand was touching his face. Her heart beat fast and her hands started shaking. She rubbed the salve in as quickly as she dared and backed away, wiping her hands on a nearby napkin.

"There," she said. "That should help a bit."

William smiled at her, deepening the flush in her cheeks. "Thank you very much."

"Take the salve home, William," Mrs. Boutwell instructed from the stove. "Put it on every two hours. And when you get home, put some ice on your cheek."

"Yes ma'am. And thank you."

William stood and put the stool back where it belonged. Clara handed him the jar of salve, her face still hot. She folded her hands over one another to stop their trembling.

"I'd like to invite your entire family to the Valentine's Day dance my parents host," William said, looking from Clara to Mrs. Boutwell. "We have been hosting one for as long as I can remember, and it's grown to be quite a large event. We would be honored to see all of you; Boutwells, Kopps, Newells, and Cutlers if you are able to come. It begins at three in the afternoon and goes until ten."

"That sounds marvelous!" Clara said, jumping up and clapping her hands, forgetting her embarrassment in a moment for her love of dance.

"It does indeed." Mrs. Boutwell glanced over her shoulder and smiled at William. "I don't know who all will be able to attend, but you can count on my husband, Clara, and I."

"Excellent! There will be a potluck supper, so you can bring something to contribute if you wish. And if not, I'm sure there will still be plenty of food." William bent down to Clara's ear. "Though I'm sure none of it will be as delicious as your fine cooking."

He winked and smiled, and Clara felt as hot as a radish.

"I'm sure we'll be able to contribute something," Mrs. Boutwell said. "Thank you for the kind invitation! We will look forward to it. Can we expect you for supper on Wednesday night, as usual?" She shot William a rather sly smile.

"If you'll put up with me, I would be glad to come."

"Well then, see you Wednesday."

"Good afternoon, Mrs. Boutwell, and thank you for the salve."

"I hope it helps."

Clara saw William to the door. "See you tomorrow."

William had his scarf over his face, but Clara knew by the glimmer in his eye that he was smiling.

"I always look forward to it," he said, momentarily squeezing her shoulder. Clara smiled back despite her pounding heart. She watched him walk down the pathway from inside the glass, then joined her mother in the kitchen.

"A Valentine's day dance sounds wonderful, doesn't it?" Mrs. Boutwell asked.

"Oh yes! I'm excited already, and it's three weeks away!"

Mrs. Boutwell chuckled. "That young man certainly is kind."

"He is." Clara's face turned up in a smile.

"He's just perfect for my little Clara. I can't think of a better son-in-law—except for Frank, Wesley, and Lewis, of course."

"Mother!" Clara protested, her face burning. "It isn't as if he's proposed!"

"I should hope not. Not until he asks your father. But you needn't be ashamed to admit you like him, Clara. There is nothing wrong with that. Both your father and I highly approve of William and are hoping that we can call him our son-in-law someday."

Clara's back was to her mother, and she leaned against the counter, staring at the pattern in the wood. "You…you are serious?"

"Certainly. Your father and I both love William dearly, as I assume you do."

Silence fell.

"You do love William, don't you?" Mrs. Boutwell asked, coming up behind Clara and putting her arm around her shoulders.

Clara kept her gaze fixed on the countertop. "Yes," she said softly. "A little, at least."

"Then what's wrong?"

Clara took a deep breath and scratched at a bit of flour paste with her fingernail. "It's just that," she hesitated, "I cannot bring myself to believe that he would take a fancy to me. I'm so much younger than he is. Seven years, Mother!"

"Why is that bad?"

Clara took a moment to gather her thoughts. Her reasons were slightly silly and childish. Would her mother laugh? "Well, for one thing, he would likely die of old age before I did, and I'd hate to be left all alone in the world."

A breathless grunt came from Mrs. Boutwell, and Clara's chest pounded. "Well, Dear, you are thinking quite far ahead into the future. Lord willing by that time, you will have many beautiful children to care for you, so you won't truly be alone."

Clara sighed. "How can he think of me as anything but a child? I'm only just seventeen! How can I know if he cares for me as anything more than a sister? It seems ridiculous that he should think of me in any other way."

Mrs. Boutwell stroked Clara's curls off her brow and laid her head on her shoulder. "Do you truly believe that he thinks you a child?"

Clara chewed on her lip for a moment. "No."

"You have given him no reason to treat you like a child. It does not surprise me in the least that an older man has shown interest in you."

Clara rested quietly on her mother's shoulder, her thoughts flailing. Her hands fidgeted with a string on her apron and she gazed into the distance, far past the oak cupboards.

"I'm just a bit frightened, that's all." Clara sighed and shifted her feet. "I don't think I'm ready to be married. In my mind, I'm hardly older than little Jimmy."

Clara felt a kiss planted on her hair and her mother's arms tightened. "I didn't feel ready to be married when your father and I wed, and I was nearly twenty-four. If a girl waited until she felt ready, I fear a good many girls would be old maids."

A grin tugged at Clara's lips.

"But, Clara, it really isn't up to you when you are ready for marriage; it's the Lord's decision. You can choose to ignore or accept it when he gives it to you."

Mrs. Boutwell stood Clara upright and laid gentle hands on her shoulders. Clara gazed into her mother's eyes.

"If you haven't already, you should spend some time praying about this specifically. Speaking to the Lord always helps clear my mind and makes it easier for me to hear Him speak. Will you do that?"

Clara nodded, dropping her gaze to the floor. She felt a kiss on her cheek and looked into her mother's smiling face.

"Would you care to do it now?"

"Yes. Thank you, Mother."

Over the next three weeks, Clara felt like she blossomed a great deal. She had spent much time asking the Lord to guide and lead her in regard to William. She and her mother had had several more discussions, and Clara spoke to Emma again, as well. She also had a conversation with her father, and was surprised to see tears in his eyes as they talked.

"What's the matter?" Clara asked.

Mr. Boutwell pulled a handkerchief out of his pocket and dabbed at his eyes. "I'm just realizing how quickly you are growing up—no—have grown up. I can't help but feel as if I am about to lose another little girl to another fellow."

Clara wrapped her arms around her father's neck and held him tightly. "You aren't losing me, Father; William and I are just courting. He hasn't proposed, and I don't think he will for quite a long while yet."

The look on Mr. Boutwell's face told Clara that he thought otherwise.

William came to supper the night before Valentine's Day. In an animated tone, he told the family the delightful things that had happened at past dances. William was as excited about the annual dance as Clara herself was, even though he had been attending every year since he was a young child.

Clara learned that William was to be one of the four dance callers. Apparently, the ballroom to be used was so large that there needed to be a caller in each corner of the room so the dancers could hear. William said that the square dances were the only ones that got too terribly loud, so, for every other dance, the four callers took turns.

After supper, the Boutwells and Kopps, along with William, sat in the parlor while Mr. Boutwell read the Bible, as he did most every evening. William and Clara sat near each other on the settee, with a full, sleepy Maud happily cooing in William's lap. Emma and Wesley, seated on the other side of the room, enjoying the little break from their energetic daughter.

Maud fell asleep in William's arms long before Mr. Boutwell had finished reading. When he was done, William handed the sleeping baby to her father and bid the family goodnight. Clara followed him to the door while her parents went into the kitchen, and Wesley took Maud up to bed.

Clara leaned against the window frame and watched William as he walked toward the street, her heart beating in the now-familiar pattern. Her hand shook against the window, and she smiled.

Emma came up behind her. "What are you thinking about?"

Clara sighed happily. "Remember what you told me, the night of Esther's wedding? How love is a choice?"

Emma nodded.

"Well," she swallowed. "With the Lord's leading, I've decided that it's all right to love William."

Emma smiled and clasped Clara's hand. "Has he proposed to you?"

"No," Clara chuckled. "I don't think he will for a time yet. I just wanted you to know that I...that I made the choice."

Emma embraced her sister. "How exciting! Not just for you, but for the rest of us as well. We all love William as much as you do, I think."

Warmth spread up her neck and cheeks. "Maybe. I'm just glad that I let the Lord take control instead of worrying all the time."

Chapter 11

The Mitchell's Valentine's Day dance was something out of a dream. The ballroom they had rented was chock full of people. Paper decorations suspended from the ceiling…hearts, cupids, and roses. Colorful paper also graced the food tables, which were brimming with luscious dishes.

Clara heard lively fiddle music playing and William's voice, among others, chanting out calls. She stood with her back to the wall and watched in awe as the dancers swung to and fro in time with the music. Never had she seen so many people performing a square dance in such perfect time. She couldn't wait to join them.

Just as William had said, there was a caller standing on each of the four corners of the room. It amazed Clara that each caller, though they could hardly hear each other over the happy shouts and clomping feet of the dancers, kept the calls in perfect time. Each caller was responsible for four squares, and each set of four had to keep in time with the other twelve squares.

Her foot tapped along beneath her skirt. When the dance finished, she joined the explosive clapping and cheering.

"There you are!"

Clara looked up to see William hurrying towards her.

"I was afraid you wouldn't make it," he said, pressing her hand between both of his. That funny little twinkle was in his eye, and his mouth perked into a smile.

"I wouldn't miss this for the world," Clara said, smiling broadly.

"Is your family here?"

"Mother and Father are somewhere." Clara glanced behind her, but there were so many people and she was too short to see above the flurry of waistcoats and dresses. She returned her gaze to William.

"I have two more squares to call, then I'm yours for a few dances. Sound good?"

Clara nodded and blushed, and William ran off to the stage again to organize the next set of squares.

A young man Clara didn't know invited her to dance, and she gladly accepted. William was an excellent caller and she wanted to be a part of one of his dances.

Though William's calling was flawless, Clara soon found out that her partner knew little about dancing, and she ended up dragging him about the square like a rag doll. He was embarrassed, and Clara tried her hardest to keep smiling despite the discomfort of having her toes stepped on and her arm yanked.

After the dance, she thanked the young man courteously and quickly went off to get some punch before he could offer to get it for her.

Mrs. Mitchell was serving the desired drink, and the two of them talked through the next dance. Clara adored Mrs. Mitchell almost as much as she did her own beloved mother.

They were still chatting when someone touched Clara on the shoulder. She glanced behind her to see William.

"May I have the next dance?" He offered his hand.

"Certainly." Clara grinned, leaving her glass with Mrs. Mitchell and taking William's hand.

The dance was a circle dance—one of Clara's favorite kinds. They were slow and waltz-like and generally involved a lot of gliding, sliding, and twirling. William's hand rested in the small of her back, pulling her close to him as they stepped back and forth. Could he feel her heart pounding?

"You dance very well," he said as he twirled her around and caught her other hand in a complicated, pretzel-like knot.

"I was thinking the same thing about you." Clara smiled into his eyes. His face was so near to hers she could almost…

The caller spoke the next move, and she ducked and weaved around William to undo the knot they had created. Hopefully, the burning in her cheeks would appear to be from the exertion. "Why haven't you told me before now that you danced?"

"I suppose it just never came up. You've taken lessons?"

Another twist landed her in his arms again. Why did she have to fit so comfortably in them? "I took lessons for several years. And you?"

He nodded. "For what I thought was far too long."

She couldn't constrain a half-nervous, half-excited laugh. William was going beyond the caller's simple calls and embellishing them, and she responded to his spontaneous movements without fault. The twinkle in William's eye was flashing brightly, and Clara felt just as happy as he looked. The heat in her face was continuing to rise.

The song was ending. William flashed a smile. "Ready?" he asked, preparing for a skillful finale.

Clara nodded. William spun her from his hand, catching her in the other arm. Both spun around together for a full revolution, then Clara spun off William's arm, pulled back for a short beat, then was reeled in close to him, and out to the other hand for a quick, above-the-head hand twirl and curtsy in William's direction. Or at least, what she thought was William's direction—the ballroom was spinning furiously.

Breathless and laughing, Clara allowed William to lead her to a chair and fetch punch for them both.

Another dance was starting, and William had asked her to dance again. But she declined, her world still whirling and twirling. He took a seat beside her, and they watched the dancers.

"There are my parents," Clara said, discreetly pointing to a couple floating to and fro on the dance floor.

"They are almost as good as you are." William's mouth turned up in a grin as he watched them.

"I think they are far better than I ever will be." She sat silent for a moment before laughing softly to herself. "They began teaching me to dance when I was hardly three years old. I remember those lessons: all of us girls together in the parlor with mother softly singing or father humming a tune for us to dance to." A sigh escaped her. "It was so beautiful."

Clara and William danced almost all of the dances together, and, each time, Clara felt as if she were flying through the air. She and William seemed to be able to read each other's minds, making dancing effortless. It wasn't long before they noticed people pointing and watching them closely.

Mr. Boutwell danced with Clara a few times, as did William's brother, Hamilton, who was also accomplished in the art.

The dancing went on and on. Just when Clara thought her feet would slip right off, the dance was declared over and folks began to leave. Clara was prepared to stay and help the Mitchells tidy up the decorations and food and such, and she was quite surprised when William asked to take her home.

"Shouldn't we stay and help?" Clara asked, looking around at the numerous things that needed to be done.

"Mum and Father and your parents and the Evanses can take care of it."

Clara went to ask her parents permission to walk home with William, but her father waved her off before she even got to him.

"Have a good time, Darling." He winked at her, strange. Her serious father rarely winked. Nonetheless, she donned her wraps and coat and followed William out the door.

The early February air was cold and brisk, but thankfully, the snow had mostly melted and the ice was nearly gone. To Clara's surprise, William walked her to a small, half-canopy buggy and helped her into it. Then, climbing up beside her, William tucked a robe around both of them and clucked to the horse.

"Is this your buggy?" Clara asked, glancing down at the beautiful leather cushion and fine hardware.

"It's my parent's, but they let me use it."

"How are they going to get home?"

"I heard them saying that your folks would be taking them."

Clara nodded, but a frown pulled at her brows. Why was everyone was acting so strangely?

A sudden bump threw her head into the buggy-top support bar at her side, so she pushed herself deeper into the seat and rubbed her temple. This time of year was the most dreadful for travel. There wasn't enough snow and ice for a sleigh, but there was too much of it for a buggy. It made going anywhere, on foot or otherwise, quite uncomfortable.

William kept the horse in check, allowing them to observe the beauty of night in Chicago. The tall street lamps had been lit, and the warm glow that came from lamps inside of shops spilled out onto the streets. It was enchanting.

It didn't take Clara long to realize that William not driving in the direction of her home, but instead toward the banks of Lake Michigan. Though she didn't understand why they were taking such a lengthy detour, the lake *was* a beautiful sight in its half-frozen state. She let out a long, contented sigh, seeing her breath in the air.

"What are you thinking about?" William asked softly.

"Nothing much," Clara breathed. "The city is lovely, isn't it?"

William mumbled a soft agreement.

Silence fell on them, the only sound being the horse's shoes clopping on the frozen dirt. They were approaching the darkened lake. When William pulled onto the snowy beach and stopped, Clara turned to him.

"What are—?"

But William interrupted her and faced her, taking both of her hands in his.

"Clara," he began, his eyes boring through hers. "Over the past few months—ever since I literally ran into you—the Lord has been showing me all the reasons why I need you in my life. He's been bringing to light all the traits that make you the perfect wife for me."

Clara's breath caught in her throat.

"I've been praying about you and for you since I plucked you out of that dreadful puddle." A wavering laugh tinted William's voice. "Yes, I am aware that I'm quite a bit older than you are, but I love you, Clara, and I'd be honored to spend the rest of my life with you. Would—will you marry me?"

Clara was sure that William could hear her heart beating—it pounded in her ears. Her hands felt jittery, even inside of William's large ones. Was this really happening? Was he truly asking her to *marry* him?

"Yes!" she breathed, an unstoppable smile creeping over her face. "Yes, absolutely!" Unbidden, her arms flung around his neck and she held tightly, his hands pressing her firmly against him.

She was surprised to find tears dripping from her eyes onto William's woolen coat. Her heart still pounded and she couldn't pry the smile from her face. She heard, "I love you," spoken into her ear, and she returned the soft words.

"Here, I've—" William released her and reached into his pocket. "I have something for you."

Taking off his mittens, William opened a tiny box and held it so Clara could see.

"Oh, William," she whispered, gazing into the box. "It's beautiful!"

"Take your mitten off," he instructed with a smile. Clara did as she was told, and William slipped the dainty, emerald-set ring on her finger.

"Thank you," Clara breathed, holding up her hand into the light of a nearby lamp. "I love it!" Words seemed entirely inadequate. What else should she say?

"Your sisters helped me pick it."

"They did?" Clara dropped her chilled hand back into its mitten and looked at William. "That makes it even more special. Thank you so much."

William smiled, taking her hands into his once again. "Mrs. McDonald," he mused under his breath. "It will be rather strange to call you that."

Clara laughed. "You'd better not call me that! I like 'Clara' just fine coming from you."

They laughed together a moment, then William sobered. "Can we pray?"

Nodding, they bowed their heads, his hands tightening over hers.

Though simple and short, William's prayer made Clara's heart warm and her chest swell. She took a deep breath and let it out slowly. This was real. He had asked her to marry him.

"Amen."

Clara smiled into his eyes for a long moment. He bent forward and pressed a gentle kiss on her forehead, sending an warmth throughout her body.

"Are you ready to go home now?" he asked, almost in a whisper. "And tell our folks?"

Clara nodded, still unable to wipe the grin from her lips.

William squeezed her hand and chirruped the horse, holding the reins in his free hand.

"Don't they already know?" Clara questioned after a moment.

"What?"

"Don't our parents already know that you were going to propose tonight? They were all acting a bit strange."

William laughed. "Yes, they do know."

"That's why they were so eager to get us out of there," Clara mused to herself. She chuckled and her heart began beating fast again.

She was going to be William's wife! His wife, forever, until the end of their days.

"Are you cold?" William asked.

"No. Why?"

"Your hand is shaking."

Sure enough, both of Clara's hands were trembling. Sliding one underneath her and squeezing William's tightly with the other, she laughed a breathless chuckle. "That always happens when I'm nervous."

"Are you nervous now?"

"No, just excited, but my hands don't know the difference."

Chapter 12

Neither Clara nor William saw a reason to postpone their marriage any longer than necessary, so the wedding was set for March twenty-fifth...only seven weeks away.

The weeks were filled with wedding preparations and more sewing than Clara thought she would ever do in a lifetime. Altering Esther's wedding gown to fit Clara's four-foot-seven frame was the easy part. It was preparing the linens and quilts for their new home that was difficult.

With three older sisters to help prepare for, Clara had not been very good at filling her own hope chest. If Clara had spent time as a youngster sewing quilts and bed sheets, it had been for her sisters, not herself. Consequently, her hope chest contained only a silver teacup that had been her grandmother's and her own baby quilt. Not much to set up a new house with.

With the entire family of women working, Clara hoped that they could have her chest at least half-full by the end of March.

Emma, Mrs. Boutwell, and Clara set to work hemming bed sheets, piecing quilts, and making towels. Clara enjoyed sewing, but she thought her eyes would be permanently crossed from spending so much time making tiny stitches. Thankfully, she was well set up for clothing and no new dresses needed to be made.

Katie came to help with quilting whenever she could, but with her own household and two little ones, her time was limited. She did, however, bring a paper-wrapped parcel to the Boutwell's house one day, and when Clara opened it, she found it chock-full of baby garments.

"Katie!" Clara exclaimed, almost offended. "It's not likely for a baby to come along anytime soon!"

"I know, I know," Katie said. "Someone from church gave me a package of baby things before Frank and I were married, and I thought it was the craziest thing ever. But it turned out to be the best gift she could have given me."

Clara screwed up her face. How could baby things help a brand-new couple set up a home?

"Remember how sick I was with Jimmy? And how we had to move during that time?"

Clara nodded.

"I didn't have any time at all to make baby things, so when Jimmy was born, he wore what the lady had given me for the first few weeks until I could catch up."

Clara began pulling out each little garment and inspecting it. Though simple, they truly were beautiful clothes—Katie had obviously put a lot of time and thought into them.

"Thank you, Katie," Clara said, an apologetic smile tugging her lips. "These are beautiful."

Katie bounced baby May on her hip. "It was my pleasure. I'm hoping to have lots of little nieces and nephews from you and William."

William had found a house that they could rent. The house, though small, was perfect in Clara's mind. It came crudely furnished, with not much more than a table and chairs, but the Mitchells were generous and lent the couple a bed, sofa, and side table for as long as they would need it. Just thinking about making the house their own elated Clara.

A firm, familiar rap sounded at the door, and Clara's heart gave a little flutter. Her insides trembled and so did her hands…but the feeling was not so strange anymore.

"I'll get it," she called to her mother and sister, hastily throwing down the quilt they were piecing together.

Turning the knob, Clara saw William, his blue eyes sparkling especially bright.

"Good evening, Miss Boutwell," he greeted, stepping through the door. "How are you on this bitterly cold day?"

Clara felt his teasing gaze upon her and she flushed. "Just fine, thank you. And yourself?"

William didn't answer, but glanced around Clara, towards the parlor.

In a flash, Clara felt her slight figure lifted off the ground and a firm kiss planted on her cheek.

"William!" Clara gasped once on her own feet again, cheeks hot. She glanced over her shoulder to be sure no one had seen his antics. Thankfully, the hallway was empty, except for a broadly-grinning William.

"You're going to get in trouble!" Clara said softly, shaking her finger at him.

"I don't want that!" William replied in the same, teasing tone, hanging his things on the coat rack.

The wedding was just three days away. Everything was in order for housekeeping, except the last quilt Clara was finishing. This would be William's last meal with the Boutwells before he and Clara were wed. When Clara went to his house for supper earlier in the week, they had celebrated William's twenty-fourth birthday.

"Good evening, William," Mrs. Boutwell said when they entered the parlor.

"Good evening Mrs. Boutwell, Mrs. Kopp. How are you?"

The Old River Road

"Sad to lose Clara," Emma answered, smiling at them. "But other than that, we are well."

Clara had picked up her side of the quilt once again and continued stitching while William watched intently from beside her.

Maud lay on a blanket on the floor, playing with a wooden rattle. She suddenly began fussing and kicking, but, before her mother could reach her, William had scooped the baby into his arms and began playing with her.

It made Clara's heart soar to see William enjoying the baby so much. She knew that he would make a wonderful father one day, should the Lord see fit to give them children.

"Are you ready for the most significant day of your life, William?" Mrs. Boutwell questioned.

"Yes ma'am, very ready. I wondered if my turn would ever come when all my friends were married off before they turned twenty. Clara…" William turned and smiled at her. "Clara is the girl I've been praying for ever since I was a little fella."

Clara's cheeks burned and she smiled.

"Turns out that the Lord was waiting to introduce us until she was old enough."

"Well, we are very excited to welcome you into the family, even though it means you'll be taking Clara away."

"Not really away, Mother," Clara protested. "We won't be living so terribly far. Not as far as Katie and Frank."

Mrs. Boutwell chuckled. "That is true, and I should be thankful. It's just hard seeing your youngest daughter get married…my last baby. Even if it is to such a wonderful man like you, William."

Clara gazed up at William's pink cheeks. He was avoiding the eyes of the adult company and instead focusing on the baby in his lap.

The morning of March twenty-fifth was bright and sunny, despite the lingering ice and bitter cold. Clara sprang out of bed and fluttered about the bedroom to collect her clothes, but as she sat on the vanity, an unseen pressure crushed her chest, and she gazed about the room that had been hers ever since she was a small child.

She would never be coming back again.

Well, she might return to the bedroom, but it would be different. There would be no sisters here to greet her, no more midnight conversations about hair and dresses…no more sisterly memories would take place in this room. Her life was turning over to an entirely new chapter. Everything was about to change. She would be leaving her comfortable life as a pastor's daughter and beginning a lifestyle of her own, with her beloved William, of course. The change was for the better, yes. So why did she feel like crying?

Seeing her mother in tears upon arriving in the kitchen didn't help Clara any.

"I can't believe my girl is getting married," Mrs. Boutwell said in a cracking voice, wiping her eyes with the corner of her apron. "It seems like just yesterday you were a tiny little baby in my arms."

Clara went to her mother and hugged her tightly, swallowing her own tears. "I'll be fine, Mother." It was true, she would be just fine, but her new life would take some getting used to.

"Oh, I don't doubt that." Mrs. Boutwell sniffled. "You are going to be absolutely fine; it's your poor mother who will be a disaster."

"You're not worried?"

"Not in the least. My only fear—and it isn't truly a fear—is that I'm losing my little girl."

Clara chuckled, although the weight still pressed on her heart. "I'll be your little girl no matter where I live." A smile played at her lips. "Though you probably wished you could disown me at times."

That made Mrs. Boutwell chuckle, and she straightened. "I can recall a few instances when I would have been happy to say you were just a visiting cousin, but those are few and far between."

Clara laughed. "Like the time Esther and I took off our dresses and swam in only our bloomers…"

"…in the puddle in the backyard?" Mrs. Boutwell finished. "Yes, I remember. Very well."

"Or what about the time I wanted to see Father coming out of the church to know when he would be home, so I climbed the lattice onto the roof and sat on the gable watching for him?"

"And when the elders came over for supper that evening, they found you bare-legged and windblown atop the roof? Unfortunately, I remember all too well."

Laughter relieved some of the nervous pressure. Clara took a deep breath, focusing her thoughts on the happy things that were to come.

"Well, Dear, I know this is your wedding day and all, but if you want to have any food in that new home of yours for the next few days, we had better get cooking."

Around two o'clock, Clara and her parents headed down to the church. Because Clara had insisted on a small wedding, there weren't a lot of preparations to be done, and the wedding would begin in an hour and a half.

Clara had asked Esther to be her bridesmaid. Esther was the closest to Clara in age and they had spent the most time together growing up. Clara knew that William had asked his only living brother, Hamilton, to be his groomsman. A few weeks ago, he had told Clara in a cracking voice that he wished his oldest brother and best friend, George, was still alive and able to be his groomsman. Even so, there was no bitterness in his heart that Hamilton was the only brother left to stand next to him.

After skillfully arranging flowers around the church, Mrs. Boutwell assisted Clara into her gown. Emma and Esther were there as well, Esther looking as fresh as a spring rose in her baby-pink dress.

"Are you getting nervous?" Mrs. Boutwell asked with a smile in her voice.

"A little," Clara confided, grimacing as her mother tightened her corset strings. "But I'm mostly excited."

Mrs. Boutwell chuckled. "Good."

The last of the tiny buttons on Clara's bodice were secured, and her sisters helped her into the long, creamy skirt. After that, Mrs. Boutwell dressed Clara's hair just as she wore it every day—the sides pulled back and secured behind her head. Then on went the lacy veil, the point-toed shoes, and the sash.

Mrs. Boutwell, Emma, and Esther stood back and gazed at Clara.

"You look absolutely lovely, Darling," Mrs. Boutwell said, pressing her fingers to her lips. Clara thought she saw tears in her mother's eyes, but they were happy tears, and her cheeks flushed.

"Oh, here."

A bouquet of white roses was thrust into her hands. She lifted the bundle to her nose and inhaled the sweet, sugary scent.

"Now you're perfect." Esther sighed dreamily. "That dress looks far better on you than it did on me."

A gentle knock sounded at the door and it opened slightly.

"Are we ready to start?"

"Yes, Father," Clara said. Mr. Boutwell came in and shut the door behind him.

"Oh, Clara," he breathed, a wide smile crossing his face. "You look absolutely stunning."

Clara smiled, her face again growing warm. "Thank you."

Emma and Esther kissed Clara and exited the room, and Mrs. Boutwell did the same. Just her father was left, and Clara was half afraid he would begin crying.

"Please don't cry, Father." Clara chuckled breathlessly. "If you do, I am sure to start again!"

Mr. Boutwell smiled through watery eyes and embraced his daughter. "I'll try not to." He held her for a moment, Clara taking long inhales of his spicy cologne. Tears tickled her eyes, but she refused to let them fall. She was getting married! There was no reason to be sad!

"Are you ready?" Mr. Boutwell asked, straightening.

Clara gazed into his wet eyes and smiled, nodding.

She put her hand in her father's elbow and, together, they exited the room and went into the sanctuary. The organist was playing, everyone else was in their positions, and the guests were standing and turning towards the back of the church, where Clara and her father stood.

Looking towards the altar, Clara saw William in his blue Cavalry Captain uniform. His face brightened into a wide smile and he nervously clasped his hands behind his back, rocking on his heels. They locked eyes for a long moment, and Clara felt her stomach flutter and her heartbeat hasten.

When her father gave her to William, Clara left her bouquet to Esther and laid her hands in William's. They were trembling again. William winked at her with a knowing smile.

Before Clara knew it, her father had pronounced them husband and wife. William caught her in his arms, bent down, and kissed her solidly. Warm tingles coursed all the way down to her chilly toes, and she locked her arms around his neck, half afraid that he would drop her from this perilous, backwards-bending position.

When he righted her, his eyes glittered like she'd never seen before. He grinned, and gripping her hand in his, they turned and walked down the few stairs, smiling as their family and guests cheered.

The realization that she was now Mrs. William McDonald finally sunk in when she and William reached the little room in the back of the church and William picked her up, swinging her around and kissing her.

She was really his. They belonged to each other now…for always and forever.

Chapter 13

To Clara, the transition from being a seventeen-year-old girl to a seventeen-year-old married woman went smoother than she expected. Far smoother. The changes which came about when Esther was married were more profound than her own marriage. It seemed rather ironic.

Not much about her day changed after she and William were married. She awoke a half-hour earlier than normal to prepare breakfast for the two of them, then dressed, then her mother stopped by to fix her hair; just as she had done every single morning when Clara lived at home. Though she was perfectly capable of fixing her own hair, Clara enjoyed the time spent with her mother, and her mother seemed to feel the same way.

She and William walked to work and back home together. There was supper to prepare, laundry to wash, and housecleaning to do, but with just two of them, the chores didn't take terribly long.

William hadn't been entirely excited about Clara continuing to work at Singer after they were married. Clara understood that he wanted to be the provider, but she also knew that his meager salary alone wouldn't pay the rent or buy the food. For the time being, he permitted her to continue working.

On Sundays, they went to the Boutwell's home for dinner. Esther and Lewis and Katie and Frank and their little ones came along as well, making it the official, weekly family get-together. On Wednesdays, Clara and William went to the Mitchell's for supper.

William proved himself to be incredibly patient and forgiving...far more so than Clara had expected. This quality came to light mostly in the form of her cooking abilities, or lack thereof. She often forgot how long food needed to be cooked or how to know when it was done; at home, she always had her mother to ask. She was most famous for putting a loaf of bread in the oven and completely forgetting about it until black smoke rose in columns from the stove.

The third time Clara pulled a blackened, smoking loaf out of the oven, she couldn't stop the tears from falling.

"Why does this keep happening?" she asked between sobs when William came into the kitchen to find the source of the odor. "Perhaps I'm more of a nitwit than I thought."

"You are not a nitwit." William took Clara in his arms and held her tightly. "You just need more practice…and perhaps something to help you remember that you have bread in the oven."

As the weather grew warmer and spring came, William helped Clara prepare the much-overrun garden in their small backyard. Together, they planted the little seeds in the earth, mouths watering for the time when the vegetables would be ripe. Yes, vegetables could be purchased in stores, but they didn't taste nearly as good as the ones they grew themselves.

The mid-August sun was hot and miserable, but Clara felt particularly wretched. Heat had never bothered her in this way before, but now it made her nauseous and glum.

Could it be…?

She pushed back a sweaty curl from her forehead and bent to pull a loaf of crisp, golden bread from the oven. No. *Surely not this soon. I'm not ready!*

Smiling to herself, Clara realized that she hadn't burnt a loaf of bread for months. Maybe William had been right—she just needed practice.

The next day was Sunday, and Clara was busy preparing the biscuits she was to take for the family meal. William lounged in the sitting room where it was cooler. Clara hurried through cutting out the biscuits, popped them in the oven, and escaped the stuffy kitchen as soon as she could.

"Ohh!" she sighed, sinking into a chair and pushing back wet, sweat-drenched curls.

"Pretty warm in there?" William questioned, setting his paper down and smiling at her across the tiny room. The heat seemed to bother his lungs—during the hottest part of the day, he had to be careful and rest so he wouldn't take to coughing.

"Very. I sometimes wonder what is getting more cooked—me or the biscuits!"

When Clara and William arrived at the Boutwell's home the following afternoon, everyone else was there and ready to eat. Clara added her biscuits to the spread on the table and took her seat next to William.

Baby Maud was around ten months old now, and she joined her sure-footed cousins in their excursions about the property, though she remained on her hands and knees. Emma had given up trying to put the little girl in long skirts, as would be proper, and continued allowing her to wear shorter skirts while at home.

During these family get-togethers, Clara's mind was attacked with memories of what it had been like in the days before any of the sisters were married. They had been much the same, only with less people and certainly no little ones running about.

Sometimes, the entire family talked as one large group, and other times, like tonight, they separated off into their own little groups. It was lovely to be out-of-doors in the cooler air. Clara sat next to Esther, both quietly listening as their mother and older sisters talked nearby.

"Clara," Esther whispered, very near Clara's ear.

"Hmm?"

"I just found out that I'm going to have a child."

Clara gasped, her cheeks turning up in a smile. "Oh Esther, that's wonderful! When will it be?"

Esther's face flushed a deep red that displayed her elation. "We aren't exactly sure, but likely in late January."

"How exciting!" Clara burst, wrapping her arms around her sister's neck. "I'm so happy for you."

So there was to be another baby! What a joy it would be to have another niece or nephew. Of course, no one could possibly be as thrilled as Esther and Lewis would be about their child, but Clara knew that the baby wouldn't feel any lack of affection.

Perhaps now would be a good time to tell Esther that she herself might be...

No. She had no business telling anyone, much less hope herself that it was true.

"Who have you told?" Clara asked.

"Just you so far. And Lewis, of course."

"Are you going to tell Mother and Father and the girls?"

"Yes…I'm just waiting for the right time."

"Can I tell William?"

"Of course!"

Clara could see the excitement almost ready to explode out of Esther. How long would she manage to keep it a secret? If Esther could make it a week without telling anyone else, Clara would be amazed.

She and William walked home slowly that evening, watching the sunset and enjoying the cool air. They were almost to their house when Clara told William Esther's news.

"Good for them!" William said, smiling wide. "They will be wonderful parents."

"I've got to think of something to make for the baby," Clara said, more to herself than to William. "Everyone makes bibs. I want to make something that will be useful for a long while."

"You could make diapers," William teased. "The baby will need those for a long time, and they'll be very useful."

"Oh please." Clara nudged him with her shoulder. Walking up the path to their house, they laughed for a moment, then Clara grew serious. "I suppose once I've finished sewing for Esther's baby, I should start sewing for ours or I'll never be ready."

There was a moment of silence, and William opened the door. Clara went inside.

"WHAT?"

Clara jumped at the sudden elevation in his voice and stared at him with wide eyes. Why in the world was he—

A blush stole up her neck, heating even the tips of her ears. She hadn't meant to speak that thought aloud.

William shut the door behind him and seemed to be looking through Clara. "Are you serious?"

"Yes…I mean no—I mean—" Clara sighed. "I don't know for sure. I'm guessing. That's why I hadn't told you yet."

The expression on William's face was strange. For the first time ever, Clara felt uncomfortable under his gaze. She was almost glad when he bolted the door and stepped into the sitting room without a word.

Clara took her empty basket into the kitchen, her mind reeling. What had she done wrong? Was it bad that she had simply wanted to wait until she was more sure before telling William? *Dear Lord, I didn't mean to upset him!*

After removing her bonnet and hurriedly tidying up the kitchen, Clara went into the sitting room and found William seated on the couch, eyes wide, staring absently at the pattern on the rug.

She took a seat next to him, folding her legs underneath her in a very un-ladylike fashion.

"William?" Her hands wrapped his arm. "You aren't excited?" Her voice sounded pitiful even to her. She didn't mean for it to, but the choked feeling in her throat made her voice sound even more childlike.

William stirred out of his reprieve and straightened. "Excited? Oh yes. Very much."

Clara wasn't at all convinced. "Then what's the matter?"

"You. You are so…so young, and so very small." William took a deep, sharp breath. "So many things can go wrong."

The tightening in her throat eased, and she leaned her chin against his arm. He wasn't upset—just frightened. "I'll be fine. I might be small, but I'm strong."

"Yes, but Clara, you're only seventeen. Seventeen!"

"I'll be eighteen by the time the baby is born," Clara pointed out.

William muttered something under his breath.

"You've seen how small my mother is, yet she's borne five children. And lots of girls, years younger than me, have babies every day."

He still stared at the ground, shaking his head. Clara thought she saw tears sparkling in his eyes. "I don't know what I would do if I ever lost you. First my father, then my brothers, and now—"

"I'm not going to die!" Clara burst, inviting herself into William's lap and hugging his neck. His arms curled around her. "Babies are born every single day to mothers of all sizes. Most of them are just fine!"

"Yes, and *lots* of them aren't."

Clara sighed, laying her head on William's shoulder. She said nothing for a few minutes. "Will, don't you think that God knows what I can handle?" She looked up into his face. "Do you think He'd give us a baby if we weren't ready for one?"

William exhaled slowly. "No, I suppose not."

"Then why should you worry?"

A concerned smile tugged at William's lips, and he bent down and kissed her. "Because I love you and it's my job to worry."

156

Clara smiled and her cheeks warmed. "I don't even know for sure if I'm right. I think I am, but—"

"You are going to the doctor tomorrow after work." William left no room for discussion.

"But—"

"No arguments," William chided. "You are seeing a doctor tomorrow if I have to throw you over my shoulder and carry you into the office."

Clara folded her arms across her chest and scowled. "I won't put up that much of a fuss." She couldn't hold her frown for long, though. Laughter bubbled in her throat and she hugged William again. With all her heart, she hoped her guess was correct.

As it turned out, Clara didn't have to go to the doctor the following day, as the doctor was incredibly busy, and neither she nor William wanted to wait in the stuffy office.

"Let's go to the other doctor across town," William proposed, beginning to walk toward the cable car that would carry them the across Chicago.

"For goodness sake, William, it's not as if I'm sick."

"I still want you to see a doctor."

Clara's teeth clenched. She planted her feet on the dusty boards of the boardwalk, stopping William in his tracks.

"What are you—"

Clara ignored his words and pulled him toward a vacant alleyway. This had gone on long enough.

"Listen." She turned to face him, fire burning in her chest. "There is nothing wrong with me. Having a child is *natural*. It's not a disease or anything abnormal."

"Yes, but—"

"You're making a much bigger problem out of this than necessary. I feel fine, and I promise that I will tell you if I didn't. Please, can we just go home?"

She didn't break eye contact, and neither did William for several long seconds. His jaw muscles flexed.

Then, he released a gusty sigh and squinted his eyes. Opening them again, he stared at her. "I'm worried." His voice was rather breathless. "I don't want anything to go wrong."

Clara's fists eased, and some of the heat inside her cooled. "Neither do I, but even if something happened, it isn't as if we could do anything about it." She took a step closer and looked up into his downcast face, keeping her voice soft. "Some things are beyond our control."

Inhaling sharply, William gripped Clara's upper arms and pulled her into him. She locked her arms around his middle, closing her eyes. Difficult as it was, truth was truth. Not all babies were born alive.

His arms remained around her for a long while, oblivious to the numerous people traveling the street and boardwalks hardy fifteen feet ahead of them. When he finally did pull away, it was just far enough to press a lengthy, warm kiss on her lips.

"I'm sorry." He rested his chin on her hair, gently squeezing her again. Clara opened her eyes. If only he wouldn't—

She stopped. Hanging off the edge of the boardwalk, staring at them with an open mouth, was a young boy. She pulled away from William slightly, her cheeks warming. It wasn't exactly proper for even a married couple to show affection in public, but what right did that boy have to gape at them?

William turned. He stiffened when he saw the boy. "Run along, youngster."

Startled that he had been caught, the boy turned and disappeared into the crowds.

A smile came to Clara's face, and she turned to William again. He was still watching the boy.

"A man can't even kiss his own wife in this blasted city without being gawked at." William's muttered words made Clara's smile grow.

"Do you need anything—on our way home?" He gently squeezed her arms.

"No."

She took his offered elbow, linking both her hands through it. Praise God, he was finally showing some sense.

"If you're sure about this, can we tell our folks?"

Her feet clomped against the boardwalk, raising little storms of dust. "We could, but it wouldn't exactly be proper yet."

"When is it proper?"

Clara thought about that for a long moment. "I—I don't know. I suppose when it becomes obvious, but I don't really know."

"When will it be—obvious?"

A giggle escaped Clara. William glanced at her with a half-offended expression. He held his hands out in a helpless manner.

"I'm sorry—I know very little about all this. Having no nieces or nephews and not really remembering much about when Hamilton was born, I'm a bit clueless."

Clara straightened and tried to stop laughing. "I'm sorry," she said, vainly attempting to wipe the smile from her face. "It just seems rather funny…" She broke into a laugh again and William put his arm around her shoulders. He was smiling, too.

They walked in silence for several minutes. Clara dearly wished she could run to her parent's house right now and tell them. But it wasn't proper for babies to be talked about much until they were born.

Chapter 14

Clara woke up with a start. The sun had risen and was shining through the window. William would awaken soon and would want breakfast.

Suddenly, Clara realized how badly her stomach churned and her mouth salivated. She needed to run for the washbasin, or...

Scurrying out of bed, Clara barely made it before her stomach turned inside out. It flipped again and again. She remained huddled over the bowl for several minutes, moving away only to wipe the mess from her mouth.

Where did I get this illness?

After a few minutes, the nausea slackened enough for her to empty the washbasin into the slop pail in the kitchen.

"Clara?" A husky voice came from the bedroom.

"I'm here," she replied, setting the basin on the kitchen table. Her stomach churned, and Clara found herself retching again.

"Are you all right?" William was at her side now, pulling off her hot nightcap and tucking her long braid under her nightgown to keep it out of the way.

The gagging stopped, and Clara nodded miserably, keeping her eyes trained on the washbasin.

"Did you eat something that didn't agree with you?" William asked.

"I don't know." Clara swallowed down the bitterness in her mouth. More than likely, she had caught the stomach flu that always traveled the city during the hot months. That, or maybe—

Maybe this was morning sickness. Esther had said that the constant nausea and frequent vomiting is what had alerted her to the fact that she might be expecting.

Clara was almost certain that she and William were going to be parents, but this confirmed it in her mind. She hadn't eaten anything that wouldn't agree with her, nor had she been near anyone with the stomach flu.

Remembering William's presence behind her, she swallowed again and spoke. "There's bread on the counter for breakfast. Can you make your own lunch, too?" Though it was Saturday, he had to go to Singer and do some extra work because of a mechanical break-down in the factory yesterday.

"Of course. Do you want to sit down?"

"Not yet."

He pressed a wooden bowl in her arms, kissing her temple and squeezing her shoulders. "You can go back to the bedroom. There's fresh water in the pitcher in there. I'll clean this up."

She nodded gratefully, slowly making her way to the bedroom and sitting at the vanity. She stayed huddled over the bowl for what seemed like an agonizingly long time, until the nausea began to ease. It didn't ease much, but at least she wasn't gagging on her own tongue now.

Clara threw a shawl over her shoulders and tried to straighten her frizzy hair. It was useless, though. Her mother could fix it later when she came.

William already had his lunch packed and was eating breakfast when Clara came and sat at the table.

"Feeling better?" he asked, reaching across to take her hand.

Clara smiled and nodded slightly, though the sight of William's bread made the nausea worsen momentarily.

"You still look a bit green," William said, stroking the back of her hand with his thumb. "Can I get you anything?"

"Some tea would be lovely," Clara said, pulling her shawl tighter about her shoulders.

"Tea it is, then."

As Clara sipped from the hot, steaming mug, she felt William's concerned eyes on her. Looking up, she saw worry written all over his face.

"I'll be fine," Clara said, a half-smile coming to her lips. "I think it's morning sickness. It's normal."

"How can being sick like that be normal?"

"Mother says that it's to be expected—I don't know why it happens. Just things changing, I suppose."

William raised an eyebrow. "How long does it last?"

Setting her mug on the table, Clara licked her lips. "A few weeks—sometimes just a few days. It depends."

"Will you be all right today?"

Clara nodded emphatically. "From what my sisters said, the nausea sometimes eases as the day goes on. And Mother is coming over today."

William finished his bread and rose to put the plate on the counter. He came over to where Clara sat and hugged her for a long moment. "I love you." He bent down and kissed her.

Clara smiled. "I love you, too. I'll be fine…don't worry about me."

William scoffed. "That's like asking Hamilton to stop eating."

When Mrs. Boutwell arrived an hour and a half later, Clara hadn't moved from her spot at the table. Nearly all the tea was gone, and she had picked up a book to read, but that was all.

Mrs. Boutwell greeted her with concerned smile. "What's going on?"

Clara froze. Should she tell her mother? She and William hadn't discussed the matter of who-to-tell-when very thoroughly.

"I was a little sick." The way her mother's face twisted, Clara knew she'd need to come up with a better answer than that. "Just some nausea. It was probably something I ate."

Mrs. Boutwell still frowned. "Do you have any ginger tea?"

Clara nodded towards the cupboard. Her mother went to the stove and brewed a mug of the tea, setting it in front of Clara.

"That might help a little."

Clara doubted it. Her mouth was salivating again.

"Try to drink some while I get a bath ready." Mrs. Boutwell began filling pots with water and setting them on the stove to heat. Then, she disappeared into the bedroom and came back with one of Clara's house dresses.

Clara stared at the grey tea, willing her stomach back down. She tried a swallow. It tasted good, but sat like a rock. Within moments, she dashed out the door and huddled over the slop bucket.

Mrs. Boutwell was there when the vomiting eased. She offered a cool, damp rag and helped Clara back to the table.

"You don't feel terribly warm," she said, pressing Clara's forehead with her hand. Despite the misery, Clara smiled. She would always be her mother's little girl, no matter how old she got.

"I'll be okay." Clara straightened and gripped her tea mug, as if to prove her point.

Mrs. Boutwell hesitated, then went outside to get the clothes-washing tub from its nail on the side of the house. When the water was warm enough, she dumped it into the big aluminum tub and helped Clara undress.

The warm water felt wonderful against her clammy skin, even though the outside air was rather hot. She slid down, letting it lap against her shoulders and drench her hair.

While she washed, Mrs. Boutwell got a batch of bread baking. She also made muffins and biscuits. The sweet smells of them baking set Clara's stomach rolling again. Soon after she was dressed, she again had to dart for the slop bucket.

Will it never stop?

Not wishing to go back inside to the luscious, nauseating smells of baking, she made herself comfortable on the doorstep. Though hot, at least the outside air was scentless…for the most part.

Mrs. Boutwell lowered herself on the step beside Clara. "Had you eaten something that wasn't agreeing with you, it would be long out of your system by now. And there is no fever, so you can't have the flu. I'm thinking that there is another cause of your illness." Her cockeyed smile was all-knowing. "And I think I might know what it is, too."

Clara couldn't resist smiling. How had she thought that she could keep the secret from her mother? "I wasn't entirely sure until today, but now…"

She felt herself squeezed tightly into her mother's arms.

"How exciting! How long have you suspected?"

"A few weeks."

Her mother kissed her cheek several times, and when she pulled away, Clara saw tears glistening in her eyes.

"What's the matter?" Clara asked, a little laugh escaping her throat. *She* was the one supposed to be experiencing rapid emotional changes.

"Nothing. Nothing at all." Mrs. Boutwell dabbed at her eyes. "It's just hard to believe that my youngest baby is going to have one of her own."

Clara awoke in the middle of the night to a peculiar wheezing sound. It almost sounded as if a sick animal were in the bedroom, but she knew that was not possible.

Pushing herself up, Clara surveyed the room. Other than William, seated on the edge of the bed, nothing seemed out of place.

What's going on?

Clara returned her gaze to William and listened carefully. The sound was coming from him! His position didn't appear comfortable, leaning over the side of the bed as he was. Whatever was wrong?

"Will?" She pushed off the blankets and slid over to where he sat. Her heart beat fast in her chest, and all

167

threads of tiredness vanished in an instant. "Are you all right?"

In the moonlight, William's face was pale. His eyes focused on the floor, unmoving. "Yeah," he managed between wheezes.

"What's the matter?" Clara asked, reaching her hand up to his shoulder. She touched his forehead, but it wasn't unreasonably warm.

"Just—just having a hard—time getting my breath." William voice was as wheezy and brushy as the sounds coming from his chest.

"You're ill!" Clara burst. "You are sick and I didn't notice!"

William took Clara's hand in his, squeezing it firmly as if to silence her.

Clara stopped talking, but she thought that her heart would burst out of her chest. What was going on? Why wouldn't he let her speak?

After what seemed like hours, William's body relaxed and the wheezing stopped. His grip on Clara's hand relaxed, too.

"What is the matter? Why couldn't I talk?" Tears burned in her eyes. "What is going on?"

"Shh," William soothed, pressing her hand affectionately. "It's nothing. Just a touch of asthma. I've had it since I was an infant. That happens occasionally, the shortness of breath. Especially when it's hot."

"Why didn't you tell me?" Clara asked, her chest squeezing. "I could have done something to help!"

William's eyes sparkled dully in the moonlight. Dark bags lay under them, as if he had been awake for days. "I didn't think to tell you; it's been a part of my life for as long as I can remember. It's normal to me."

"There is nothing normal about not being able to breathe properly!" Clara insisted, her voice coming out at a higher pitch than usual. "You must see a doctor!"

"I've already seen several doctors," William said. "There is nothing they can do for me. It's just typical asthma. There is no cure for it."

No cure for it. Clara's mind was spinning. How had William not told her of this before?

"Don't fret, Sweetheart. I'll tell you more in the morning." William kissed Clara and stroked her cheek. His tired grin sparkled in the moonlight, and Clara attempted a smile back.

"I love you," she whispered, in half desperation. Could one die from this disease…asthma? Something about that word sounded vaguely familiar.

"I love you. Let's get some sleep."

She left her hand in his as she travelled the short distance to her side of the bed. He lay on his back, propped up on folded-in-half pillows to make them taller. Clara pressed close to him and curled atop the quilts.

Squeezing his cold hand, she stared through the dim glow of moonlight into William's face. His eyes were closed and his mouth open to breathe. Had she not known better, she would have thought him to be asleep. But no—his thumb bumped along her knuckles in a gentle, soothing motion. How could she possibly go back to sleep now?

The sun would be rising soon, rising to a Saturday. William would be home for two days. There would be plenty of time for him to explain his asthma.

She was choking. That word; asthma. It meant something. Dark clothes, a narrow coffin, shovels in the dirt...

Clara awoke with a scream. She pressed her hands to her sweaty face, elbows resting on her knees.

Asthma. Asthma had killed her uncle Harold. She had been just a little girl when it happened, but the memories were burned into her mind.

And William—her own darling husband—suffered the same disease! Would he die like her uncle had?

Sobs rattled through Clara, though she tried to muffle them for William's sake.

Asthma. Why did it have to be asthma? And now, with the baby on the way...

Her chest tightened. Would William die, leaving her widowed with a brand new baby?

The bed shook beneath her.

"Clara, what's wrong?" William's voice was husky with sleep. He pulled her hands away from her eyes, laying one of his hands on her shoulder.

Clara curled into him, clinging to his neck. "My uncle—" A sob hitched in her throat. "My uncle died of asthma."

William was silent for a moment, rubbing his hand up and down her arm. "I'm sorry to hear that. I didn't know."

He had missed the point. Clara scrunched her face as another flood of tears welled in her chest. "No…it was a long time ago. But—" she swallowed hard. "Are you going to die from it?"

For a brief moment, Clara thought she would be crushed by his arms.

"Oh, Clara, of course not. Don't even think of that." He kissed her hair. "Mine isn't severe—I just get short of breath like that every now and again. It goes away within minutes. Please, Darling, don't worry yourself."

On Monday, Clara went to the Mitchell's home. She wanted to speak with Mrs. Mitchell about ways to cope with William's asthma. After all, Mrs. Mitchell would likely know better than any doctor.

Mrs. Mitchell did have ideas and remedies that had worked for William in the past. She was dismayed to hear that her son still struggled with the wretched disease, as he had been free of it for several years. It worried Mrs. Mitchell just as much as Clara that his asthma had made a return, but armed with the remedies that she provided, Clara felt more prepared and

171

confident for the next asthma attack, should there be one.

As Clara passed a general store, the yellow and black poster for Washington territory caught her eye. She stared at the letters, reading them again and again.

The longing to go west was stirred up in Clara's heart. Longing for trees and vast open spaces and freedom tickled her soul and beckoned her. She smiled, thinking of all that had happened since the last time she saw this same poster…almost a year ago. She had been a young, unmarried schoolteacher the last time she saw it. But now, she was a wife and soon to be a mother. Her ideals and priorities had shifted significantly. She had duties, responsibilities. No longer did she have time to harbor unlikely dreams.

Setting her chin high, Clara sighed and continued on her way. The west would be there for her when she was ready for it. For the time being, there were other things more pressing than teaching a roomful of children how to read and write.

Chapter 15

It was nearly six weeks before Clara was able to see the doctor. And by that time, she didn't need him to confirm her suspicions; she was completely sure.

After hearing the doctor say that Clara was perfectly healthy and should have no trouble with the pregnancy, William was ecstatic. It was hard for Clara to believe that this was the same man who had been upset when he first found out that they might become parents.

"I think you should stop working at Singer now." William spoke slowly. "It just doesn't seem right—proper."

"We need the money." Clara's voice sounded small, even to her.

"I know, but you can't keep working. We aren't that desperate. I can get another job or spend more time with the militia if necessary. Not that the militia would pay much, but..." his voice trailed off into mumbles. "And your folks won't be happy with me if I let you keep working."

Clara smiled slightly. There certainly were a lot of people looking out for her. "Can I at least work until I start showing? Would that be improper?"

"When will that be?"

Clara mentally ticked off the months. "Just a few weeks, I suppose." That left her barely enough time to send in her letter of resignation.

Clara did send her letter of resignation, and, the week following, she worked her last day. It was bittersweet to leave the place she had worked for the past three years, but her co-workers weren't more than acquaintances.

What Clara was most concerned about was that her and William's daily walks together would end. It sounded like such a silly thing to be worried about, but nonetheless, Clara was disappointed. William convinced her that they could still take a walk each day, but she knew that it wouldn't be the same.

Another thing Clara was concerned about was what she would do all day. There wasn't enough work at home to keep her busy! Even with all the necessary preparations for the new baby, Clara feared the boredom and loneliness that was bound to come.

Before Clara resigned from Singer, she and William decided that it was time to tell his parents about the expected child. Mrs. Boutwell had already told her husband, but the rest of the family didn't know yet. Both the Boutwells and the Mitchells were beyond ecstatic—especially the Mitchells, as this baby would be their first grandchild.

The first Monday that Clara didn't work was a long one. She walked through the house again and again, making sure every surface was dust-free and every object in its precise place. To her dismay, everything was in order. She thought about baking, but if she made any more bread or biscuits or rolls, she and William wouldn't be able to eat them before they got moldy. She considered sewing for the new baby, but then remembered that she hadn't any material left. Esther's baby gift was finished...perhaps Clara could take it to her parent's house now.

Gathering the already carefully-wrapped baby dress, she tied a bonnet over her head and set out into the cool October air.

It was only two blocks to her old home. She enjoyed the brisk walk down the quiet street. As a gentle breeze tickled her face and toyed with her skirt, Clara felt a childish urge to run. A smile crept over her face, but she checked herself.

She would not run. She was a married woman. She was going to be a mother. Running down a city street would be entirely unacceptable.

Reaching her parent's home, Clara didn't bother knocking and waltzed herself through the door.

"Mother?" she called into the quiet house, unable to make herself stop smiling. Fresh air still had the same effect on her as it had when she was a little girl.

"I'm in the kitchen, Dear." The greeting was the same as when Clara had lived there.

Pushing open the door, Clara deeply inhaled the fragrance of the kitchen. She set her parcel on the butcher block and went into her mother's open arms.

"You made it longer than I thought you would," Mrs. Boutwell said, straightening her apron and tucking back a strand of hair, all the while smiling at her daughter. Clara sensed a lilting tone in her voice.

"What do you mean?"

Mrs. Boutwell chuckled. "It's almost lunchtime. I expected to see you here hours ago."

Clara still didn't understand. Why would her mother expect to see...?

"There was nothing to do at home and no one to talk to," Clara protested, hastily untying her bonnet strings. "And besides, I needed to bring Esther's gift over."

"And you assumed Esther would be here?"

Clara opened her mouth, then snapped it shut again. She felt redness creeping into her face.

Esther didn't live here anymore. Of course. She lived five blocks away.

Before Clara thought of a response, she was enveloped in another hug.

"I'm only teasing you, Darling. I'm very happy you're here. And you're in luck; Esther is coming over for lunch!"

Clara's defenses fell and she returned her mother's embrace.

"Of course, I can't really tease you," Mrs. Boutwell said, straightening and looking into Clara's eyes. "I was worse than you the first year your father and I were married. I was at my parent's home nearly every day."

Mrs. Boutwell chuckled, and Clara smiled. Her mother had been a girl her age once. She knew what it was like.

"How are you feeling, Dear?" Mrs. Boutwell turned to the stove and Clara sat on a stool, leaning against the counter.

"Just fine." She couldn't resist glancing down at her stomach. The bump wasn't noticeable under her dress, but Clara could feel it with her hands.

"The sickness?"

"It's getting better."

"Tiredness?"

"A little."

"Have you felt movement?"

"No. I hope it will be soon, though."

Mrs. Boutwell glided to the counter and picked up a bread knife. Then, turning to a freshly-cooled loaf, she carefully sliced five pieces.

"Mother!" a chipper voice called from the walkway.

"I'm in the kitchen."

Esther burst through the kitchen door, a wide smile on her rosy-red cheeks. Clara stood to greet her bubbly sister and smiled at her growing belly. Esther's face was absolutely radiant.

"Clara-darling, how are you feeling? Has the sickness gotten better yet? Oh, when I had it, I couldn't bear the smell of food cooking! Poor Lewis had to get his own meals for a few days! Stand straight, Clara! Let me look at you!"

Clara chuckled at her sister's constant stream of chatter. Not much had changed since they were children.

"I'm feeling wonderful, and yes, the sickness is much better."

"Good. I was so dreadfully ill for those few weeks—it was terrible. But it is gone now, thank goodness."

Esther greeted her mother with an embrace. Clara took the parcel into the parlor to give to Esther later and found Emma and Maud occupying the room. Maud was playing on the floor with her toys and Emma sat on the sofa, knitting.

Maud giggled gleefully and crawled after Clara. And, once she reached her, she put her arms up and grunted.

Clara pulled the baby onto her hip and pressed kisses all over her sweet little face.

"I've missed you since yesterday!" She hugged the grinning one-year-old to her. Emma smiled at the pair.

"She sure loves you, Clara."

Clara and Maud locked eyes for a moment, then the baby laughed again and threw her chubby arms around Clara's neck.

"I love her," Clara stated, seating herself near her sister. Emma held knitting needles and yarn in her lap.

"What a beautiful sweater." Clara brushed her fingers along the fancy stitches that made a lovely twisted pattern in the dark blue yarn. "Who is it for?"

"It's for whichever one of you has a baby boy," Emma said, a playful smile on her lips.

"And if we both have boys?"

Emma chuckled. "Then I will be buying more yarn."

"Lunch is ready," Mrs. Boutwell called lightly from the dining room. Clara stood and clasped her little niece close to her. Maud wiggled excitedly as Clara seated her in her high chair at the table. Emma tied a bib around her daughter's neck and handed her a piece of bread, which the baby instantly began to gnaw.

The mealtime talk consisted of babies and sewing and the coming winter. Had Katie been there to join them, it would have felt almost like old times with just the four sisters.

After eating, Clara presented Esther with the gift, which she eagerly tore into. There were gasps as she pulled a carefully stitched, beautifully embroidered baby dress embellished with ribbons and lace.

"Oh, Clara, this must have cost a fortune! And it must have taken you months to make it!" Esther gently fingered each delicate embellishment.

"Nothing is too expensive for my little niece or nephew. And I had a lot of time on my hands."

Clara was glad that her gift was so graciously accepted. She had enjoyed making the little dress, but doubted she would ever make something so fine again. It *had* been a lot of work.

Before the week was over, William and Clara made a trip to the dry goods store to purchase the makings for baby things. Warm flannels, calico, yarn, diaper materials…it seemed like so much for a person who would start out so tiny. Clara was extremely excited, yet she desperately wished that there was a way to know if the child would be a boy or a girl.

I suppose it doesn't matter, Clara told herself, selecting gender-neutral colors. *Hopefully the tiny things I make now will last through all of the children we will have.*

On the way home, William carried the rather large parcel under one arm, and Clara hooked hers through his other elbow. The Chicago streets were busy, as usual. People bustled here and there, paper-boys called out on the street corners, and the saloons would occasionally spit out a man.

"What will we name the baby?" Clara asked in the midst of a silence.

"We can't name it until we know what it is," William said, with a bit of a chuckle.

"Yes, but I think we should at least have some names picked out that we like," Clara protested. "Though some people do it, I don't think a baby should go unnamed for weeks and weeks, waiting for the parents to choose a name."

William nodded. "That's true. What do you like?"

Clara knit her brows together. "I think we should name boys after our fathers. And girls, after our mothers. Keeping names in the family is important to me."

"How many children are we planning on having?" William teased. "That's five names right there—my folks and yours."

"And I hope we have to use every one of them." Clara stuck her chin up and smiled giddily. "If the Lord sees fit, I want a whole houseful of children."

"We might need a bigger house, but I agree with you."

At home later that night, Clara began knitting a pair of booties. She had knit plenty of socks before, but nothing as tiny as these would be. She hoped they would turn out without too many dropped stitches or a purl where a knit was supposed to be.

Clara was concentrating very hard when all of a sudden, she felt a small flutter. A gasp escaped from her lips and the needles fell from her hands.

"What's wrong?" William asked, nearly throwing his paper across the room.

"I…I think the baby just moved," Clara said, a smile creeping over her face. "I've not felt that before."

William grinned. "I'm sure it won't be the last time," he said.

Clara laughed, picking up her dropped needles. "No, likely not."

Clara curled up against William as he read from the Bible. They were reading in Genesis, one of Clara's favorite books. The story of Joseph was the one Clara enjoyed the most.

William was reading wonderfully when he abruptly began wheezing and gasping for breath.

Asthma!

Sitting up and pulling the Bible from her husband's hands, Clara scrambled to her knees. William's face was pale in the lamplight and his eyes, dilated. Everything Mrs. Mitchell had told Clara came flying into her mind.

"Sit forward and put your hands on your knees," Clara instructed. Slowly, he did so.

She placed her hands on the back of William's neck and rubbed vigorously, massaging the tense muscles in his neck and upper back.

"Breathe slowly. Inhale through the nose, big exhale through the mouth. Inhale…exhale. Inhale…exhale."

William followed all of her instructions, though it seemed like he wasn't even hearing her. Clara rubbed and rubbed his neck until her hands hurt, but still, she didn't stop. That, along with the controlled breathing, seemed to be chasing the asthma away.

Within five minutes, William's wheezing stopped, though Clara continued rubbing his neck and coaching him through slow breathing. At last he straightened and leaned into the couch cushions, closing his eyes.

Clara then realized how badly her hands hurt and how violently they shook. Her heart was stuck in her throat and she was unable to keep the tears from spilling out. These bouts of asthma were so frightening—how could William be so calm?

"Thank you, Sweetheart," William whispered, his eyes still closed and his breathing labored.

The dam holding back Clara's sobs broke and she tossed her arms around him, laying her head on his chest and listening to the terrible rattling of his lungs. His arm encircled her weakly.

Dear Lord, please take this affliction away from my husband! Her tears spilled onto William's shirt. *And God, please, don't take him away from me!*

The relief of the attack being over, Clara shut her eyes and forced herself to relax. Mrs. Mitchell said that it did little good to get worked up when William had an attack—it only worried him more.

Her eyelids were heavy and William's arms warm. Had his chest not rattled so, she could have imagined that it was a perfect evening.

When Clara awoke, she found William gently stroking her hair and whispering her name. Opening her eyes, Clara saw that the lamp had burned out and it was completely dark in the sitting room.

"Let's go to bed."

Clara didn't argue. She allowed herself to be taken into the bedroom, and, once there, she quickly donned a nightgown and sloppily braided her hair. Crawling underneath the cool sheets, Clara reached across the covers and took William's hand in hers. She prayed that it be a long while before another bout of asthma overtook her husband.

Chapter 16

Thanksgiving came, along with a chilly skiff of snow. The Mitchell's hosted a dinner for the entire Boutwell family, and it was quite the feast. The most exciting event was not the delicious plum pudding or perfectly roasted turkey, but an announcement from Emma and Wesley. They were expecting another child! Clara thought it rather comical that three of the four sisters were expecting babies at the same time.

Clara's eighteenth birthday arrived and was celebrated with a small family party. However, family gatherings could no longer be reported as 'small,' and there were even more members on the way.

As the weather grew colder and the Christmas season came upon them, Clara was completely at a loss of what to give William. When she asked him about it, he reported that he was having the same challenge.

"Why don't we buy one gift that we will both use?" William suggested.

"Like a new dish set?" Hope swelled in her chest. "Ours is so terribly cracked."

William nodded slowly. "Would that mean that my supper won't drip from the cracks onto my lap anymore?"

Clara laughed. "I believe so, yes."

"All right, sounds wonderful to me. Where should we look?"

"I don't know," Clara said. "We could ask our parents. They will likely know."

Mrs. Mitchell did have a suggestion for where they could find new dishes, and when William took Clara to the store she had suggested, Clara immediately picked a set with pink and blue flowers. It wasn't too fancy— nice enough for company but practical enough for everyday use.

After making the purchase, William asked that the dishes be wrapped and delivered. The storekeeper promised delivery by Christmas Eve.

Clara and William walked down the boardwalk, which had been swept of snow but still held lingering patches of white. The sun had set, leaving the sky a deep blue. The lamplighter was doing his job, and shopkeepers were coming out to light the lamps near their doors. A distant echo carried the tune of *Angels We Have Heard on High*.

Taking a deep breath of the frosty air, Clara let it out slowly as a smile crept over her face. What a beautiful life the Lord had given her—tucked away in a safe cocoon of loved ones in the great city of Chicago.

"What are you thinking about?" William asked. Clara raised her eyes to meet his and felt that all-too familiar flutter in her chest.

"I was thinking about how wonderful it is to be alive," Clara said, sliding her hand from his elbow to his mittened hand and squeezing. "Amidst all the busyness and excitement of city life."

William smiled again, his eyes shining in the small bit of remaining sunlight. "I cannot believe that just last year, you and I were merely courting. It seems like forever ago."

"It does?" Clara let her breath out slowly. "I think this year has gone by remarkably fast."

William considered that for a long moment. "The days were long, but the year was short," he said. "All in a very good way."

Clara chuckled. "Will…" she smiled for a moment, wondering if she should ask the question at all. "When—how—did you know that I was the one you would marry?"

A warmth came over William's face. "From the moment I plucked you, soaking wet, out of that muddy puddle and all you could say was, 'My books'."

Laughter bubbled up inside of Clara. "I suppose that was a rather ridiculous thing to say."

"Quite the contrary. I was so embarrassed and humiliated that I had been so careless, and you were so forgiving and sweet about it. That's when I knew that you were the one for me. No doubt, any other girl would have thrown a colossal fit."

On Christmas morning, William and Clara dressed hurriedly and made their way to the Boutwell's home to spend the day. As Clara attempted to button her coat, she realized that her baby bump was quite unmistakable now, especially with her small frame. It would be just three short months until their baby would arrive. Clara left the coat on its hook and donned a thick shawl instead.

Mrs. Boutwell had outdone herself with breakfast. Cinnamon rolls, oranges, cranberry bread, roasted ham...Clara's mouth watered as she set the table.

Only Katie's family and the Mitchells were absent from breakfast, but they arrived not long after. Everyone gathered in the parlor as the fathers handed out gifts.

Jimmy and May were by far the most excited, and Clara enjoyed watching as Katie vainly tried to calm them and quiet their shouting. May received a lovely little rag doll made with love by her grandma and Aunt Emma, and Jimmy received a beautiful miniature animal set and Noah's ark.

Clara was handed a large, soft package. Carefully tearing away the paper, she couldn't contain a gasp as she pulled out a small, baby-sized quilt. "Oh, it's so beautiful!" she breathed, running her fingers along the careful stitching and colorful blocks.

"We girls and Mother each did something on the quilt," Emma said softly, a smile gracing her lips. "And Mrs. Mitchell helped, as well."

Tears pricked Clara's eyes as she rose to hug each of her sisters, her mother, and William's mother. The quilt itself was absolutely beautiful, but the time and love stitched into it meant far more.

Clara and William received a great many baby things, including a beautiful maple-wood cradle, little knit caps, blankets, and clothing. Clara was delighted when her parents gave her a large bolt of sturdy calico to make herself a new dress of, one that would fit from now until the child was born. If she made it right, the dress could last through all of her pregnancies.

Since she and William had already bought their gift for each other, the only thing under the tree for them from one another was a sweet, love-filled note. Clara hoped that no one was watching as she read hers; she could feel the flames creeping about her face. She tucked the note back into its envelope and glanced up at William, her heart pounding and chest fluttering. She hid her trembling hands in the folds of her dress while he smiled at her, eyes twinkling. He bent down for a quick kiss while no one was looking.

Clara noticed that Esther, while cheery and bubbly as ever, seemed rather tired. She couldn't be blamed though; the child within her demanded more room every day, and she was losing her stamina.

Esther had told Clara that her baby wasn't very active. It was a rare treat for her to feel it kick or move.

Clara almost scoffed at that—if only her child would hold still for a moment! Though Clara enjoyed the near-constant reminders that the baby was alive and healthy, she also enjoyed her sleep. And trying to rest with an active little one somersaulting, kicking, and stretching inside her was frustrating and painful.

After supping and reading of the Christmas story, the families packed up their gifts and headed towards their different homes. Clara and William's baby cradle and bedding would be picked up the following day.

Though it was bitterly cold outside, William and Clara enjoyed their trek home. Clara never grew tired of the snow crunching under her feet or seeing her breath in the air. It seemed so magical, so utterly beautiful to see the lamplight reflecting off of snow and ice. The cold did seem to aggravate William's asthmatic cough, though. Hopefully, the fire in the stove would revive quickly.

Before stoking the fire, Clara headed into the bedroom to change into a loser dress. Her best gown was uncomfortably tight; the baby certainly was growing.

Clara bent near the large, blackened stove and dug around with the iron poker to find the hidden coals. She could hear William bustling around in the sitting room. What could he possibly be doing to make so much noise?

"Clara, come in here for a moment!"

"Just a minute!" Clara scrunched her face against the billowing ash as she tossed more wood on the coals. Satisfied that the fire would grow, the iron door creaked closed, and she wiped her hands on a nearby apron.

"Yes, Darling?" Clara questioned as she stepped through the door, her eyes adjusting to the dimly lit sitting room. William must have just lit the lamps.

He said nothing and just stood in the center of the room, grinning like a child and rocking on his heels. What in the world was he up to?

Then, she saw it.

"Oh, William!" she gasped, moving towards the stunning wooden rocking chair. "It's beautiful! However can we afford it?" Clara's excitement was dampened for a moment, and she took her hands off the smooth finish of the chair to gaze into William's eyes.

"Don't worry about that," he chided, grasping her about the waist and pulling her towards him. "I promised myself long ago that if I were ever blessed enough to have a wife and children, there would be a chair to rock the baby in."

Clara felt soft kisses placed on her head, and her hand wandered back to the satiny-smooth finish of the chair. "You shouldn't have." A smile crept to her face. It *would* be much more comfortable to cuddle and nurse the baby in a rocking chair rather than the hard, lumpy sofa.

"But I did, and there's nothing you can do about it." William ran his finger down Clara's nose with a tender smile.

"All right then," Clara sighed. "I might as well enjoy it."

William released her and Clara lowered herself into the chair, kicking it into motion with her feet. A few gentle sways eased her tired muscles. She could almost fall asleep.

Suddenly, the baby gave a sharp kick that caused Clara to gasp. "I suppose the baby likes it, too."

At the end of January, Esther gave birth to a beautiful little boy. He was tiny and wiry. The doctor attending the birth said he was a bit early, but not to worry; he was assuredly healthy and shouldn't suffer any complications.

Much to Clara's relief, Esther came through the birth surprisingly well, giving Clara confidence for her own delivery.

The doctor was washing up in the Cutler's kitchen as Clara dressed her nephew on the table. He had just been given a bath and was ready to curl up with his mama for a long nap.

"You are an aunt?" the doctor addressed Clara.

She smiled and nodded.

"I see it won't be long before your own little one comes along." The middle-aged doctor's kindly smiled warmed Clara's heart.

"Just another two months."

"Congratulations. I know that I am not your doctor, but please do heed my advice and give yourself plenty of rest in the coming months. I have discovered over the years that younger women tend to overdo activities and pay for it in the end."

Clara fished her nephew's tiny hand through the sleeve of the dress. "I will, Doctor. Thank you."

"Take care of yourself and enjoy your little nephew." He winked at Clara, gathered up his bag of instruments, and exited the house before Clara had a chance to walk him to the door.

She returned her focus to the tiny little human beneath her hands. She forced a pair of booties onto his worming feet, pulled his long dress down over them, then securely swaddled him in a blanket.

Esther was eager to see her little son, holding out her arms for him when Clara entered the room. Clara carefully lowered the bundle to Esther's side and watched as tears formed in her sister's eyes. Esther—teasing, excitable Esther—was dumbstruck by the little form, squiggling and grunting in the blankets. She wound his tiny hand around her finger and kissed his head again and again, while Lewis spoke softly to his wife and son.

Clara smiled at the little family, her heart swelling. She could hardly bear to wait for her own child to be born.

Ivy Rose

Chapter 17

The remaining two months were not as long as Clara had feared. She kept busy knitting caps and sweaters for the baby, and, because knitting was not her strength, it took quite a long while.

Much to Clara's dismay, William had two asthma attacks in that time. She blamed it on the sour weather. Though she was getting better at coping with and treating the dreadful bouts, they never failed to strike fear into her heart that lasted for days. Whatever would she do if William died, as her uncle had? He was practically all the world to her.

The maple-wood cradle was placed in the sitting room for the time being. It would eventually be moved into the bedroom, but the baby would be sleeping in the big bed with her and William for the first few months. Clara made up the cradle with the bedding and quilt. She couldn't help but steal a peek at it every few minutes as she knitted in the rocker.

It won't be long now. Her hands rested over her bulging tummy.

Mrs. Boutwell continued to come every day to do Clara's hair. Clara was perfectly capable of doing it herself, but she much preferred allowing her mother the chore. And besides, Clara loved the time they spent together. She wouldn't have changed that for anything.

At last, the day Clara had been both dreading and eagerly anticipating arrived. She was preparing breakfast on a Saturday morning when the first pain came on. Excusing it as nothing more than a typical twinge, she carried about her work. But when another pain came within ten minutes and then another, worsening in length and intensity each time, Clara knew that the little one was on its way.

She had no desire to stop baking, though, and knowing that it would likely be hours before the baby arrived, she braced herself for each contraction and fought through it.

William was sitting at the table reading aloud while Clara baked. In the middle of a sharp pain, she heard his voice anxiously calling her name. She held up her hand to silence him until it passed.

"What's the matter, Clara?" William asked, coming up behind her and placing a hand on her shoulder.

The pain began to ease and Clara managed a smile. "I think—the little one is starting to come," she said breathlessly.

William's eyes widened and his mouth fell. He stumbled over his words for a few seconds, then managed to say, "You'd best get into bed."

"Not yet," Clara pleaded. "My bread is in the oven, and you must go fetch Mother. I don't want to burn the bread, and it is highly unlikely that the baby will make an appearance for several hours yet."

"You're sure?"

Clara laughed lightly. "I'm sure. Go get Mother, please? I'd feel more comfortable with her here."

William stood dumbstruck for several moments. He raised a hand to scratch his head, then lowered it. "Will...will you be all right by yourself?"

"I'll be fine," Clara said, smiling and pressing his hand between hers. "Really, I will." She rolled onto her tiptoes and kissed him. "Go on."

William left immediately, and Clara sat at the table. She might as well wait until the bread was baked.

He must have sprinted all the way to the Boutwell's home, because he returned with her mother faster than Clara thought possible.

Mrs. Boutwell came in the door with a slightly concerned frown, but her face relaxed into a smile seeing Clara comfortably seated at the table.

"How far apart are they?" she questioned, drawing a chair beside Clara and placing a hand over her tummy.

"About five minutes."

"And how long do they last?"

"A little less than one."

Mrs. Boutwell pressed on Clara's belly in a few places, then nodded in satisfaction. "Perfect! You are coming along just fine. No need to summon the doctor just yet, William," Mrs. Boutwell said, grinning up at the nervous, jumpy husband. "And please, bring more wood in."

When William had stepped outside, Clara turned to her mother, gripping the back of the chair. "Is it supposed to hurt this much?"

Mrs. Boutwell laughed a little. "Yes, and it will get much worse before you can see your little baby."

Clara's mouth dried. She'd known that labor wouldn't be easy, but this…

Her mother's hand rested on her shoulder. "Don't focus on the pain. Keep praying, and think about the treasure you will get when this is all over."

Nodding dumbly, Clara turned back to the table, clutching a fistful of her dress in her hand.

She stayed at the table while the bread and muffins finished baking, and Mrs. Boutwell prepared the bedroom. William loaded the wood box and took his seat across from Clara.

Her back tingled with the feeling that she was being watched. Clara lowered her hands from her face to find William staring at her with wide eyes, his hands clenched together and pressed firmly to his lips.

"I'm going to be fine," Clara said, extending her hand to him. "There is nothing wrong with me. You've heard the doctor say that I'm perfectly healthy."

William desperately clutched Clara's small hand between his large ones and pressed kisses on it. She felt the agitation in his muscles.

"'Trust in the Lord with all thine heart,'" Clara prompted.

"'And lean not unto thine own understanding.'" He managed a smile. "I'm trying. I really am."

The hours wore on, and Clara's pains grew steadily closer together and more intense. Mrs. Boutwell finally insisted that she get into bed, and Clara didn't argue. She was ready to meet the child she had carried for the past nine months.

Eventually, the doctor was summoned, and not long after he arrived, Clara gave birth to a baby boy.

"An energetic little fellow if I do say so myself," the kindly doctor said, glancing over to where Mrs. Boutwell bathed her tiny grandson. The baby did not want to be bathed and ensured that everyone on the block knew it.

It cut Clara's heart, not to mention her ears, to hear his shrill cries. She was most thankful when her mother quickly dried him and placed him in a diaper, not bothering to dress the squalling child before handing him to Clara.

Once on his mother's chest, the little boy quieted and soon began to suckle. Clara couldn't stop the tears from coming as her trembling hand brushed over her son's wispy hair and felt his warm little body against hers. Her heart throbbed.

He really was hers—hers and William's. So innocent, so completely helpless, relying on her for every single aspect of his life. Such a miracle he was…everything about him was so perfect. From the little bits of hair on his head down to the tiny toenails on his soft, red feet. Clara felt a teary smile slowly growing on her face.

The doctor didn't stay around long. He said that both mother and baby had come through beautifully and that Clara could be up in two weeks if she felt ready.

"Which of the dozen names we like will he be called?" William asked in a near whisper, sitting in a chair at the bedside, caressing the baby's small, wrinkled feet.

Clara broke out of her thoughts and smiled at William. He wasn't watching her, though; he was watching every movement and twitch of his little son. Without words being spoken, Clara saw how much he already loved the baby. The look on his face made her heart pound harder.

"Well, if Mother Mitchell is all right with it," Clara smiled lovingly at her mother-in-law, "I'd like to call him Archibald Ronald."

Tears came to William's eyes and his chest heaved. Archibald Ronald. It was the name of William's father, the one he had been born to. The one who died in the War.

Mrs. Mitchell's reaction was similar to her son's, but she managed a small smile. "I more than consent," she said. "His grandpa would be very proud to have such a handsome young fellow as his namesake."

Looking back to William, Clara saw him struggle for control. Doubt settled in her mind. Perhaps she shouldn't have mentioned that name. After all, William was the only surviving son of Archibald McDonald, and to have his first son named after his father…perhaps it was too much.

"It's perfect," William eventually said in a husky voice, rubbing his thumb and index finger over his eyes in one motion. "We can call him Archie."

"Little Archie," Clara breathed, returning her gaze to the baby in her arms. Did he look anything like his namesake grandfather?

Once young Archie had satisfied his belly and curled in his mother's arms for a nap, tiredness crept over Clara like a gentle wave. The excitement of meeting her son was wearing, and exhaustion from the labor beginning to set in. Mrs. Mitchell offered Clara a bit of supper, but she declined. Her eyes refused to stay open a moment longer.

Mrs. Boutwell took Archie and dressed him in a warm flannel nighty. Then, after wrapping him in a blanket, he was passed between his grandmas until William asked to hold his son. Clara fell asleep with her hand in William's, watching him cuddle their sleeping child.

When Clara was awakened a few hours later, she found Archie cuddled up beside her, just beginning to squirm inside his blankets.

"He wants to be fed," Mrs. Boutwell lovingly prompted, helping Clara sit up and arranging pillows behind her. Clara unbuttoned the front of her nightgown and lifted the baby into her lap. When he was quietly eating, Clara yawned and rubbed her eyes. She was still quite tired and greatly desired to go back to sleep.

"Can you drink something?" Mrs. Boutwell asked, holding a mug in front of Clara. Clara nodded and took the mug carefully so as not to slosh it over herself and the baby. Raspberry tea it was…a very strong brew. Clara drank half the cup and handed it back, her bleary eyes cooperating more fully now. She glanced about the room.

"Where's William?"

"He's taking his mother home—he will be back shortly. Do you feel like eating anything?"

Clara nodded. "Just a bit, though."

Mrs. Boutwell disappeared for a short moment, returning with a plate of bread and oatmeal. She sat in the chair beside the bed and offered the plate to Clara. Clara took the slice of bread and butter off the plate and took a bite, careful not to drop any crumbs on herself or the baby.

"How do you feel?" Mrs. Boutwell asked, her voice soft.

"Very tired and sore."

"Those will fade in time. You did absolutely wonderful—even the doctor said so. He told me that he was quite surprised that you did so well, being as young and small as you are."

Clara smiled. "I was praying a lot."

"So was I," Mrs. Boutwell said. "As were the rest of the family. Your father is eager to meet his newest little grandson. If you feel up to it, he would like to visit tomorrow."

"Of course I'll feel up to it," Clara said. "I am always eager to see Father."

William arrived back just as Archie finished nursing and Mrs. Boutwell was settling Clara and the baby back down again. Clara knew that her mother would be staying overnight—for a week, if necessary. William had set her up in the spare room, just as they had arranged months ago.

Clara was thankful that her mother was there. Exhausted from the rather lengthy labor, she didn't awaken during the night when little Archie wanted to eat. But thanks to Mrs. Boutwell's sharp ears, the little fellow didn't skip a meal and Clara rested easily.

"A strong-willed little one," Mr. Boutwell noted, cradling his newest grandson in his arms and smiling at the baby's scrunched face. "Much like his mother."

Clara smiled, gazing down at her folded hands and feeling heat spread over her face.

Mr. Boutwell crossed the room and laid the baby in his mama's arms, pressing Clara's head gently against his chest and kissing her. "I wouldn't have it any other way," he whispered, "and I know that you won't, either."

Clara looked at Archie's sweet little face and grinned. She could hardly believe that he was truly hers.

Each of her sisters visited her that Sunday. They all said that Archie was a handsome baby for one so young, and Clara had to agree. All babies were beautiful, of course, but Archie really was particularly handsome and not just to her eyes.

The Mitchells also visited. Clara thought that William might just burst with pride as he showed Archie off to his grandpa and uncle Hamilton.

Seventeen-year-old Hamilton was afraid to hold young Archie at first, but soon warmed up to the idea of being an uncle and held his tiny nephew. Mr. Mitchell was nearly bursting. Clara had a feeling that all of Chicago would know just how beautiful her son was before morning, if Mr. Mitchell had anything to do with it.

Mrs. Boutwell stayed with William and Clara for two weeks after Archie's birth. During that time, Clara and William celebrated their first wedding anniversary. It wasn't much of a celebration then, but William promised that they would have a larger celebration once Clara had fully recovered from Archie's delivery.

The first day on her own after Archie's birth, Clara felt that she managed quite well. Fitting his care around her typical household duties was not as difficult as she had expected, and Archie was a good baby. He slept when he was supposed to and was otherwise happy…so long as Clara could change his diaper fast enough and would sit down to nurse him the moment he was ready. If she didn't, he made sure everyone knew that she was not properly doing her job.

Clara kept him in bed with her and William at night. It was far easier to feed him when he was already beside her rather than if he were in his cradle. And besides, she enjoyed having him close to her. William seemed to enjoy it as well, and sometimes, Clara would lay Archie between them so that they could both watch his little chest rise and fall with each breath.

"I can't believe he's ours," William said on one such night, his head on the pillow, eyes fixed on his little son. "It is amazing that God would trust us to care for and raise this little person. Why us? What did we do to deserve him?"

Clara smiled. William's eyes sparkled in the moonlight as he watched Archie, and Clara could see the faint lines of concentration on his forehead.

Reaching across the cool sheets, Clara slid her hand inside William's.

"I don't know why." She had been wondering the same thing herself. "God has blessed us immeasurably."

Chapter 18

Time went by fast after Archie was born. Before Clara could blink, summer was upon them in all its power yet again. Archie was four months old, and very active for one so young. Clara had her hands more than full keeping him entertained.

In July, Emma delivered a sweet baby girl whom she and Wesley named Hazel. Maud, not quite two years old, was puzzled about the little stranger who had invaded her life and was not happy that the new baby took so much of her mama away from her.

Life settled into a fairly normal schedule for Clara and William. Every morning, while Archie slept, the two of them arose and Clara prepared breakfast as quickly as she could, giving them time together in the Word before William left for the day. When he arrived home near suppertime, Clara greeted him with an enthusiastic kiss and excited smile. He would lift her off the floor and spin her around, similarly to how he did the day that Clara passed the teacher's exam almost two years ago. Then, he would look for the baby, and, should he find him sleeping, he would softly kiss the little forehead, or should he be awake, he would toss him into the air and caress him like the precious treasure that he was.

To Clara's relief, William only had bouts of asthma when the weather was particularly cold or hot. It relieved her to know the reason behind the attacks and not be fumbling for answers about why they continued to happen.

One chilly Sunday, soon after Thanksgiving, the family was gathered at the Boutwell's home. Voices of the children in the parlor filtered into the dining room. The peaceful chatter was interrupted when Katie set her glass down on the table with a rather unladylike *clunk*. Clara watched as she and Frank exchanged a glance, and Frank nodded. Something was going on.

"We wanted to tell you some news," Katie said, her eyes flashing. But behind that flash, there was a spark of sadness. "We're expecting again—"

She didn't get any further than that before the dining room exploded with laughter, well-wishes, and clapping. Katie smiled, but her voice dulled as she went on.

"And after much prayer and consideration, we've decided to move out to Washington territory, where Frank's family is."

Clara's heart stopped. Katie was moving? Leaving? All the way to Washington?

Silence reigned in the dining room.

Katie went on. "We'll take the train out. Frank's family already has a big homestead for us with lots of land to farm, so we won't be alone. The homestead is near Spokane—one of the biggest cities in the territory."

After several seconds, Clara found her voice. "When are you leaving?"

"The second week of February."

Two months. Two months, and her sister was leaving for good. They wouldn't see her again; Washington was too far away to make visits.

The morning of Clara's nineteenth birthday, she awoke from a frightening dream to the winter sun shining in the window. Her breath came in short pants, her forehead damp.

Glancing to one side, Clara felt more than saw Archie's warm body as he slept against her. Turning to the other side, her eyes focused on William. He was facing her, eyes closed, snoring softly. His short-cropped blonde hair shimmered gold in the sunlight.

Remnants of the dream still flitting about in her mind, Clara groped around for William's hand under the quilt. Limp as it was, she slid her hand into it. Her heartbeat slowed just by the comfort of touch. He really was here…he was alive. Asthma hadn't taken his life, as it had in her dream.

Clara startled when she felt his fingers intertwining with hers, fearing that she had awakened him. But no…another look at his face told her that he was still sound asleep. A small smile grew on her lips and her chest warmed. How was it that even in sleep, he knew to squeeze her hand so?

Within a few minutes, William's eyes began to open and he shifted positions. His eyes settled on Clara.

"Good morning, Darlin'," he whispered. "Happy birthday."

Clara tried to reply but, no words would pass through her tight throat. His smile melted into a concerned frown.

"What are these for?" He reached a hand up and brushed her wet cheek.

Clara brought her own hand up and rubbed her face. She hadn't realized that she was crying. "Nothing," she said quickly. "Only a frightening dream."

"Are you all right?" William asked with meaning, squeezing Clara's hand and pressing it to his chest. She hadn't kept her horrid dreams a secret from him.

Nodding, she took a deep breath and forced a smile. Every few months, the dream would make a terrifying appearance. "I will be."

210

Because it was Saturday and William could stay home, there was no need to rush to get breakfast. Clara had no desire to get out of bed.

The fire in the stove had been banked last night, causing the bedroom and the kitchen to be cold. Clara didn't want to get up and liven it, and apparently, neither did William. He laid on his back, eyes closed, still clasping Clara's hand in his. His thumb rubbed back and forth over her knuckles in a soothing, calming motion.

"I don't want to build up the fire," William said after a little while, confirming Clara's thoughts. His eyes were still closed and a faint smile played at his lips.

"It's not going to get any warmer in here without one," Clara teased softly. "And if I move, Archie will wake up." It was a pathetic excuse, she well knew, but it made William chuckle.

Within a few minutes, Archie began to wiggle. As soon as he lifted his head and grunted sleepily, Clara pulled him over her body and settled him to where he could nurse. William grasped Archie's little foot under the quilts and played with it.

Archie hadn't slept in the big bed with them since he was a very little baby. Normally, he slept in the cradle at Clara's side. But because the weather had grown so cold, she wanted him close to her.

A shiver from Archie made Clara's heart catch in her throat. Had the baby gotten too cold anyway? Perhaps the quilts hadn't been covering him completely.

"Are his feet cold?" Clara asked William, groping around for Archie's tiny hand.

"No...they're toasty warm."

His little hand and fingers were perfectly warm, as well. She pulled the eight-month-old's body closer to hers and rubbed his back, wondering why he had trembled so. He wasn't feverish nor chilled. Perhaps it had simply been a shuddering sigh. Clara willed her heartbeat to return to its normal pace.

"If you build up the fire, I'll make pancakes for breakfast."

William chuckled. "How can I say no to that?"

In a flash, he jumped out of bed and sprinted into the kitchen. Clara heard a bit of clambering, and the door of the stove squeaked twice. Then, William bolted into the bedroom and dived under the quilts, shivering.

"Those p-pancakes had better h-have sugar in th-th-them."

Saying good-bye to Katie, Frank, and the children was one of the most difficult things Clara had ever done. She and Katie promised to write to one another, but Clara still was worried. As exciting as it was and as much as she wanted to go west herself, so many things could go wrong. And with Katie's baby on the way...

Frank promised that they would be living near his family, which he had quite a lot of, when they arrived in

Spokane. Katie wouldn't be alone when it came time to deliver.

Surprisingly, Katie didn't appear frightened in the least about any part of the move. In fact, she was excited.

Was her sister crazy? Didn't she know all the problems that pioneer families could have?

But then again, hadn't Katie been the first one to tell Clara about the Oregon trail and the beautiful Pacific Northwest when they were both little girls? Hiding underneath a proper lady was an enthusiastic adventurer. Clara only hoped that the enthusiasm wouldn't wear off too quickly.

Archie grew and grew, and his personality was exactly as his Grandpa Boutwell had predicted: strong-willed, just like his mama. Clara certainly had her hands full with him. There were a few times when she got one of William's belts and tied the toddler to his chair so she could have a few moments rest.

Even as an active sixteen-month-old, Archie was surprisingly happy being rocked in the chair. If he was particularly cranky or obstinate, Clara would sit in the rocker with him and read aloud from whichever book she was reading. Then, and only then, Archie would sit perfectly still, oftentimes sucking his thumb as he cuddled into Clara.

For the most part, Archie was a happy little boy. Only around eighteen months of age—near Clara's

213

twentieth birthday—did he really begin testing the limits. A few times, if Clara couldn't get his breakfast fast enough, Archie would get it for himself. So, scaling the drawers, he opened the bread cupboard and helped himself to various breads and an occasional muffin.

He also enjoyed exploring Clara's sewing basket. She watched him from behind the kitchen door as he thoroughly emptied the basket, throwing the contents of it onto the floor of the sitting room. It was difficult for Clara to do nothing as he played with the sharp pins, but her mother had said that natural consequences were oftentimes better than punishments.

Soon enough, Archie stuck himself hard with a pin and came running to Clara, crying and holding up his bleeding finger. Though it cut Clara's heart to do so, she gently chided him for playing in the forbidden sewing basket, before administering a comforting hug and kiss. His little baby eyes held sorrowful remorse, and, from that day forward, he regarded the sewing basket quite warily.

Another year-and-a-half passed swiftly by. Archie was now a bouncing, tumbling three-year-old and the joy of his parent's lives. His excited, never-ending baby chatter warmed Clara's heart, and she could see by the softness on William's face that he thought the world of his little son.

The young McDonalds were overjoyed to have another little stranger join their family. This child was also a boy, born just three weeks after Clara's twenty-first birthday. She and William decided to name him after Clara's father—Newton James.

Baby Newton was quite the opposite of his older brother. He was quiet and snuggly. Getting him to cry after birth proved to be quite the challenge. Newton was a perfectly content and quiet baby, which was a welcome change for Clara after boisterous Archie.

Archie adored his new baby brother and showed himself to be protective of the little one. Clara was immensely thankful; she had feared that Archie would resent his little brother, as Maud had when Hazel was born.

William's asthma steadily grew worse over the next two years. Clara's hands grew strong from massaging his neck and back during the dreadful attacks, and she became accustomed to the smell of Potter's herbal smoke. Potter's came in a small tin, and when William's asthma worsened to the point that he nearly fainted, Clara would make a fingertip sized pile of the loose, dry herbs on an old plate and light it with a match. The herbs would burn, creating a potent-smelling smoke that never failed to stop an asthma attack in its tracks and allowed William to breathe more freely.

Though it was confusing to Clara how inhaling such strong smoke could help one's lungs, it certainly did help William's.

Archie and Newton continued to grow into beautiful children. Archie was very much the leader, oftentimes getting himself and Newton into dreadful scrapes. And Newton—quiet, gentle Newton—was always ready for a hug or kiss from his parents or grandparents or aunts or uncles. He could sit on someone's lap for hours at a time.

Both of the boy's favorite activities was being read to. Clara would sit in the rocker with them on her lap as she read various books. She hoped that by doing so, she could instill a love of reading upon her children, as her mother had done with her.

Around Thanksgiving time of the year 1891, William's asthma had become so acute that he was beginning to lose weight, color, and appetite. He had an attack at least twice a week, if not more. It pained Clara to see her once strong and healthy husband declining into a state of invalidism.

She was completely at a loss of what to do. Mrs. Mitchell, who also was gravely concerned about her son's health, was out of ideas. Clara had begged William to see a specialist, which he consented to, but the only recommendations the doctor could give was to see a different doctor, who recommended another doctor, and again and again…

As the months wore on, Clara became increasingly concerned as William continued to decline at a rapid pace. Her ever-present fear of losing him to asthma became a far-too-real possibility. Some nights, Clara would lie in bed, watching his wan, sunken face in the darkness, clasping his cold hand in hers and praying that the Lord would spare his life.

I don't know what I would do without him, God.

A young widow with two small children, in the great city of Chicago? What could she do?

Two weeks before her and William's sixth wedding anniversary, Clara took William to see another lung specialist. It cost a very pretty penny to see this particular doctor, but Clara knew that her husband was dying and was willing to do anything in her power to save him.

She had taken the boys to stay with her parents during William's appointment, as she wanted to have the freedom to pay attention to every word without the little boys being there to pull her away.

After a lengthy clinical exam of William, the elderly doctor crossed his arms and sighed. Clara felt William's hold on her hand tighten.

"I will not lie to you, Mr. McDonald," the doctor said. "You are a very sick man. There isn't anything I can do for you. As sorry as I am to say this," the doctor glanced quickly at Clara, "I estimate that you have two, or possibly three months to live."

Clara's heart stopped, drying her mouth and freezing her fingers. Breathing seemed senseless to her shocked brain.

Three months?

The shock was entirely beyond tears. Clara wanted to cry, but she simply could not. Bile rose in her throat. *Three months.*

How could doctors, even specialists such as this man, estimate such morbid matters?

The doctor spoke again. "The only thing I can recommend is that you get away from the city. If you have any hopes of living to see your thirtieth birthday, you must get far, far away from Chicago into a dense forest somewhere. Going north into Michigan is an option, but I would strongly recommend that you go west. As far west as you can manage. The air is far cleaner there than it is here, and I have heard that it has remarkable effects on those with weak constitutions."

Chapter 19

Clara wasn't sure when or how she and William arrived back home. She felt completely numb, desperately wishing that tears would come and relieve the pressure building in her chest.

Once inside the privacy of their own home, Clara could think a bit more clearly and was able to gather her frazzled thoughts.

"Three months!" she finally burst, as William helped her out of her coat. She gazed up into his face. It was pallid and emotionless.

William took her by the hand and led her to the sofa, pulling her down beside him. His breathing was labored, but steady. Looking into his dull blue eyes once again, Clara's tears burst forth. There used to be a fiery spark in those eyes.

She cried and cried, resting her head on William's chest and holding his neck. He said nothing, but from the way his chest heaved Clara thought that he might be crying, too. Shudders attacked Clara, ravaging through her body until she was shaking as violently as if she were feverish. William's arm was securely around her, pressing her to him with a strength Clara didn't know he possessed anymore. Without a doubt, the thought that lingered in William's head was the same as the one in hers. *What are we going to do?*

Hours must have past. The next time Clara looked up, it was dark outside and a knock was sounding on the door.

The boys.

In her shock, she had forgotten about them entirely. Unwinding her arms from William's neck, she rose to answer the door.

Her mother and father stood there, each with a boy in their arms. Smiles resounded on all four faces, but both Mr. and Mrs. Boutwell paled when they saw Clara.

"Did you have fun with Grandma and Grandpa?" Clara asked in as steady a voice as she could manage, reaching for cuddly Newton. The toddler nodded and laid his head on Clara's shoulder, while Archie jumped here and there, telling of everything they had done that afternoon.

When Archie had bounced out of earshot, Mrs. Boutwell put an arm about her daughter's waist and pulled her close. "It isn't good news?" she questioned softly.

Clara shook her head slowly, running the back of her hand across her eyes. Her father's shoulders visibly slumped and his face grew even paler, and her mother squeezed her tighter.

A firm wedge rose in Clara's throat. For a moment, she was afraid that she might vomit.

"What are we having for supper, Mama?" Archie questioned, coming back into the entryway and grasping the folds of Clara's dress.

"Supper." Clara blinked. "I forgot about supper." What could she give the boys to eat? She was not hungry in the least, and it was doubtful that William was, either.

Newton began fussing a little and tugging at her bodice.

"I'll fix something for supper, Darling," Mrs. Boutwell said. "You can tend to Newton and try to relax."

Clara nodded numbly. Take care of Newton. She could do that. Going into the bedroom, Clara set pillows behind her and leaned against the headboard, cuddling Newton and kissing his downy head as he nursed.

She could hear her father playing with Archie in the sitting room and pots clanging about in the kitchen. Occasionally, William's voice interjected something into Archie and Mr. Boutwell's play. But his tone—it hardly sounded like William. Such dejection and despair

Clara heard—nothing like the man she had known for the past six years.

It pained Clara dearly to hear William speak, yet she savored every word, wondering if it would be one of his last. Tears welled in her eyes once again and her hands trembled.

Dear God, spare his life!

Mrs. Boutwell prepared a simple, yet nourishing meal, which Archie scarfed down easily. Newton, quite obviously sensing that not all was well in his world, was clingy and refused to be set down. Clara forced herself to eat a few bites of the stew, though it made her nauseous. She noticed that William also forced down spoonful after spoonful.

Clara's parents stayed to clean up after supper, and wouldn't listen when she said that she could finish.

Archie began to eye the adults in a curious, half-frightened manner. Clara attempted to wear a smile, trying assuring her small sons that everything would be all right, but it was in vain. Everything *wasn't* all right.

Newton put up quite a fuss when it was bedtime, and Archie wasn't his typical agreeable self, either. In the end, Clara and her mother put both boys in their parent's bed. With each other for company, the little boys were soon sound asleep.

When all four adults gathered in the living room, Mrs. Boutwell finally asked what the doctor had said.

Clara struggled to find the necessary words, but none would come. A hard lump had caught in her throat and refused to leave.

But she didn't need to speak…William was doing it for her. He briefly explained all that the doctor had told them without a quaver in his voice. How did he do it? Her emotions were all upside-down and backwards.

Mrs. Boutwell's breath caught when William mentioned the part about having only three months to live. Clara was having a difficult time keeping her tears from flooding again.

"Would you be willing to go out west?" Mr. Boutwell asked when William finished.

He nodded assuredly. "I'm willing to do anything."

Clara saw tears in her mother's eyes, and her father was pressing clasped hands to his lips as he often did when nervous.

"If I arranged for you to go out to Spokane to be with Katie and Frank, would you go?" Mr. Boutwell's question was weighty and full of meaning, and his eyes were steely.

"Absolutely."

"Even if it meant leaving Clara and the boys here?"

William faltered, and Clara's throat constricted. If William only had three months to live, she wanted to be with him the entire time! Was her father insane?

William's grasp on her shoulders tightened, and he firmly nodded. "Even if it meant leaving them behind."

Clara opened her mouth to protest, but Mr. Boutwell held up his hand.

"Listen, Clara. It would be foolish for you to go with your husband now. You have no place to live out there. It is far easier for a single person to find a roof to put over their head than four people, much less small children. I can easily arrange for William to go to Spokane, and, if you decide that you like it there," Mr. Boutwell glanced meaningfully at William, "Clara and the children can come later. Are you willing?"

William nodded, but Clara hesitated. *She* wasn't willing! There was no way she would be separated from him during what could be the last months of his life.

But what other option did they have? They couldn't afford four train fares at the moment, nor would it be wise to go to a new city and have no place to stay. William could either stay here and die, or go west without them and *possibly* recover.

Clara managed a short nod as well. If it might save William's life, she could manage. She would manage. She had no other choice.

Before the week was over, Mr. Boutwell had purchased a train ticket and placed it in William's care. He also found a large carpetbag for William's belongings, which Clara dutifully packed full of clothing and photos and notes, as well as a good many tears.

A letter had been sent to Katie and Frank, telling them that William was to be arriving around the twenty-second of March—just three days before Clara and William's anniversary. No one expected the letter to travel much faster than William himself, so William didn't anticipate that anyone would be waiting at the station to meet him.

A friend of Clara's from church, who had been visited the west several years prior, recommended that William take something of value along with him to sell in the case of an emergency. The young McDonald's didn't have many valuable items that would fit in William's bag. The only thing that would work was a silver tableware set that had been a wedding gift. Clara had only used it a handful of times, and though she desperately wanted to keep the silverware, William's well-being while in Spokane was far more important. Multiple doctor visits had stripped them of almost every penny they owned.

Late one night, after the boys were in bed, William pulled the worn leather bank-book from the shelf and set it in front of Clara. He sat on the opposite side of the table and flipped the book open.

"Even with all the doctor visits, we aren't in debt."

Clara nodded slowly.

"But we don't have any money left. There will be a small pension from the militia, but it isn't much."

"We'll be all right." Clara swallowed, pasting on a brave face. "I'm still a certified teacher. I can get a job."

"No!" William's voice rang through the house, and Clara jumped a little. He cleared his throat. "No." It was much softer this time. "I don't want you to work. If you ever need help, my parents have more than enough funds. They are, and forever will be, happy to help in any way."

His eyes bored through hers. Clara fought to keep the tears away.

"Clara, promise me that you won't go back to work while the boys are young. No matter what happens. Promise that you would ask my parents for help first."

Her brows knitted and her eyes fell to the table. She didn't want to be a beggar. She would far rather work than ask family members for money.

His thin hand clasped over hers and tugged gently, pulling her eyes upwards.

"For the boys' sake, Clara, please stay home with them."

His voice pleaded, but not as much as his eyes did. She nodded slowly.

For the sake of their children, she could swallow her pride. Though hopefully, the western air would cure William, and she wouldn't have to.

Clara couldn't keep the tears from falling as William hugged both of the children goodbye at the train station. Though neither Archie or Newton understood exactly what was happening, they clung to their father's neck, no doubt sensing that something terrible was going on. After several minutes of consoling words, William set both boys on their feet and Mrs. Boutwell took their hands, distracting their attention away from their parents.

Reaching up, Clara clasped her hands behind William's neck and buried her face in his chest. He held her tightly against him, lightly kissing her hair and forehead. Clara's heart burned, sending daggers of pain through her gut and tears leaking from her eyes.

He's leaving. She hadn't ever been separated from William for more than an ordinary work day. And even then, he was nearby. But this—all the way to Washington—it was such a long way. And in his feeble condition, with no promise of recovery…

"You'll be all right." William stroked her hair. "I'll send for you as soon as I get a house."

"The boys and I will be fine," Clara said into William's shirt. "I'm worried about you."

"Don't be." William squeezed her tighter. "The Lord is in control. Take care of yourself and the boys. Don't make yourself sick because of me."

Clara straightened and looked into William's face, nodding and forcing a smile. "I'll be praying for you."

William kissed Clara's lips, then released her and stepped aboard the train.

The train lurched forward, and Clara's stomach lurched with it. She waved and smiled through her tears as the enormous beast picked up speed and carried her husband off. Far off…all the way to Washington.

With William gone, the days felt long and empty. There was a steady stream of friends and family to help and comfort Clara, and she tried to be pleasant to them, but it did little good. The only times she felt at peace was while praying or reading her Bible, when she was able to focus on the Lord instead of her beloved husband, a thousand miles away, who could very possibly die without her seeing him again.

A week after William left, Clara received a wire from Spokane. It was dated March twenty-fourth.

ARRIVED SAFELY STOP ASTHMA LITTLE BETTER STOP LOVE AND MISS YOU STOP WILLIAM

For a ten-word limit, William had done quite well. The 'asthma little better' part concerned Clara greatly. Did it mean that his asthma was not better or was a little bit better? Clara sent a five-word wire back, as she had no money for anything more.

MISS YOU STOP PRAYING LOTS STOP CLARA

"Mama, why doesn't Father come home?"

Clara's needle stabbed her finger, causing her to gasp and wring her hand. Archie sat on the floor at her feet, his upturned blue eyes full of question. His eyes were even bluer than William's.

William.

"He can't, Darling." Clara swallowed. "He's with Uncle Frank and Aunt Katie. Remember?"

Newton shuffled around his blocks, scooting closer to Clara. "'Tan we go see him?"

She shook her head. "He's a long way away from here."

"Is he coming back?" Archie pressed both chubby hands on her knee.

"I'm not sure."

They'd had this conversation before. Trying to explain the situation to a five and two-year-old was challenging.

The boys went back to their blocks, and Clara sucked on her bleeding finger. It wouldn't do to get blood on Newton's trousers.

Several quiet minutes passed. Then, Archie's voice came again, soft and hesitant. "Does Father still love us?"

Clara dropped the mending to her lap before she could stick herself again. Her heart pounded, and her throat swelled to see Archie's brimming eyes.

"Oh, Baby, of course he does." She tossed her sewing off to the side and pulled Archie into her lap. His head rested against her shoulder, arms twined around her neck. She closed her own tearing eyes and rocked him side to side, rubbing his back as it hitched with sobs.

How could Archie even doubt his father's love? But, of course, the five-year-old couldn't see the deep pain in William's eyes as they said good-bye at the station. He didn't know that William would rather die slowly in Chicago just to be with them than to leave with hopes of possibly recovery.

Newton wiggled up to the space beside Clara, looking about ready to burst into tears himself. She pressed him to her, dropping kisses on his head.

God, for their sakes, please restore William's health!

Clara spent much time in prayer, asking the Lord for His peace and asking Him to protect William from the wretched disease that poisoned his body. Each day she waited for word from William. Just a short letter—a small telegram even!—would be welcome. If there were only a faster and more sure way of communicating long distances.

It was three weeks before another wire came from Spokane. Clara tore the envelope from the messenger boy and ripped into the paper.

WITH NEWELLS STOP READY FOR YOU TO COME STOP WIRE ARRIVAL DATE

Clara read the message again and again. A frustrated scream welled in her throat. Why didn't he say anything about his asthma? Was he asking her to come just so that they could be there when he died?

Mr. Boutwell took care of purchasing Clara's ticket west. He also purchased a large trunk for Clara and the boys' belongings.

It was a beautiful trunk. The green canvas cover was accented by strong, brown-leather rims and straps, connected with brass corners and buckles. Clara carefully packed her dresses, aprons, quilts, the boys' clothes, the baby clothes she hoped she would need again…and amidst the clothing, she packed fragile items such as their dish set and mantle clock.

She was adamant that the baby cradle, rocking chair, and desk be shipped to Spokane with them, so her father arranged for that. Clara's best friend, Martha, had a brother and sister-in-law who lived in St. Paul, where the train bearing Clara and the children would be stopping, forcing them to stay the night and transfer trains. Martha arranged for Clara and the boys to spend the night with them.

The night before Clara and the boys were to depart, she lay in bed, awaiting sleep, staring into the darkness. Her heart fluttered as it dawned that she was really, truly, going west. Granted, this was not the way she thought it would ever happen, but here she was.

She couldn't help but shed a few tears over the thought of completely uprooting her life and moving into the wild west, though Katie's letters had fairly convinced Clara that the west was not as wild as she had hoped.

What condition would they find William in? Had he sent for her only because he didn't want to die all alone in a strange place?

Nightmares taunted Clara all night long. The graveyard, the slender coffin, the little boys pressed against her side, Newton tugging at her hand with tears running down his little face…

She jumped violently, shaking the bed. The sun shone through the windows, making her blink.

"Mama!"

Newton's desperate voice at her side made her heart leap again. He pulled at her hand, crying softly. How long had he stood there, trying to wake her up?

"Oh, Darling." Clara reached down and pulled him into bed beside her. He nuzzled into her chest, rubbing a soft hand up and down her cheek. "I'm sorry, Baby."

Lingering tears dripped to the pillow, but the aching in her throat eased. As much as she wanted to, giving up wasn't an option. With or without William, the boys needed her. If not for herself, she had to remain strong for them.

The train didn't leave until five o'clock in the afternoon, and the morning dragged on even longer than the night had. Clara scurried here and there, hoping that she hadn't forgotten anything. Her head pounded terribly, but it wasn't just from a lack of sleep. Nauseous waves had taunted her all day. Headaches and nausea were her typical signs of pregnancy, but she pushed the thought away with a vengeance. Now was *not* a good time for a baby.

Her parents arrived early to help her finish packing and keep the boys out of trouble. Their presence helped soothe her frazzled emotions.

The entire family, including the Mitchells, were at the station to see Clara off. She bravely contained her tears and managed to speak in a smooth, even tone, but inside, her heart was being ripped in two. Terrified, lonely, frightened...many doubts and fears began creeping into her head and refused to be pushed out.

Clara hugged her mother the longest. Her dear, darling mother, who had faithfully washed and styled Clara's hair almost every day since the moment she was born. The woman who had taught her everything about keeping a household and being a good wife and raising children. What would she do without her mother just around the corner to ask questions?

Chapter 20

Clara squinted her eyes to keep the tears from leaking out. For the boys' sake, she must remain composed. This trip would be traumatic enough for them without their mother having a nervous breakdown.

"You can do this," Mrs. Boutwell whispered into Clara's ear. "You can do this for your husband. I know you can stay strong."

Pulling away, Clara saw tears in her mother's eyes, yet a smile graced her lips.

"We love you and are always praying for you."

Clara nodded, drawing a deep, shuddering breath. Prayer and reliance on the Lord was the only thing that could relieve the pain.

The trunk and large luggage had been stowed away in the boxcar, leaving Clara with only a small carpet bag of necessities to tote around. Newton was especially clingy. She held him on her hip, grasping the carpetbag with the same hand, and keeping a tight hold on Archie with the other.

She put on a brave smile for her family, then turned and boarded the train, fighting the swelling in her throat. She handed the tickets to the conductor and walked aboard the train.

She chose a seat so that they could see their family, still standing on the platform. Archie waved and waved, and Clara lifted her hand in salutation as well. Bless them all, they were smiling and waving as if it were a homecoming, instead of what it truly was…a far away, long departure, possibly for the remainder of their lives.

Clara watched the figures on the platform until they were too small to see. Then, after a silent prayer for peace and strength, she turned her gaze to Archie and watched as his head swiveled around and around, surveying the finery of the first-class car Mr. Mitchell had helped to pay for. The five-year-old seemed at a loss of words…something Clara never deemed possible.

Newton sat contentedly on Clara's lap, sucking his thumb and watching the scenery out the window. Clara watched, too, as Chicago began to fade into nothingness and they rattled along the Illinois plains.

Exhausted from the emotions flying about in her and a significant lack of sleep, she felt the tense muscles in her back relaxing and her headache beginning to ease. The soothing rattle and clacking of the train was a beautiful melody to Clara's ears.

"Mama."

Something softly poked Clara's cheek.

"Mama." The baby voice was whispered and pleading, and a gentle pressure was felt on her cheek again.

Opening her eyes, Clara saw that it was dark in the car except for two glowing lanterns on either end. The sun must have set long ago. How long had she slept?

"Mama, p'ease."

Looking down, Clara saw little Newton gazing at her with soft, pleading eyes. He gently pulled at the front of her dress.

Clara glanced around at the other passengers. She supposed that it was far from proper to nurse one's child in the middle of a first-class car such as this, but she didn't have much of a choice. And besides, most of the passengers were dozing in their booths.

Bending down and pulling a small blanket from the bag at her feet, Clara threw it over her shoulder and covered Newton with it, then proceeded to unbutton the front of her dress.

When Newton was settled, Clara suddenly realized that Archie was no longer in the seat across from her. Her heart stopped. Where could the child have gone?

A soft snore from her side whipped Clara's head down to the velvet seat, where Archie lay, curled like an infant. He had kicked his shoes off and nearly had his head in Clara's lap. She supposed that he would have if Newton weren't already occupying it.

Clara reached down and pulled a second blanket from the bag, spreading it over Archie. It was quite chilly and drafty in the car, and she didn't want the boys catching a cold.

To her surprise, both little boys slept soundly until sunrise. Clara herself slept fitfully, as it would be improper for her to lie down across the seats as the boys were doing. Her head continued to loll forward or to the side, making it bump into the window of the car.

In the morning, Clara brought out some of the food her mother had packed. She was about to begin eating, but Archie surprised her with a rather loud, "Aren't we going to pray?"

Clara stopped her hand midair. "Yes, I suppose we should." It seemed rather strange to pray out loud while on a train, but Archie was right—God certainly didn't care where they were.

Taking the boys' hands, Clara closed her eyes and bowed her head. "Dear Lord, thank You for keeping us safe on our journey thus far. Please be with William— Father—and heal him of his asthma. Thank You for this food. Amen."

Clara glanced around at the other passengers in the car, but to her surprise, no one was paying them the slightest bit of attention. She chuckled to herself. What exactly had she expected?

Even being confined as they were, Clara was so proud of the boys and their behavior. Not once did either of them have a fit about needing to stay in the rather small booth. They contentedly played with the few toys Clara had thrown in her carpet bag and sat patiently while she read to them.

Thankfully, Clara's nausea wasn't as terrible as she had feared it would be, though she did have to run to the lavatory twice.

Why now, God? The thought of another child excited her, but now wasn't exactly the best time for one.

Once the train arrived in St. Paul and the passengers exited, Clara was tapped on the shoulder by a smiling, dark-headed woman. She didn't appear much older than Clara herself.

"Clara McDonald?" she asked, her voice sweet and excited.

Clara nodded and smiled.

"I'm Ida Porter, Martha's friend. And this is my husband, Carter."

"Pleased to meet you," Clara said, holding out her hand.

"The pleasure is ours," Mrs. Porter said. "If you give Carter your luggage tickets, he will gather your things and meet us at the hack."

Clara dug into her carpet bag and pulled out three tickets. "I warn you, we have some odd luggage," she
239

said, blushing as she remembered the baby cradle, rocking chair, and desk.

Mr. Porter took the tickets from Clara's hand with a grin. He tipped his hat and set off to the boxcar.

It was a short distance to the hack the Porters had hired. The driver helped the ladies in, handing the little boys up after them. Archie wore a look of amazement on his face and he gingerly touched the fine velvet of the deeply padded seats. Newton, on the other hand, clung to Clara, surveying his surroundings from a secure place inside his mother's arm.

Clara gazed out the hack's window into the bustling St. Paul street. It reminded her very much of Chicago. A lump arose in her throat.

Chicago. Mother, Father, Emma, and Esther—

Mrs. Porter was looking at her with a caring, perplexed smile.

"Pardon me," Clara said. "My mind was wandering."

"No problem." Mrs. Porter smiled kindly. "I was asking how your trip has been thus far."

"Very nice," Clara said, nodding. "My parents and friends did all of the hard work for me. All I've needed to do is pack and keep the boys with me."

"I wanted you to know that we've been praying for you and your husband ever since Martha first told us about your situation. And our prayers will continue."

"There's the trunk!" Archie pointed, diffusing the situation before Clara dissolved into a puddle of tears.

Her emotions seemed to be taking high mountains and deep valleys, not pausing in between. *Pull yourself together!*

Clara followed Archie's finger and saw the green trunk being carried between two men, one of which was Mr. Porter. Behind them were three more men carrying the rocker, cradle, and desk. Clara blushed.

"What a lovely cradle," Mrs. Porter breathed. Clara wasn't entirely sure how she could see it in the dim twilight. "And that rocker. My goodness, they are stunning."

Clara smiled out the window, the memory of when William first brought those items into their home flooding her mind. "I simply couldn't leave them behind," she said with embarrassment. Bringing a rocker, cradle, and desk out west, especially when traveling by train, was not a normal or typical thing to do.

The following day at noon, Mr. and Mrs. Porter took Clara and the boys back to the station to catch their next train. In the few hours they had spent together, Clara had found a kindred spirit in Ida Porter and deeply regretted that they lived so far apart.

For the next two nights, Clara and the boys lived in another small booth. The boys did so well, as Clara often told them. Not once did she have to discipline either of them for unruliness, for which she was exceedingly thankful.

It wasn't hard to see the difference in the landscape as the train carried them further and further west. The land grew flat, then mountainous, then flat again. Clara liked Montana the best. She wished that there was more time to look around while the train was stopped at a station. Something about the quaint, sleepy towns drew her in. Such a drastic difference from Chicago. But Clara rarely got off the train. She had heard far too many stories of passengers being left in little towns such as these because they failed to board again before it departed.

After another pass that led out of Montana, the train twisted and turned through the beautiful north Idaho mountains. Those eventually led into the Washington mountains, and soon there were more and more patches of flat land.

Clara began to see homesteads dotted along the land. Signs of civilization were getting thicker and thicker, until she saw bumps of what must be Spokane in the horizon. Her fear of the unknown was mingled with excitement as the train rolled into the station.

She was finally out west.

Clara and the boys stepped off the train onto a wet platform. The station wasn't much more than just a platform—nothing at all like the beautiful stations in

Chicago and St. Paul. According to what Clara had heard, the larger junction of the Northern Pacific Railway was further down the line.

Rain was coming down hard, and grey clouds spread as far as the eye could see.

"Ow!"

Clara jumped and stared at her little son at her side. He yanked his hand from hers and wrung it.

"Mama, you're squeezing me!"

"I'm sorry." The words came without conscious thought. Clara's eyes darted here and there, looking for a familiar face. Where was William? Frank, even? They had said that they would be here.

Two young fellows unloaded Clara's trunk and the furniture, setting them on the platform. Clara asked that they be taken under the roofed area, to protect them from the rain. Then the train whooshed out of the depot, tooting its whistle loudly.

There was no one around, just strangers, and not very many of them at that. Clara had expected Spokane to be a larger city. But this...this was barely a town.

"I'se cold, Mama," Newton said, a shiver going through his body, and he wrapped his arms around Clara's neck.

Clara blinked slowly and shook her head to clear her thoughts.

"Come here, Archie." She ushered the little boy towards the small roof covering and sat on the bench provided.

Where were the men? Her father had said that Frank would be meeting them with a hack! Clara's mind reeled. She had been promised that there would be someone to meet her at the depot. But where were they? Her father had specifically said in his telegram on what day Clara and the boys would be arriving. April twenty-eighth.

April twenty-eighth!

Panic seared Clara's chest. Today was the twenty-seventh. The train must have been faster than expected.

The cold, hardness of the bench seeped into her. What could they do? The boys would be getting hungry soon, as would she. Fishing around in her pocket, Clara pulled two coins out.

Twenty cents. That was all she had. The last of their funds. Every dime had been spent on doctor fees.

Oh, Lord, help me know what to do!

Clara replaced the coins and attempted to control her breathing. Whatever could she do with twenty cents? There was no conceivable way that it could buy a meal for the boys, much less for herself. And no one would be coming to fetch them until tomorrow.

What could she possibly do? She had heard of people sleeping in train depots, but not on a cold, spring night with two young children.

It wasn't long before darkness fell. The rain continued to pelt down steadily, making the platform slick. Her time was running out.

Chapter 21

A place to sleep—that's what they needed first. Clara took a deep breath and stood up, swinging Newton onto her hip.

"Where are we going, Mama?" Archie asked, trotting after her as they walked down the empty platform.

"Going to speak with the ticket agent," Clara said, holding her chin erect. She was smart. She could figure something out. Pushing open the door, Clara exhaled.

"Good afternoon, Ma'am," the ticket-man said with a bubbly smile. "What ken I do for ye?"

Clara managed a small smile back at the curly-headed, middle-aged man. His Scottish brogue reminded Clara of the one William sometimes slipped into when he was excited.

"Can you tell me the name of a quiet hotel near here?"

Archie perched his hands on the rather tall desk and pulled himself up, standing on his tiptoes. The ticket-man's eyes fell to Archie's big blue ones.

"The Commercial Hotel is a fine one," he said, returning his gaze to Clara. "Jest up the road a ways."

"Can I leave my luggage here until morning?" Clara questioned. "And may I bring it inside? Some of it is rather fragile."

The man didn't answer for a long moment, his eyes moving slowly from Clara's to Newton's to Archie's.

"'Course, 'course!" he exclaimed. "Will ye be needin' help?"

"I would appreciate it." She set Newton on his feet. "Stay with your brother, Newton. Mama will be right back."

Newton took Archie's hand and nodded solemnly, and Clara followed the ticket-man back out the door. She dragged the rocker inside while the man took the cradle and desk. She took steps to help him bring the trunk in, but his voice stopped her.

"Nay, nay. I can fetch the trunk. Can't have ye harming yerself, Dear." The man grinned at her as he stepped out the door.

Once the trunk was safely inside, the man stepped behind his desk once again. "Might I have a name so thet when ye wish to fetch yer things, ye won't be questioned if I ain't here?"

"Certainly. It's McDonald. Clara McDonald."

The man scribbled that onto a slip of paper, then studied it for a long moment.

"McDonald, is it?" he asked. His eyes met Clara's. "Do ye happen to be related to a young lad by the name of William? Rather tall, with blonde hair and blue eyes."

Clara's heart leapt in her throat. "Yes!" she cried. "He is my husband. Have you seen him?"

"I believe I have…'bout three weeks ago, it was. He was wantin' a ticket to Chicago. Had only been here a week and said he was so homesick and was a' headin' home." The man chuckled to himself. "I suggested that he stay awhile longer…I thought he might turn out likin' it here. 'Parently he did, as I havn't seen hide nor hair of him since."

Clara's heart pounded. She closed her eyes for a moment and swallowed. "How did he look when you saw him? Meaning…was he sickly-looking at all?"

The man furrowed his brow and was silent for a long moment. "Nay, I don't believe he was. He looked perfectly healthy to me. A bit sad, but seein' as what he had left, I cain't say that I'd blame him." He winked.

Hope soared in her chest. William was all right. Or, he had been, three weeks ago. Surely, if he had survived the trip out, he would still be just fine now.

"Thank you for your assistance," she said to the ticket-man. "We will be back tomorrow to fetch the luggage."

He nodded and waved to the boys.

Taking Newton's hand in hers and bidding Archie to follow her, they set out into the dark wetness of Spokane.

It didn't take them long to get to the Commercial Hotel, which turned out to be far more grand than Clara had hoped. She gazed upwards at the four story building, feeling as if it were crushing her.

No. She wouldn't let this defeat her. Clara marched herself inside the lobby, dripping wet.

"May I speak with the manager?"

The young lobbyist nodded and left down a long hallway. Within moments, a sharply-dressed older man came from a back room. Clara feared that he would turn his nose up at her and the boys, dripping as they were on the pretty rug, but he did not. Instead, he extended his hand and smiled.

"Is there something I can do for you?" he asked, eyes full of compassion.

As briefly as she could, but without sparing too much information, Clara explained her plight to the kindly manager. She asked if they might have a room and something to eat.

"You can keep my rings until my husband arrives to fetch us in the morning," Clara said, preceding to pull the rings off her fingers—the emerald engagement ring and ruby wedding band.

"I'm sure that won't be necessary," the manager said, holding his hand up. "Isaac." He turned to the lobbyist. "Please show this young woman to one of our large rooms, and see to it that she and the young fellows get a good meal in the dining hall."

The manager smiled at Clara. "If you need anything, please do not hesitate to speak to me."

Tears stung Clara's eyes. She hadn't expected this much kindness. Her voice cracked. "Thank you so very much."

"It's my pleasure." He took her hand and shook it lightly.

Isaac showed Clara to a room that was insanely large. It had two beds and a couch, as well as a vanity and water closet. Electric lights were mounted on the walls.

This is fit for a queen!

"The dining hall is located downstairs to the left of the lobby."

Clara voiced her thanks, and Isaac left.

Archie and Newton stared at the finery of the room in complete awe. Clara wasn't much better. This was one of the finest places she had ever seen, in little tiny Spokane! The room even had electric lights, which were incredibly rare in Chicago. It seemed rather ironic.

"Well, boys," Clara sighed, setting the carpetbag on the vanity. "Let us change into dry clothes, then we will go eat in the dining hall." She made a silly face as she said 'dining hall', making Archie giggle.

The meal proved itself to be outstanding. She wasn't sure if it was the chef's cooking abilities that made the roast beef and potatoes so delicious, or the fact that she and the boys had lived on sandwiches for the past four days.

Clara was far more tired than the little boys were and getting them ready for bed proved to be a challenge. Once she got them into one of the large beds, curled beside each other, it wasn't long before their little eyes closed and they breathed steadily.

Lying down in the second plush bed, Clara smiled to herself. It was as if she were lying on a cloud. Her eyes drifted shut, but her mind was far from quiet.

She fell into a shallow sleep, troubling thoughts tumbling around in her head. William had been killed in a train crash; no, a wagon crash, her father lay abed with a broken leg, her mother stood in the kitchen of their old home, calling to Clara for help…

Clara awoke with a start, jerking upright in bed. Sweat beads danced on her forehead, and her breath came in short pants. Would the nightmares ever stop?

Oh, God. Clara slowly shut her eyes and leaned back on her hands. *Please, don't let any of those horrid things be true!*

Newton awoke Clara the next morning by crawling into bed with her. Checking the clock on the night table, Clara saw that it read seven A.M. She released contented sigh and kissed Newton's head, cuddling him closer to her. Archie was still sleeping soundly in the other bed.

Would there be someone to pick her up at the station this morning? How far was it to Katie and Frank's homestead? To William? She was more than ready to see him again. The separation, though it had been only for a month, felt like years.

Clara and the boys ate breakfast in the dining hall once again. When they were finished, she gathered up their belongings and went to find the manager. She thanked him profusely for his kindness and again offered to pay him once Frank or William arrived.

"Certainly not, Mrs. McDonald," the manager said. "I enjoy helping others out and do not expect anything in return. Please, do not deny me this small pleasure."

Clara reluctantly agreed, bid him farewell, and exited the hotel.

Despite the torrents of yesterday, the sun was now shining brightly over Spokane. Clara could see far more of the city now, though there truly wasn't much to look at. Spokane was far smaller than she had anticipated.

They made their way back to the depot to see if Frank or William had arrived yet, but no one was waiting for them. Clara left her carpet bag with the Scottish ticket agent and, taking the boys' hands, set out to see the sights of Spokane.

It took them all of fifteen minutes to see the extent of the town, even with the little boys' short legs. Monroe street was the main roadway, featuring a general store, butcher, shoemaker, and dressmaker—all of the typical things. Clara walked down the muddy dirt street, steering the boys away from the puddles, and followed it all the way to the bridge.

She grimaced. The Monroe street bridge spanned the width of the Spokane river, which in itself was not large, but the canyon it had eroded was large indeed. There were people walking across the bridge, horses, wagons...no one seemed to notice that the bridge had a definite sway to it or that it creaked rather loudly. Clara was sure that the remaining rusted bolts would give way momentarily and the rotten beams would fall into the river below, taking the people with it.

"Can we walk on the bridge, Mama?" Archie asked, turning sweet, inquisitive eyes to her.

A shudder jostled through Clara. "No. Absolutely not. We should be heading back to the station in case Father or Uncle Frank come to get us."

With that, Clara left the creaking Monroe street bridge behind them, and they travelled back towards the station.

Clara spent her remaining twenty cents on a large bundle of dried fruit. She had no idea how long it would be before someone came to fetch her and the boys, and she was already hungry.

They sat in the train depot for a few hours, munching dried apples and enjoying the spring air. Clara could not stop herself from taking large inhales of the pure, sweet, western air. It was even better than she had imagined it. Surely, such air, along with so many people praying, had improved William's health.

"Clara?"

She snapped her head towards the voice and saw her brother-in-law standing near.

"Frank!" she cried, embracing him. "I'm so glad to see a familiar face!"

Clara was surprised to find tears rolling down her cheeks. Perhaps she'd been more concerned than even she had realized.

"Your train was early?" Frank asked, pulling Newton into his arms. "You weren't supposed to arrive until later."

Clara wiped a tear off her face. "Yes, we came in yesterday afternoon. The kind hotel manager allowed us to sleep there for no charge."

Frank poked Newton's tummy and nose, and the little boy squealed. "I'm so sorry. If I'd known..." his voice trailed off. Of course, there was no way he could have known. He cleared his throat and went on. "William will be so glad to see you, Clara. He's terribly homesick. He was planning on coming in later to pick you up himself, but now, we get to surprise him!"

"I'm so glad he's with you. We feared that Father's letter wouldn't reach you before he arrived."

"It didn't," Frank said. "William had been in town a week and half before we received the letter stating that he was coming. You can be sure that I rushed into town and picked him up that very day. And a good thing, too...he had no money whatsoever, and when I

253

found him, he was standing in the middle of the street, attempting to sell a case of silverware." Frank chuckled. "He has a funny story about that, but I'll let him tell it."

Clara gulped. "How is he feeling?"

Frank grinned. "Perfect. You'd never know it was the same man."

Air rushed out of her lungs as if someone had punched bread dough. William was all right. He was alive. Healthy even, from the sound of it.

"Surprise Father!" Archie jumped up and down, his eyes twinkling. "Can we go now?"

Frank ruffled Archie's hair. "Archie? Is this the little tot who couldn't walk when I saw him last?"

Clara nodded, smiling.

"Can we see Father now?" Archie begged, tugging Frank's hand.

"Not yet, little fireball. I've got a few things to pick up at the store, then we'll head out." Kneeling down and lowering his voice, Frank said to the boys, "There might be a stray peppermint stick or licorice whip for you boys, as long as you've been good and helpful to your mother."

The boys' eyes gleamed, and Clara laughed. "Oh, Frank, you'll spoil them. The last thing they need is candy."

"A little candy never hurt anybody, Sis." Frank winked at Clara. Setting Newton on his feet, he said, "Now boys, I need your help. Archie, can you carry that carpet bag? That's a boy...I know it's heavy. Newton, hold tight to your Mother's hand and don't let her fall down. The hack is right over there, with the black and chestnut horses. I'll be over with your trunk in a moment."

Clara followed Archie down the steps, smiling to herself. It had been five long years since she'd seen her brother-in-law, but he was just as she remembered him. Only, much more tan and muscular.

She looked about for a hack, but all she saw was a small, primitive wagon, with a front bench and a second bench behind it. There was a chestnut horse and a black one.

Ivy Rose

Chapter 22

"This must be it," Clara said, a confused sigh escaping her. This was nothing like the expensive, luxurious hacks she had seen in Chicago.

Shrugging, Clara sat Newton on the rear bench, helped Archie hoist the carpetbag over the edge, and gave him a hand up.

Frank soon came off the platform with the Scottish ticket man, holding Clara's green trunk between them. Clara moved out of the way as they situated it in the wagon, and, once it was in, Frank lifted her onto the front bench. Her legs couldn't have reached the step had she wanted to get in by herself. And there wasn't even a seat pad on the wooden bench.

Frank and the ticket man brought out the furniture and carefully secured them, as well. Then, Frank took a seat beside Clara and clucked to the horses.

"I just need to grab a few things at the hardware store, then we will be on our way to the prairie."

He made the hardware store a quick stop and came out with a licorice whip for each of them.

Clara's heart shuddered with every step the horses took as they went across the Monroe street bridge. Frank said that it was the only bridge across the river, and it had already burned down twice. Clara didn't wonder at that. Her knuckles were white against the seat when they arrived safely on the other side.

Frank kept mentioning 'prairie,' but it seemed impossible that a prairie could even exist amidst these mountains. "Just how far is it to the prairie?" Clara asked.

"Depending on the conditions, four to six hours."

Her mouth dried. "I had no idea you lived so…remotely." Never had she lived so far from civilization. Not that Spokane could really be considered civilization, but it was better than nothing.

Frank cocked his head. "It isn't too rural. We have our own store and church and schoolhouse, and there are quite a few other families on Wild Rose. William sure seems to enjoy it there, and I hope you and the little fellows will, too."

The further they travelled out of town, the more beautiful the land became. Gently rolling hills, hundreds of thousands of pine trees in sight, blooming lilac bushes and blossoming cherry trees…even the air smelled sweet. A red-tailed hawk circled high above. Clara's lips tugged into a smile. The posters she had seen in Chicago hadn't captured even half of this beauty. Perhaps it was worth living so far outside of town.

The boys kept up a constant chatter as the horses drove on and on, and Clara occasionally asked Frank questions. He seemed to know the owners of every homestead and ranch they passed by.

"Just over that hill there is our homestead," Frank said, pointing to the swell of land in front of them. Clara's grin broadened and her pulse quickened. She was so close to seeing William.

When they crested the hill, a gasp escaped unbidden from Clara's throat.

A long, wide prairie stretched out before her, bordered on all sides by tall mountains. Neatly planted fields sprouted green, still showing the rich soil beneath them. Some of the fields weren't yet planted, but the beauty of the soil, darkened from last night's rain, mingled well with the green. Cabins and barns dotted the horizon and sprang from a sea of yellow…roses?

"I was hoping you'd get here before the roses went away for the summer." Frank smiled at her. "See why it's called 'Wild Rose Prairie'?"

Clara thought it was the most beautiful thing she had seen. Except for the fields, the entire prairie was a glowing carpet of gold. A gentle breeze carried the scent of the roses, along with the earthy smell of fresh rain. She inhaled slowly. *Nothing* in Chicago could even come close to this natural beauty.

Frank drove the team up to a log cabin and called out for Katie, who came running. Clara stood stiffly, accepting Frank's arms to help her down, and embraced her oldest sister. Five years of just letters and no hugs. How had they done it? And now, though Katie would be close, the other sisters were far away.

Though Clara was overjoyed to see her sister and Clara May and young George, whom she hadn't yet met, her eyes roved about, searching for the lanky form of her husband. He didn't appear to be anywhere on the homestead.

"He should be here any moment," Frank promised. "He must have gotten hung up at Old Jerry's."

Clara didn't have a chance to ask who Old Jerry was before Jimmy, now a tall nine-year-old, came barreling out of nowhere. He looked about to throw his arms around Clara, but stopped short and folded his hands behind his back, gazing sheepishly at the ground.

"Jimmy! Oh, you've gotten so tall! How are you?" Clara embraced the boy, and he returned her hug.

"Just fine, Aunt Clara!" His eyes fell to the little boys. "Is *that* Archie?"

"'Course I'm Archie!" Archie slapped his hands on his hips. "Why do people keep saying that?"

Clara rested a hand on her little son's head, joining her sister in laughter. "Because, silly boy, you were a little baby last time Aunt Katie, Uncle Frank, and your cousins saw you."

Archie nodded slowly, narrowing his eyes at the relatives he was too young to have memories of.

Katie tapped Clara on the arm, smiling mischievously and pointing into the fields.

Clara followed her finger, seeing nothing but yellow roses and prairie grass at first. But then her eyes settled on a figure, walking in their direction. The loping, long-legged gait told her who it was.

Almost without conscious thought, Clara set off on the path through the just-sprouting wheat field, towards the bobbing figure. Her lips felt like they were going to crack, she was smiling so broadly. That and the drying prairie wind. Picking up her skirts, she hurriedly jogged toward him.

William must have seen her, too, as his figure began bobbing faster and faster as he ran towards Clara with a strength and stamina she hadn't seen in years.

I can't believe it!

When he reached her, strong arms encircled Clara and her feet lifted off the ground. The world spun, and he kissed her firmly. His hand pressed her head tightly against his chest. Though his heart pounded from the run, there was no rattle in his lungs. And by the strength with which he was hugging her, Clara knew that he was feeling himself again. Better than himself.

"You have no idea how much I've missed you," William said, his voice husky.

Clara laughed breathlessly, closing her eyes and breathing in his scent. It was different than she remembered, with more sweat and dirt. But still, it was *his.* Tears leaked out of her eyelids. "I've been so terribly worried. You never said how you were in the telegrams."

William pulled away and they locked gazes. The sparkle was back in his sky-blue eyes. How badly she had missed it! She could almost forgive the lack of information in his telegrams just to see him well. Almost.

William kissed her again and again. Clara couldn't get enough of looking at him. She had prepared herself to find him in the same condition in which he had left Chicago, or worse. But nothing could have readied her for this. She hadn't let herself even hope that he could be such a picture of health.

Eventually, Clara's ears picked up on the gleeful shouts of the boys. She glanced back towards Katie and Frank's house, the smile refusing to leave her lips. William glanced at the house too, but he broke his gaze in a moment and turned back to Clara, smiling wide. Together, they began walking towards the house, his arm draped over her shoulders and Clara's arm around his waist.

The little boys were running as fast as their short legs would carry them. Clara giggled as Newton pumped his chunky little legs to keep up with Archie's longer ones. Newton tripped and fell into the soft dirt a few times, but each time, he would simply stand up and keep running, not even bothering to brush himself off.

William knelt down as the boys came near and caught them in his arms. Clara smiled, watching their embrace. Her heart was soaring as high as the ravens above her.

He's all right. He's healthy. This isn't a dream.

The little McDonald family took their time getting back to Katie and Frank's home. There was so much to talk about! The boys hardly let their parents get a word in edgewise, but Clara didn't mind. Her brain still stuttered, and she couldn't make her eyes believe that William truly stood before her, rosy cheeked and muscular. Perhaps not muscular when compared to Frank, but for a man who had been on his deathbed four weeks ago, the change was remarkable.

"How was your trip out?" William asked Clara, talking over the boys. He tightened his grip around her shoulders, as if to ensure that she really was beside him.

"Wonderful. Father made it so easy for us. The only difficult part was when our train came into the station yesterday at five o'clock."

William's eyes widened and his jaw bobbed a few times. "What did you do?"

"I left our luggage with the ticket man and headed towards the hotel he recommended—the Commercial. I talked to the manager and offered him my rings until you or Frank arrived, as I only had twenty cents left. He was kind enough to give us a large room and two meals in the dining hall and refused to accept any payment."

William laughed breathlessly. "You…you did that? I didn't know you had it in you!"

Clara gave him a sideways glare.

"I take it back," William said, laughing and squeezing her. "Let me just say that I haven't seen that side of you in a good, long while."

The remainder of the evening was filled with talking and laughter and more fun than Clara had had in a long time. By itself, the relief of knowing that William was all right was invigorating. She almost forgot how tired she was amidst all the excitement.

The Newell's two-bedroom cabin on the prairie seemed tiny to Clara, but Katie said that it was quite large compared to most other cabins. Jimmy, May, and George gave up their bedroom for Clara and William. Archie wanted to join his cousins in sleeping on the floor in the main living area of the cabin, but Newton was perfectly content to sleep on Jimmy's narrow cot in the same room with his parents.

Clara was afraid that she wouldn't be able to settle down and sleep, but after seeing Archie cozily tucked in beside his cousins and Newton curled in Jimmy's bed, Clara climbed in beside William and sighed contentedly. The bed was nowhere near as fancy as the hotel bed had been, but it was comfortable and warm.

Clara desperately wanted to stay awake and talk, but she soon found her eyes closing without permission and felt William stroking her cheek gently, whispering that they could talk more tomorrow.

"You're sure?" Clara questioned sleepily, closing her hands over his. Even in her half-awake state, she could feel the strength and roughness in William's hands. No traces of the weakness asthma had given him.

"I'm sure," he chuckled. "Go to sleep."

The following morning, Clara awoke not to Newton curling beside her, but to soft kisses brushing against her face. She dragged her eyelids opened and blinked. When the fog before her cleared, William's face hovered above hers.

"Good morning," he said softly, his eyes twinkling.

Clara smiled and rubbed her face. "Good morning. What time is it?"

William glanced away for a moment. "Nearly eight o'clock."

"Eight!" How terribly rude of her to sleep so long! "I need to help Katie with…"

William pushed her back into the pillows. "Katie doesn't need any help. *You* need to take care of yourself—the train ride alone will tire anyone out."

"I'm fine," Clara protested. Despite the churning in her stomach, she felt more rested than she had in days—weeks, even. She glanced about the bright, sun-lit room and saw that Newton was just beginning to stir in his bed. "Is Archie awake?"

"Likely so. Jimmy, May, and George are quite early risers. One has to be, here on the prairie."

"I should get up, too," Clara said. How could she have slept so long? She pushed herself up and leaned against the wall, rubbing her hands over her face.

William chuckled softly. "We aren't homesteaders yet, Clara. We don't have our own animals to care for like Katie and Frank do."

"Will we...someday?" Her eyes sought his face.

"I suppose so, if you decide you like it out here. If not, we can find a place in town. That's the main reason I didn't buy any land before now."

Clara's mind replayed images from the trip out in Mr. Carter's hack. It had all been beautiful, but the moment the hack crested the hill and she had seen Wild Rose prairie, a bizarre sense of belonging attacked her, like Wild Rose was the home she had never been to.

"Of course I want to." She rubbed her eyes again. "Don't you?"

William nodded. "Lord willing, I can find a vacant plot of land soon and we can settle down."

Silence fell. True silence. No noisy streetcars or clomping of horses hooves on hard-packed dirt. Newton's bed creaked slightly as he squirmed about, and a few pots clanked together in the kitchen.

Silverware.

"William, did you have to sell the silverware when you got here?"

His face puckered slightly. "I'm not much of a salesman."

Clara raised an eyebrow. What did that have to do with it?

"You see, I'd been in Spokane about a week and a half, without hearing from Katie and Frank and without knowing where they even lived. I missed you so badly that I went to the station to buy a ticket home. The Scottish agent begged that I give myself just a little more time before heading back. I didn't have enough money to get a ticket anyway, but by no means did I want to stay. So, I took that fancy silverware case and started walking up Second Avenue."

Newton interrupted, clambering into William's lap. His sleepy grin warmed Clara's heart, as did the way he said, "Fa'ver." She smiled at her little son and squeezed his toes. "Did you sleep well?"

Newton nodded, rubbing his eyes.

"I walked up and down that street," William continued, "as well as a few others, for hours and hours."

"Nobody wanted it?" Why wouldn't anyone want such a lovely set? She hadn't seen any silverware sets anywhere close to as beautiful as that one in Spokane's shop windows.

William ducked his face into Newton's hair. "Well, no one really saw it."

"What?"

He sighed, yet a boyish smile played about his lips. "I couldn't work up the courage to knock on a door."

Clara couldn't resist slapping him. Gently, of course. She smiled, too. There was a reason that their boss at Singer had put him in engineering instead of sales. "What did you do?"

"Well, that's when a certain Frank Newell came upon me. Apparently, the letter your father had sent finally reached them that morning. Frank begged me to come up here with him, promising that he would help me find some work so that I could save up enough for that ticket." William chuckled. "Old Jerry took me on right away, and by the time I had enough for a train ticket, I kind of liked it here."

"So you sent the wire for us?"

William nodded. "I did, even though I don't have a house ready. Was your father all right with that?"

"He didn't say anything."

He smiled, leaned forward, and kissed her. "I missed you and the boys so much I couldn't stand it any longer. We'll be able to find a house soon…I've been asking all the neighbors and they're on the lookout, too."

Chapter 23

Clara's first day on the prairie was packed full of surprises. It started when she saw how far it was to the nearest water pump. Katie told Clara how fortunate they were to even have a pump. Most families had a single, bucket-drawn well.

Katie's kitchen wasn't much different than the one Clara was used to. The stove was nearly identical, which drew a sigh of relief. She was half afraid that she would have to learn how to cook over an open fire. Katie had a root cellar under the house, in which she stored canned goods, milk, butter, cheese, vegetables, and various meats. Clara hadn't ever seen so much food in one place, except a store.

"How do you eat all of this fresh food before it spoils?" Clara gazed around the dimly lit cellar. Goosebumps arose on her arms. The air underground was quite cool—almost cold.

"It doesn't spoil quickly," Katie said. "We go through the milk products the fastest, of course, and the meat has been either dried or smoked. With the winters we have here, one must be prepared."

Clara's heart skipped a beat. What was different about winters on the prairie?

"The roads to Spokane are impassible during most of the winter months," Katie continued, ushering Clara up the cellar steps. "Even though the Hazzard's still keep their store open, they can't restock regularly, if at all. The folks out here are on their own when it comes to winter months."

"Hazzard's?" All morning, Katie had been speaking so quickly that Clara couldn't catch all the names and places and people of the prairie.

"The Hazzard's have a store and post office just a half mile from here."

"Oh." If she and William were to make their home on the prairie, she needed to learn the names of the locals.

Archie and Newton had been chasing their cousins around the farm all morning. Clara felt bad for Jimmy and May having the little ones tagging along as they did their chores, but the older cousins seemed to be enjoying it. Clara knew without a doubt that Archie was going to love living on the prairie. He could be as loud as he wanted and had plenty of room to run about without being scolded.

"Your children are so sweet," Clara said, turning away from where the five cousins were chasing

270

chickens around the yard. She watched as Jimmy scooped Newton over his shoulder and tickled him, causing her little son to scream in glee. Her heart soared seeing her shy baby being boisterous and adventurous.

"Yours must be as well, or mine wouldn't be having such fun." Katie shot a sisterly grin towards Clara as she pulled a loaf of bread from the oven.

"I hope we are able to find a home soon, somewhere close by so they can enjoy each other."

"Frank and William have been looking ever since William first came."

"And they haven't found anything at all?"

Katie slowed in her bustling, her back to Clara. "No," she said, a touch sadly. "The land is pretty well taken up on the prairie."

A lump rose in Clara's throat. She had hoped that their new home would be near to Katie's. She had so much to learn about pioneer life and didn't want to do it all by herself.

"But sometimes, folks get tired of living so far away from the city and leave, selling their homesteads." Katie's tone held more hope. "We may be able to find you a home that way."

Clara couldn't imagine why anyone would want to live closer to a city. Sure, it was lovely if that was all one knew. But after this taste of country living—small and short as it had been—she was ready to give up city life for good. If only the rest of the family could come join them…

Heavy boots clomped against the wood floor as Frank and William entered the kitchen.

"Old Jerry needs us for a few hours," Frank said, helping himself to the jar of cookies. "We'll be back for supper."

William took the spare cookie from Frank, squeezing Clara's hand on the way by. "See you later."

"Who is this Jerry fellow?" Clara asked when they had left.

"A rancher who lives a mile and a half away. He and his wife Jule—" Katie laughed lightly, and Clara saw a strange look come over her face. "They...they kinda took us under their wing when we got here. Like us, they had just arrived on Wild Rose, but they've been pioneering since they were first married thirty-five years ago."

"Why do they move around so much?" Clara asked.

Katie laughed again. "Jule reminds me of you, Clara—always hungry for adventure, yet she doesn't go aimlessly hunting for it. And, like you, she isn't afraid of trying something new. She and Jerry have the most wonderful relationship. They've taught Frank and I a lot, not only about pioneering and farming, but about our relationship with each other."

"They sound wonderful." Clara brushed at a bit of flour that had fallen from the table onto her dress. "I'd like to meet them. You say William and Frank work for Old Jerry?"

"Yes, they do. He only runs his sawmill for a few months out of the year. When William arrived, he was running it and offered Will a job right off."

"What exactly does he do there?" Clara asked. William would have been terribly sick and weak upon arrival. "Sharpen blades?"

Katie chuckled. "No, Clara, he stacks the timber."

Clara thought her jaw would come disconnected from her skull. "He what?" Had she heard Katie wrong?

"He stacks the timber. That's been his job since he started."

"But how—he was so…" William had been on the brink of death, and yet, hardly a week after arriving in Washington he was stacking timber?

"We were even more surprised than you are right now when William told us he had come because the asthma nearly killed him. Though I'm sorry to say it, we almost didn't believe him. He was so…so healthy."

"Bu—"

"We realized after a while that he still was rather sickly after his week in Spokane. But we didn't notice it at the time."

All those years of suffering, that money spent on doctors and remedies—and one week in clean air had cured him. Clara shook her head. *You're amazing, Lord.*

Katie and the children showed Clara the remainder of the farm and property, which they were quite obviously proud of. It *was* a beautiful plot of land—a half-quarter section, which was 80 acres.

When Newton became tired and fussy, Clara took him indoors and nursed him while she and Katie talked. After being separated for five years, they had a lot to discuss. Katie told Clara all about their local pastor and the lovely church that had recently been constructed.

"Is there a school?" Clara questioned.

"Not yet. There aren't enough children on the prairie yet to summon a teacher."

"You teach Jimmy and May here, then?"

Katie nodded. "I don't have to teach them much. Once I taught Jimmy how to read, he started devouring every book he sets eyes on. And May asks Frank and I to create arithmetic problems for her to solve." A warmth settled in Katie's eyes and she chuckled. "We're blessed to have children who want to learn."

The children were inside playing a game and supper was on the table by the time Frank and William arrived back. Much to Clara's embarrassment, William swung her in his arms, pressing his lips against hers.

"William!" She glanced around, cheeks burning, but no one was watching them. The children appeared entirely oblivious. In fact, Frank was kissing Katie in a similar manner.

William chuckled, not releasing his hold. "We aren't in the city anymore, Ma'am." His lips brushed her ear. "And besides that, I've missed you just a little this past month."

"Just a little?" Clara scolded, smiling. After glancing around again, she gave him a peck on the cheek.

"Supper's ready!" Katie announced, and the children tossed away their game. William returned Clara to her feet, and they took their seats around the table, joining hands for prayer.

During supper, Frank and William talked about the different places where the McDonalds might make their new home.

"There is a lot of railroad land around," Frank said. "They'll be auctioning it off here soon, and it always sells for hardly more than dirt."

Clara glanced at William. He was silent, no doubt contemplating this proposal.

"How far away would that put us from you?" Clara asked, trying valiantly to conceal the tremor in her voice. Being away from the family in Chicago would prove itself hard enough. Surely they could find land somewhere close to Katie and Frank.

"Not more than a mile or two," Katie said.

A mile or two? Clara swallowed the chunk of bread that had turned to rock. It might as well be ten miles.

Within four days, William and Frank had discovered a homestead on a piece of railroad land that would be going up for sale. The owners didn't want it to go to auction, as they received more money selling it privately.

"Two bachelor brothers have been on it for the past two years," William reported to Clara as they prepared for bed. "It's got a beautiful, large house on it. Two floors! Can you believe it?"

Clara smiled at William's near-giddiness. "Why are the brothers leaving?"

"They ran out of money."

A sliver of fear crept into her heart. She and William didn't have much money to start with. Was it truly so hard to make it out here? Katie and Frank seemed to be doing wonderfully.

"How much are they asking for the land?" Clara asked.

"Dirt," William stated. "They just want to be rid of it. I seriously think that they would give it to us if we asked them."

Absently, Clara twirled a lose curl around her finger and stared at the chinked log wall. The thought of having their own homestead was frightening and exciting all at the same time.

"I thought we could go look at it tomorrow." William's statement was more of a question.

"Of course." Clara's eyes remained glued to the chinking. But she saw far beyond the dusty, mud chink. She was seeing all of the horrid images that had ravaged her mind ever since William's asthma had taken a turn for the worse.

The casket, the tears, the fresh grave. How was it that the man Clara was sure would die was now able to work in a saw mill and was going to be purchasing his own land to farm? Why had God spared William's life? Why was He being so merciful?

"Hey."

Clara was suddenly aware of a soft hand on her shoulder. She jumped slightly and turned her face up to meet William's.

"You all right?"

"Why did God give us this second chance?" she murmured, a pommel pounding in her chest. "What have we done to deserve this incredible mercy?"

William's other hand went on Clara's shoulder and squeezed. "I don't know." His voice was thick. "I don't understand, but I thank Him for it every day."

The house turned out to be even grander than Clara had dreamed possible on the rural prairie. In comparison to the things she had seen in Chicago, the two-story home truly didn't hold a candle to any of it, but she hardly cared.

There was a cellar and a well directly behind the barn, which in itself was small. A large plot of ground had been tilled into a lovely garden, ready for planting. Clara barely refrained from jumping up and down like a silly schoolgirl when she saw that. She had always wanted to have a large garden.

The two bachelor brothers—and an odd pair they were—truly were asking very little for the property. William arranged the terms of payment with them on sight.

Clara thought that her heart might beat out of her chest when William shook hands with the brothers after settling on the price. This house was so much better than their home in Chicago. Not only was it bigger, but—

In honesty, this house was actually quite run down compared to their lovely home in the heart of the city. But something about this house already felt more homelike than the Chicago dwelling ever had.

On the two-and-a-half mile walk back to Katie and Frank's home, Clara couldn't keep a smile from her face, and William babbled on about how perfect the house would be for them and how they wouldn't have to add onto it, even if they had ten children.

"Ten children!" Clara laughed. She loved children without question, but ten seemed like an awful lot—especially after seeing how busy life was with just Archie and Newton. And it would just get busier with this third baby, which she still hadn't told William about yet.

"Why not?" William asked, catching her hand in his. "That house could actually hold them all, far better than our little closet in Chicago could."

Clara laughed. "No reason, I suppose, except that is a lot of little ones."

"I suppose it is." William almost seemed disappointed. "Well, I guess we will just wait and see how many the Lord sees fit to give us."

The McDonalds moved into their new home just days after signing the bill of sale written up by one of the brothers. The brothers were eager to leave and Clara was eager to move in, so the arrangement worked beautifully.

Since they had come west by train, instead of by wagon as most families had, Clara and William had few belongings to put in their new home. Thankfully, the brothers had no use for their furniture and left it in the house. A table and chairs and two medium sized beds was the extent of it, along with a few pots and pans deemed too cumbersome to strap onto horses.

Clara set the rocker by the hearth and tucked the cradle in a corner. If her estimations were right, it wouldn't be terribly long before the cradle would again be in use. When she told William her news the previous night, he had picked her up and swung her around the bedroom. Thankfully, the clatter hadn't woken anyone up.

Katie had added two crates of preserves to the wagon bearing the McDonald's belongings, along with some fresh bread and milk. Clara carefully stored these items in the pantry and put the milk in the cellar. She had to smile when she saw the lone jar of milk sitting on the wooden shelf. Such a difference it was from Katie's well-stocked cellar.

The little boys seemed disappointed that the barn held no animals. Katie had promised Clara a flock of chickens as soon as the chicks were old enough to be separated from their mothers. Clara and the boys would have to work hard to get the small chicken coop ready for its new residents.

Clara cooked a small supper their first night in the new house—eggs from Katie's hens, bread, milk, and salt pork. It wasn't much, but it was filling, and everybody was too tired to care much.

"Dear Lord," William prayed as the little family joined hands. "Thank You for giving us this beautiful house to live in. We are blessed to have such a big, well-built house on this large property, and to have bought it for the price we did. Thank You for this meal Mother has prepared for us. Amen."

William smiled as she echoed his "amen." Chills ran through her body. How blessed they were! William was healthier than he had ever been before, and they lived on the prairie, within two miles of Katie and Frank, just as they had hoped.

What had they done to deserve such blessings?

Chapter 24

Old Jerry had informed the McDonalds that his saw mill was only functional for a few months of the year, so they weren't surprised when he shut it down. Even so, it left William out of a job.

Finding no employment nearby, William left for Spokane early one morning. Being a fairly large city, there had to be some employment there. He left at two in the morning, awakening Clara with a gentle kiss.

"I'll be back by tonight." His words soaked into Clara's groggy brain.

They had no horse, so William would be walking to town and back.

When Clara arose several hours later, she knelt by the bedside and prayed that William would find work quickly without trouble. "You've brought us this far, Lord," she prayed, speaking softly. "And we know without a doubt that You won't leave us now."

Moving downstairs, Clara starting by reviving the fire in the stove. Today was baking day, and she had quite a lot of it to do. In Chicago, she had baked several times a week in little bits, having no place to keep the goods from spoiling. But here, the lovely root cellar kept goods fresh for far longer.

Archie and Newton soon awoke, wolfed down their breakfast, and hurried outdoors to play. At times, Clara wondered how they could play outside day after day after day on the same plot of land; they were not allowed to enter the dirt fields that surrounded the house on all but one side. Did she really *want* to know what they were doing?

She let the kitchen door remain open to let in the crisp, sweet air. Leaning against the doorframe, she closed her eyes, inhaling slowly. If she weren't busy keeping the house in order, she would be out with the boys, laying in the prairie grass and wild roses, watching the puffy clouds go by, not caring who was watching her.

Clara sang to herself as she kneaded the bread and mixed up muffins. She couldn't keep the smile from her lips. Something about the spring air made everything seem all right. Everything except...

Please, God, help Will find a good-paying job.

Archie's little barefooted steps came slapping into the house.

"Someone's comin', Mama!" he gasped excitedly. "And it's not Aunt Katie!"

"Archie! Even if it was Aunt Katie, we would be very happy to see her."

"Come look!" Archie grasped Clara's floury hand and dragged her to the porch, evidently not hearing her rebuke.

Following Archie's finger, Clara stared out into the grass—far out—and her eyes met four bobbing figures. They were still rather far away, but Clara saw the tallest figure raise a hand and wave. Smiling, Clara waved back.

A bit of flour fell from her hand onto Archie, and she gasped a little.

"Oh dear, I'm not in any state to have company!" she muttered to herself, attempting to brush the flour off her apron. It did nothing, as the flour already on her hands merely smeared what was on her apron and dress.

Running back inside, Clara dunked her hands in the wash basin and scrubbed to get the flour paste out from beneath her nails. She then took her apron off and shook it fiercely outdoors, watching as the figures drew nearer. It was a woman and three children and an infant, Clara could now see, and her heart skipped a beat. Who were they and what homestead did they come from?

When the figures finally drew close to the house, Clara stepped outside to greet them.

"Welcome!" Clara said, extending her hand to the young woman. "I'm Clara McDonald. My husband and sons and I have recently moved here from Chicago."

The woman's sapphire-green eyes were flecked with black, but to Clara they were flecked with spunk. Her hair was the reddest Clara had ever seen. Such a stunning contrast to the green-gold prairie.

"My name is Mary Ann Trolan." Mary Ann took Clara's hand for a brief moment and shook it. "And these are my children: Jimmy, Danny, Margret, and Alice."

Clara gazed at the baby in Mary Ann's arms and smiled. She was just as bright-eyed as her mother and siblings, though she couldn't be more than six months old. Both of the boys, and the girl, standing at Mary Ann's side had carrot-red hair and more freckles than tanned skin. They grinned impishly at Clara and flashed their blue eyes at her.

"We live in the adjoining homestead." Mary Ann gestured behind her to where a small cabin was visible. "The Butcher brothers told us that a new family was moving in. I apologize it has taken me so long to come over to meet you."

"Don't apologize," Clara chided. "I have been busy settling in, or else I would have come visiting you."

Mary Ann smiled and shifted the baby in her arms.

"Please, won't you come in?" Clara gestured towards the house. "I've put the coffee on."

"Thank you," Mary Ann said, starting towards the house.

"Can we play here, Mum?" her oldest boy asked.

"If it is all right with Mrs. McDonald."

Clara nodded to all five children, who were examining each other from a distance. That wouldn't last long, though. It would be a matter of minutes before Archie began talking the Trolan childrens' ears off.

"What are your little boys' names?" Mary Ann asked as both women mounted the steps into the kitchen.

"Archie and Newton," Clara said, glancing at the lump of bread dough on the table. It was kneaded enough. "They are five and two." She took the dough and formed it into a pan, then set it on top of the stove to rise once more.

Mary Ann seated herself at the table and sat little Alice upright in her lap. "Jimmy is eight, Danny is five, and Margaret is three. This may be exciting." She flashed a knowing smile out the door.

"How old is Alice?" Clara questioned, bringing the coffee pot and cups over to the table and pouring herself and Mary Ann a cup. There was some residual flour on the table, but it was hardly noticeable—or so Clara hoped.

"Nearly eight months," Mary Ann said, gazing down to the baby girl in her lap. "I am glad to have the older children around to help keep track of her. She started crawling early."

Clara and the baby locked eyes for a long moment. Clara smiled at the little one and was rewarded with a happy grin that lit Alice's entire face.

"She's darling!" Clara exclaimed, and Mary Ann laughed delightedly, pride spilling out of every pore.

"Dan and I like her pretty well."

"Dan is your husband?" Clara questioned, carefully sipping her hot coffee.

Mary Ann nodded. "He wanted to come and meet you, but he couldn't be spared from the fields. And I figured that your man wouldn't be here anyhow. With Old Jerry's mill done for the year, he must be looking for work."

How did Mary Ann know so much about them? Clara hadn't ever talked to this woman before! "Yes, that's right," Clara said. "He's in Spokane right now."

"You folks won't be farming?"

"We will, but we have no money to purchase the things we need to do so. I think a garden is the only planting we'll be doing this year."

"You don't have a team?" Mary Ann questioned.

Clara shook her head. "Not yet. After paying for the doctors William saw in Chicago, then the fares out here, then buying this house, we have mere pennies left."

Mary Ann's face melted. "I know how it feels, especially with little ones."

Clara nodded. *Three little ones.* "Yes," she said. "But we trust that the Lord will provide. He always has."

"Indeed. If you ever need anything—and I truly mean it—please tell us." Mary Ann smiled, and Clara saw the caring soul deep within those sapphire eyes. "I don't know how it is in a big city like Chicago, but out here, everyone helps each other. It's just how we do it. Not that anyone has much to give, but with everyone giving and sharing what they can, we get along fine."

Clara's chest swelled. Mary Ann was a perfect stranger, yet she was offering everything she had.

"Thank you," Clara breathed. "I cannot tell you what that means to me, especially after what we've been through recently."

"Reliance on the Lord is everything," Mary Ann said. "He has brought Dan and I through many difficult times in our married life. Not our relationship with one another, but with the things that have happened to our families since our wedding. But onto merrier subjects…" Mary Ann smiled brightly and Clara wondered if the woman was capable of being angry. "You seem awfully young to have seen such hardships already. If I didn't know that you had a five-year-old, I would age you at eighteen."

Clara chuckled, fingering a curly lock that rested in her lap. Even now, she hated wearing her hair up and let it stream about her shoulders and back. "I'll be twenty-four this November."

Mary Ann scoffed. "Why, you are hardly more than eighteen! Dan and I got a rather late start on having a family—we're in our forties."

"There's nothing wrong with that." Clara smiled. "My husband is much older than I; he turned thirty-one this spring."

Mary Ann stayed nearly all afternoon. Such a kindred spirit she was! Clara felt like she were talking to one of her sisters, not a woman who had been a complete stranger only hours ago.

Clara was sad to see them leave, and invited them back anytime. Mary Ann extended the invitation to her home as well, and Clara promised to take her up on it.

"They's nice kids," Archie said, watching Mary Ann and the children walking back towards their home. "They teachded us some Indian things, like making bows and arrows, but the arrows don't have any sharp rocks tied to them; they're just sticks. They also teachded us how to find frogs in the garden and by the creek. Did you know that frogs live in the creek, Mother? They do, and they lay little black eggs under the…"

Clara grinned as Archie chattered on and on about the things the Trolan children had "teachded" them. She was glad that the children had played so well with each other.

Scooping Newton into her arms, she kissed his cheek, and he twined his arms around her neck. It was past his usual naptime, and Archie wouldn't suffer from a bit of a rest, either. She took the boys into the kitchen and helped them clean up, fed them a slice of bread and butter, and settled them in bed for a short nap.

Mary Ann's visit had significantly helped pass the time while William was away, as well as keep Clara's mind off him. It was nearly four o'clock. Hopefully, he would be home soon.

The boys ate an easy supper of bread and salt pork, along with some of Katie's tasty canned green beans. Darkness fell, and Clara lit the hearth fire to ward off the chill of the spring air. Then, she took both boys in her lap and read to them from a child's storybook that had been hers. Within a few months, it would become more difficult to hold them both on her lap. Thank goodness the baby wasn't needing much room yet.

When Archie and Newton were comfortably settled in bed, Clara finished tidying up the house and went back to the sitting room, taking the Bible with her to the rocking chair. She lit the kerosene lantern on the table and pulled it towards her.

Frank had told her that when he and Katie first arrived on the prairie, and for a few years after, kerosene was an unknown luxury. Household lamps were constructed with a dish, grease, and old rags. He said though that type of lamp didn't give off the wide light of the kerosene lanterns, the little bit of light was better than none at all.

The hours wore on, and Clara's heart quickened. Why wasn't William back yet? Could he have been attacked by a wild animal?

She nearly screamed when she heard boots clomping on the porch. Closing her eyes and swallowing, she pressed a hand against her chest. Of course, it was only William. Standing carefully, Clara went to the kitchen to greet him.

"Are you all right?" Clara asked, stepping into his open arms. Praise God, he appeared unharmed.

William held Clara tightly to him and kissed her. "I'm fine, and I found a job. I'll tell you more tomorrow."

"Do you want any supper?" Clara moved towards the stove where she had green beans still sitting in a pan.

"No, thank you." William pulled his boots off and hung his jacket on a peg on the wall. "I ate while I walked."

William caught Clara's hand and together, they made their way towards the bedroom. Clara peeked her head into the room where the boys slept, making sure that they were still covered. They appeared comfortable, so she quickly jumped between the cool sheets of her own bed.

William sprawled on the mattress beside her, not remembering to remove his trousers or belt. Clara reached across in the darkness and felt that his shirt was only halfway unbuttoned. It wasn't necessary to awake him. Walking twenty miles would tire any man, especially one who was still acquiring endurance. She grasped the extra quilt folded at the end of the bed and threw it over him. He would be plenty warm.

"Washington Water Power?" Clara repeated. She didn't bother swallowing the oatmeal in her mouth.

Across the table, William nodded. "It's the biggest power company in Spokane—probably in all of Washington."

"That isn't saying much," Clara reminded him.

"I know, but it pays well."

Clara was about to ask another question when she saw William staring intently at his oatmeal and fidgeting with his spoon.

"The bad thing," he began, slowly, "is that I need to stay in Spokane to work."

Clara stopped chewing, and her napkin paused midair. William's eyes remained plastered to his bowl.

Stay in Spokane? Had he truly just said that?

"I should have asked you, I know," William was saying. "There were no other jobs available, and I needed to tell the hiring man right then if I would take the job."

Saying nothing, Clara tried to sort out each word as they pummeled into her brain.

"Clara?"

The soft-spoken word pulled Clara's gaze towards her husband's face.

"I can stop working there anytime." He sounded almost apologetic. "This isn't a permanent arrangement."

Clara nodded. "How long will you have to stay in town?"

"I believe I can leave on Sunday afternoons, be in town all week, and return on Saturday afternoons."

A week? That was better than being gone a solid month, as Clara had feared. She found herself nodding slowly.

They could do this. They'd already done far more difficult things.

So why was her throat caving in?

Chapter 25

"Mama!"

Clara pulled her hands out of the wash tub and put them in the small of her back. How it ached from bending!

"I'm right here, Darling," Clara said, grimacing as her muscles protested each movement.

"Aunt 'Tatie comin'!" Newton cried gleefully.

Clara stepped out from behind the clothesline and waved at her sister as she trudged through the grass. None of the children were with her, which was unusual. Typically, the cousins came visiting at every chance they got.

Archie ran across the yard a few feet away, with thirty squabbling pullets tripping after him. No one could deny that the chickens were ugly. Their adult feathers had yet to grow in, leaving them looking like someone had shaved patches of their bodies. But Archie loved the little critters and they followed him around like dogs. Clara only hoped that they would start laying eggs soon.

"Washing day, is it?" Katie questioned with a smile, embracing Clara.

"Indeed. I'm nearly through."

"Let me finish."

Katie grasped the trousers in the wash tub that Clara had been scrubbing and began running them over the washboard. Clara drew a breath in protest, but it was too late.

"Thank you." She sank down onto the grass and untied her apron. She wished she could remove the calico skirt she wore. Even without a petticoat it, felt as heavy as winter wool. Pushing back a sweaty curl, Clara turned her face upwards to the clear blue sky. It was only June. What would August be like?

"Little one giving you fits?" Katie asked knowingly.

"That and the heat," Clara said, wiping her face and neck with her apron. "Summers always seems hotter when there is a baby involved."

Katie chuckled. "How much longer?"

Clara swallowed, her tongue sticking in her mouth. It was *so* hot. "November. I'll be glad to finally meet it."

"As will I. I've missed living near my little nieces and nephews for the past few years."

Katie was almost done with the laundry when Clara realized that her sister hadn't yet said what she had come for.

"Come for?" Katie questioned. "Oh! I wanted to tell you that Hazzards are planning another Fourth of July celebration. There has been one for as long as we've been here, and they are great fun. Everybody brings something to add to the meal. There is a pie contest and games for the children, and then fireworks after dark."

"Fireworks? I didn't think anyone around here had the money for fireworks."

Katie smirked. "The show is nothing like the ones we used to see in Chicago, but it is still fun to watch."

Clara thought the celebration sounded like great fun, but she was saddened to hear that the Fourth of July would be on a Friday. William wouldn't be able to attend.

"Where is it?"

"The grounds between the cemetery and the church. That's where all of our celebrations are held."

"I'd like to come." Though Fourth of July was nearly three weeks away, she was already looking forward to a much-needed break from the daily grind. And besides, it would give her a chance to meet other nearby families who weren't able to come to church every Sunday.

The Fourth of July celebration, though rather small and insignificant compared to anything they had attended in Chicago, was far more fun and enjoyable. The neighbors were all so kind—many of them already felt like family to Clara. Never in the city had neighbors been such close friends. But on the prairie, the only options were to be friends or enemies. And who didn't like a friend to turn to when things went sour?

John Dunn, a confirmed bachelor of at least thirty-five, had organized a rather entertaining game of baseball. Though many of the other men were participating, as well, none were as enthusiastic or as ridiculous as Mr. Dunn. He happened to be the McDonald's nearest neighbor, living hardly a mile away from their doorstep. Clara had talked to him a handful of times, but had never she seen him playing with the children like this.

As much as she tried to stop it from happening, Clara's thoughts drifted to William many times throughout the morning. She knew that he wasn't working today, but he would be on Saturday, making it impossible to come home for one day, before returning on Sunday.

The neighbors had started gathering near the cemetery grounds early in the morning, and folks filtered in and out as the day went on. It was nearly eleven when Clara, seated in a chair in the shade of a tall scrub bush, felt two rough hands captivate her shoulders. She turned with a start, and barely refrained from squealing when William's glittering eyes met hers.

She stood and hugged him tightly, not caring who was watching. "What are you doing here?" she asked, pushing away just enough to see his face.

"I'm surprising you." A mischievous, boyish smile tugged at his lips.

"But how? Why—"

William chuckled and, glancing around for a moment, quickly brushed his lips against hers. "Don't ask questions, just thank the Lord. My boss is being generous. I'm home tomorrow and Sunday, as well."

Clara smiled and praised God in her heart for this unexpected pleasure. William pressed her close to him for another long moment, then knelt down and opened his arms for Newton.

For the past three months, ever since William had gotten the job with Washington Water Power in April, he had only been home a combined twelve days. It was desperately hard to have him gone so much, but they managed. The fact that he had two entire days off was a wonder.

Though some of the neighborhood men invited William into their conversations about farming and such, William kindly refused and stayed near Clara and the boys. Archie and Newton were glued to their father, even amidst the temptations of the neighbor children and their exciting games. Clara herself left him only when it was time to serve the pies.

The afternoon went by far too quickly for Clara's liking. She wanted it to last forever—that feeling of security with her husband, children, and newly-found friends. The only thing absent from the picture was her parents. Clara still missed them dreadfully. To her own shock, she oftentimes found herself musing, *I'll just go ask Mother,* only to realize that Mother was a thousand miles away.

They had received letters from Chicago, all bearing news of health and safety to the loved ones who resided there. But it just wasn't the same from the days when the Boutwell family lived in such close proximity.

Pulling herself out of the sad thoughts, Clara cuddled Archie nearer to her as the family sat on the grass in the darkness, waiting for the fireworks to begin. William's arm was around her waist, and he held a very sleepy Newton in his lap. Clara couldn't contain a smile.

True, she missed her family in Chicago. Life was difficult on the prairie. But, without a doubt, this was the place the Lord wanted them to be.

August seemed to drag by. Or perhaps it was Clara who was dragging. It was far too hot to be indoors, yet out of doors was miserable as well.

No sewing was required for the new little one since Clara had saved everything from Archie and Newton. Clara almost wished the child would need more clothes. For the first time she could remember, she wanted to sit still and sew.

Mary Ann came over at least one time a week, if not two. Though they had only known one another for a few months, it seemed as if they had been friends their entire lives. Even the children got along well, with very few spats between them.

Clara often waited up for William to arrive home on Saturday nights. She missed him so badly and wanted to see him the moment he arrived, even though he was exhausted and didn't do much but kiss her and fall into bed.

Though she would never admit it, having William gone was far harder for her than she let on. She despised not being able to see him every day. And the little boys—they needed their father around! But Clara said nothing to William. It wouldn't accomplish anything to do so—she knew he hated it just as much as she did.

Harvest time came and went. Katie taught Clara how to can, preserve, and dry the various vegetables so that they would last all winter. Clara already knew how to do some canning, but Katie was an expert. When they finished, her cellar wasn't nearly as full as Katie's, but it would provide them with food for many months.

One chilly Saturday in mid-November, Clara sat in the rocker, waiting for William as usual.

One o'clock a.m. He was *always* back by eleven p.m.

Dear God, keep William safe!

William had never been this late before. Horrible thoughts flitted through Clara's mind. With a great effort, she pushed them away and prayed for his safety again and again.

Pushing herself up, Clara went to the door and peeked out. There wasn't anything to see…just blackness. Blackness and bitter cold.

Sighing, she pulled a chair up to the sitting room window and stood on it. The curtains must be closed, but she couldn't reach them without a boost.

Despite her worry, a smile crept into Clara's face as she fingered the fine, lacy curtains. Katie teased her about having such lovely linens out on the prairie, but Clara loved her curtains and wouldn't have exchanged them for anything. It was true that they weren't entirely practical, but their stunning beauty made up for that.

Without warning, the chair beneath Clara gave way. She was sprawled on the hard floor, flat on her back, before she could even grip anything.

The fall knocked the wind out of her lungs, but Clara recovered quickly. She lay there a moment, her heart pounding and her breathing fast. *The baby!* Had it been hurt? No…it couldn't be. She hadn't fallen *that* hard.

Gingerly, Clara began moving her limbs. Nothing was especially painful. She carefully pushed herself into a sitting position and stared at the chair that had given her such a ride.

One of the legs had splintered, and another had cracked. The seat part was disconnected from the legs. Clara frowned. She should have known better. This chair was made by the Butcher brothers and had never been entirely sturdy.

Groaning as she picked her cumbersome, heavy body off the floor, Clara gathered the remnants of the chair and tossed a few pieces in the quavering coals. Firewood was always in short supply because William couldn't chop enough for one week on Sunday afternoons. At least the broken chair would give them some heat.

William didn't arrive home until six o'clock the following morning. He came in with baggy eyes and sluggish steps.

"It got dark so fast," William explained, holding Clara close. "I had to wait until I could see the road. I slept in the bushes at what I thought was the side of the road."

"I'm just happy you're safe," Clara mumbled into his shirt. She took a shuddering breath. "I was so worried."

Clara readied the boys for church, and, after breakfast the family set off towards the small church house. William was exhausted; she elbowed him twice during the service so he didn't fall asleep and topple off the bench.

Her heart was heavy as they bid William farewell later that afternoon. Trying to keep a smile on her lips, Clara and the boys waved at his fading figure until he was too far away to see.

A gusty sigh escaped her. Another week was beginning.

A sharp pain suddenly attacked Clara's abdomen. She narrowly escaped falling into a nearby chair and, instead, grasped it so tightly that she got a small splinter in her finger. The pain eased within moments, and Clara stood again.

Should she go and fetch Katie? Or send the boys to John Dunn's, so he could get Katie? If the little one was to make its arrival now, she was going to need help. But no; it had taken hours for the pains to be consistent with Archie and Newton. She had a bit of time still.

If only William were here!

Clara finished washing the breakfast dishes and was about to fetch the broom when another pain started. A startled scream escaped her lips at the severity of it, and she leaned against the wall for support.

Dear Lord, something is wrong!

The pain lasted so long Clara wondered if it would ever ease. Finally, it did, but another came within a few minutes and she knew she must get in bed. How could Katie be beckoned? Clara didn't think she could manage to fire two rounds from the shotgun; their agreed emergency procedure.

Clara's heart beat fast, partly from the pain, and partly from fear. She didn't want to deliver this baby by herself, and she certainly didn't want the boys in the house when the pains became severe.

The boys! She slowly made her way into the spare room where, thankfully, both Archie and Newton were playing with slates and slate pencils.

"Archie, Darling, I need you to run to Aunt Katie's as fast as you can," Clara said, leaning heavily against the doorframe. "Mother is sick and needs Aunt Katie to help her. Newton, can you go with your brother? Can you run very fast?"

Little Newton nodded his head seriously.

"Go very, very quick. And tell Aunt Katie to hurry as fast as she can."

Archie sprang to his feet, his face paling, and grabbed Newton's hand. Clara feared what her countenance must be if even Archie noticed something.

"We'll run fast, Mother. Very fast."

The boys dashed out of the house just before another contraction seized Clara, and she knew she must get to bed immediately. This baby was wasting no time.

Clara moved as quickly as she could into the bedroom. She began to unbutton her dress to change into a nightgown, but realized that she didn't have time. Crawling into bed with a quiet moan, Clara prayed that Katie would make it in time.

But Katie didn't make it in time. Inside of twenty minutes, Clara had birthed a baby boy, unattended and alone.

Chapter 26

The baby boy, perfectly formed and wiry, was completely still. For one terribly long moment, Clara thought he was dead. But then, his chest rose and fell. Once.

Tears came to Clara's eyes, and she took the little baby into her lap. There was nothing nearby to wrap him in, so she set him in the folds of her skirt and cleaned him as well as she could with them. Her body ached fiercely from the fast labor, but that was the least of her concerns.

Something was wrong. Her baby was entirely motionless; his fingers didn't even flutter. Breathing was the only movement he made, and even that was irregular and sporadic. Clara prodded him all over, attempting to entice him to cry.

It didn't work. He wouldn't, or couldn't, cry.

She lifted him carefully under the arms and supported his head, gazing into the sweet baby face that was so still…so horribly still. Surely, he would be just fine. How could he not?

Her heart lodged in her throat and tears came rapidly, deep sobs racking her already-sore body. She pressed the little child to her chest, allowing herself to fall back onto the pillows.

Why didn't he cry? Or move? If only her mother or Katie were here, they would know what to do! They could help him.

Please God, let him live. Don't take him.

Clara was unsure of how long she lay there with her little son before Katie came bursting through the open door, panting and red-faced. Her hands clamped over her mouth, and a muffled, "Oh, dear Lord!" met Clara's ears.

Katie wide eyes roved the bed. Clara tried to speak, but her tongue was as rough and hard as sandpaper. What could she say, anyway? Words seemed futile.

"What's wrong?" Katie knelt down and pulled Clara's hand away from the baby's face. Gently, she touched him all over, apparently checking for anything physically wrong with the infant. Clara allowed Katie to inspect the baby, but she couldn't keep her tears from coming and her mouth refused to form words.

"Clara, talk to me," Katie urged, her wide, green eyes reeking desperation. She pulled back a lock of Clara's disheveled hair. "Tell me what happened."

"The pains…they came—so—so fast," Clara said through hitching sobs. "He can't cry. He—he doesn't move."

Katie flipped the baby onto his back and prodded him even more. Clara could feel his breathing, which was far more steady now. But still, no movement at all. Not even a fluttering eyelid or a waggling finger.

Katie stared at his little body for a long moment, her face drawn up in thought. Then, she gently slid him into her own arms. "Unbutton your blouse."

The words didn't penetrate Clara's numb mind easily. What did Katie want?

"Your shirt," Katie prompted, cradling the baby in one arm. "Unbutton it."

Clara's fingers fumbled with the buttons, and Katie helped with her free hand. Then, very carefully, she laid the baby on Clara's bare skin.

Clara's heart leapt at the warmth and weight of her little one. She half wondered if Katie was doing this for the baby's benefit or hers. Whichever it was, the clenching in her throat slowly began to ease, her breathing slowed, and the hitching sobs beginning to lessen. Maybe everything would be all right. It *had* to be.

Katie arranged a blanket over Clara and the baby, then set to cleaning up as best she could. Clara watched through blurry eyes. What had caused labor be so quick? Nothing seemed awry during her pregnancy. Granted, the baby hadn't moved as much as Newton had, but Clara frequently felt flutters. According to her estimations, he was only around three weeks early. Not early enough for him to be so very, very small like he was. His head was nearly swallowed up in her hand, which in itself was petite.

When Katie finished, she brought Clara a glass of water and helped her sit up slightly to drink it.

"Will he be all right?" Clara asked, her tight throat easing enough for words to slip through. A little urging reminded her—warned her—that babies frequently died. It wasn't something that would happen to her baby, though. Was it? She exhaled, her muscles trembling as she did so.

"I don't know, but we can't give up." Katie's tone was taut. "He's still breathing."

He was. Barely, but he was. Clara kept her hands cupped over his rump and head, relishing the warmth of his fragile skin. *Let me keep him, God. Please.*

Time seemed nonexistent, yet it flew by. Clara ached for William. He had been at her side during Archie and Newton's births. If he were here to pray with and comfort her, it would make the situation more bearable. Perhaps someone could send a wire, telling him that the baby had come, as they had previously arranged. She doubted he would be allowed to leave work, but at least he would know.

Katie and Clara tried to get the infant to nurse, but to no avail. He made no recognition that anyone was even touching him, much less that he should suck and swallow.

Only a few hours had passed since his birth, and Clara hadn't budged except to drink from the cup Katie offered her, which consisted of red raspberry tea and some other bitter herb she didn't recognize.

Her heart tripped over itself when the baby released a long, shuddering breath. Clara held her own breath, waiting for his to resume.

It didn't.

She turned her head to see him better and jostled him slightly, but there was no response. A dagger pierced her heart and twisted, sending sharp pain coursing through her veins. It couldn't be. He had been breathing just fine a moment ago.

Her heart told her differently.

He's…he's not breathing.

How could a baby that looked so perfect not be alive? Surely, he was just sleeping peacefully. Archie and Newton had sometimes skipped breaths as newborns.

But no; he was dead. Quiet. Unmoving. She hadn't even heard him cry.

"Clara?" Katie asked pensively.

Tears rose in Clara's eyes and the sobs began again with a vengeance. But there was no relief in them. Only more pain. *Why, Lord?*

Katie pulled the blanket back just enough to see what she needed to see. "Oh, Clara, I'm so sorry." She took Clara's hand in hers and squeezed tightly.

Words seemed senseless. Clara felt stray teardrops fall on her arm occasionally. Her tongue stuck in her mouth, dry and cold.

Clara's mind felt numb for the remainder of the week. Yet even through the hallowing numbness, there was a sharp, aching pain. Recovery from the baby's birth was far more difficult than it had been with Archie and Newton, which only added to her emotional struggle. At least with the older boys, she had a newborn to care for and love on during the difficult days.

Katie promised to stay with Clara as long as she was needed, stating that young May was perfectly capable of cooking in her absence. Clara half wondered if she would ever be ready for Katie to return home.

Nights were the hardest for Clara. She desperately wished that William were here to share in her grief. Frank had sent a wire to the company the day of the baby's birth, but they had received no reply. Clara wondered if William was even given the message. If he had gotten it but not been allowed to leave work, she knew without a doubt that he would have at least replied. But he hadn't, which meant he still knew nothing about the baby and wouldn't learn until he returned on Saturday night. And she would have to tell him.

Clara spent much of her time sitting with her back against the maple tree, gazing at the tiny cross Frank had constructed for the baby's grave. With a chilling November wind in her face, Clara felt a small sliver of relief.

Oh Lord, please give my heart peace and keep my faith in You strong. This is so hard for me…so terribly hard. I don't understand why You would take away my sweet little baby, but You did, Lord.

Tears drew in Clara's eyes yet again, and her eyelids felt sandy. How could she keep on living when one of her children was lying, though peacefully, beneath the prairie dirt? Would the deep, sharp ache ever leave?

Newton came out of the house, walking slowly and rubbing his eyes. Silently, he straddled his mother's body, laid his head on her shoulder, and placed his thumb in his mouth. Though she and William had decided not to tell the little boys about the baby until it was born, her grief was affecting them almost as if they knew about their lost little brother.

Clara put her arms about Newton and kissed his head. She needed him as much as he needed her. No— more than he needed her.

It was late Saturday evening; William would be coming home soon. Clara dreaded seeing him, yet she wanted nothing more than to be enveloped in his arms and cry with him. How could she possibly tell him what had happened without breaking down?

She stood at the stove, watching the coffee pot boil. Katie was still with her and, at the moment, she was putting the children to bed. It had taken several minutes for Clara to summon up enough gumption to make coffee. And she hadn't gotten any further than the water pot.

Why did the baby have to die? It wasn't as if he had done anything to deserve death. He was just a helpless, innocent little boy.

Water spilled over Clara's eyes, and the thickness in her throat worsened. She dropped her hot face into her hands, welcoming the slight coolness they provided.

"What happened?" a strangled voice croaked.

Her head whipped to the door. William stood there, his face blanched. She desperately wanted to go to him, but her feet stuck to the floor.

William gestured to her figure, and Clara's head dropped to her chest while more hot tears flooded her eyes. Her knees wobbled dangerously. If she didn't sit down, she would fall down.

It was a long moment before William's arms closed around her and pulled her tightly against him.

Clara didn't even try to contain her grief. She surprised even herself by having any tears at all after the past week. Something about William's presence, comforting her with kisses and stroking her hair, willed her to release some of the aching through tears, little as the relief might be. Clara locked her arms around him, wishing never to let go.

"I lost him," she breathed into his shirt. "He died. Just a few hours after birth."

William stiffened. "How long ago?"

"Monday." A sob interrupted her. "I was so frightened. Katie couldn't get here soon enough—"

William's arms tightened around Clara as her weeping increased. "Oh, Darlin'…" His voice trailed off.

"You should have seen him, Will," Clara said, pulling away just enough to see William's face. "He was so perfect. Every little finger and toe was there. He was a bitty little thing, but so beautiful."

Clara pressed her ear against William's chest again, and heard him swallow hard.

"Where is he now?"

"Near the maple tree. Frank made a little cross."

Unaware of how much time passed, Clara rested in William's arms, grateful for the strength they provided. She never wanted to let go. But he had to leave again tomorrow afternoon. Less than twenty-four hours.

Her arms tightened around his middle. *Lord, why are You testing us like this?*

"I'm quitting my job."

Clara jumped and her mending fell from her hands. Her eyes shot upwards to his face, which glowed fiercely in the dim lamplight. He had only been

313

home for a few hours and seemed to be in a great state of unease, and not just because of the baby.

"What?"

"I'm quitting my job." It sounded as if he were trying to convince himself.

"You can't!" Clara exclaimed. "We need the money."

William drew himself to his full height and paced in front of the hearth. "I want to work closer to home. We can't have something else happen like with the—" he drew in a sharp breath, "the baby. Honestly, Clara, if you or one of the boys were injured, it would be an entire week until I heard about it, since apparently my boss is against giving me my own telegrams." His fist pounded on the mantle. "I'll find a job somewhere else. Closer to home."

"Spokane is the only city within forty miles. There aren't many jobs to be had."

William sighed and leaned against the hearth. "Surely there has to be something else available. I'll look around tomorrow."

"Tomorrow is Sunday." Her breath hitched. "Church."

"You shouldn't go yet—it's only been a week. Do you really want to?" His voice was soft as their eyes met.

Clara dropped her head to her chest, the pressure rising in her throat once again. "I don't even want to breathe."

In a moment, William had pulled her into his arms once again. He pressed her head against his chest and rested his cheek there. Clara wondered if she would ever run out of tears to cry.

Her tears weren't tears of anger—not at all. She knew better than to blame God for the baby's death. Still, such profound sadness filled her heart, even breathing made it ache.

"You stay home tomorrow with the boys," William said. "I'll go to Denison; I heard some fellows last week at church saying that the lumber company was looking for some men."

"Denison?" Clara said, using a rough, chapped hand to wipe her eyes.

"It's about a half-hour's walk from here," William said. "Turning east at Hazzard's."

Clara hardly let herself dare to hope that he could work so close to home.

As William had suggested, Clara and the boys had a quiet Sunday at home. He left at sunup for Denison, leaving Clara alone for the first since the baby had been born.

She cooked an easy breakfast of oatmeal and bread. The outdoor air was cold, and the woodpile getting low. There were just a few small rounds left. She put one into the kitchen stove, and, with Archie's help, dragged the rocker into the kitchen and settled

Newton in her lap. Archie sat on the floor, attempting to read a McGuffey reader.

Mary Ann stopped by for a few minutes after church. She had come by nearly every day since she heard about the baby, for which Clara was thankful. Mary Ann had lost a child herself and was able to offer something that no one else could: true understanding.

William returned before supper, far sooner than Clara had expected. There was a definite spring in his step, and his cheerful whistle carried across the snow-dusted prairie.

"I got the job!" He swung Newton into the air. "In Denison! I can be home every day."

A smile crept to Clara's face; the feeling was almost foreign. William held Newton in one arm and pulled Clara close with the other. "I'll go into town tomorrow and tell the Water Works I'm quitting."

The new job was far better than Clara expected. It took them all a while to adjust to William's night shift, but Archie and Newton soon learned to be quiet in the mornings while William slept, and Clara adapted to the strange mealtimes he required.

Clara braced herself for a blast of cold wind as she stepped out the door to fetch wood for the stove. Winter had definitely begun. There was little snow yet, but the bitter cold was worse than snow. And, worst of all, they didn't have enough wood.

William chopped wood as often as he could, but there wasn't much to be had on the prairie, and he had missed the community wood trip to the mountain base a few weeks ago. Clara wondered how long they could live on the meager stack of wood, especially with colder weather setting in.

Had Clara known how to chop wood, she would have done it herself. But even if she could have, the axe was far too large for her to get a good swing. She had tried a few weeks ago with little success.

Pulling two small pieces into her arms, Clara went back into the house and threw them into the fire. She would let them burn to nearly coals before adding more.

"Bye, Darlin'." William came up behind Clara and hugged her tight, pressing his cheek against hers. "Will you be warm enough?"

Clara nodded, but a shudder passed through her before she could stop it. *Convincing.* "We'll be all right. I'll keep the boys in bed with me tonight."

William's arms tightened and Clara closed her eyes, resting her head against him. How much longer could they survive in the cold without wood? Their bedroom was upstairs, directly above the kitchen. It was the warmest room in the house. The little boys had been sleeping in there on cots for the past few weeks, but tonight, Clara didn't want to risk that. It was so cold, even in the bedroom, that it could be dangerous for the little fellows. Tonight, they would all be sleeping in the big bed with a mountain of blankets over them.

"I'll try to find some wood tomorrow," William said in her ear, "or see if I can snag some rejects from the lumberyard."

Clara nodded again. "We'll be fine. I love you."

William kissed her. "I love you, too."

Clara shivered again as William went out the door. She gripped her upper arms. It had never been this cold in Chicago. Ever.

Though it was just six o'clock, the little boys were already up in Clara and William's bed, playing with blocks under a tent of blankets. Gathering a loaf of bread and bucket of water for drinking, Clara joined them. It was far too cold to be anywhere else.

Chapter 27

Money was scarce. Yet, though the Buckeye Lumber Company was closing until January, Clara and William were able to give the boys a nice Christmas. William made a trip to the Hazzard's store and bought the boys some sweets, which were received with much glee and shouting. Clara made sweet bread and a special egg dish with some of the vegetable preserves. She had also knit each boy and William new socks, mittens, and hats. It was cold enough that the three of them put on their new clothing and wore it for the rest of the day.

The temperature continued to drop. Because wood was so scarce, it had to be carefully rationed, but the house was growing colder. William was able to chop a small amount of wood when he found it, and he had even borrowed some from Katie and Frank. But wood wasn't something that was easily shared. Prairie winters were cold and long.

A few days after New Year's, William bundled up, tied on his boots, and took the axe from its hook by the door.

"Where are you going?" Clara had her suspicions; he had already told her that there was no wood to be found within a few miles.

"To find a tree," William said, his voice taut. "We can't keep living bundled up like this."

Clara shoved hot potatoes in his pockets. "Please, don't go far." She gazed into his eyes and gripped his arms. The snow was deep and cold, and the prairie seemed to stretch on forever. She couldn't lose him.

"I won't," he promised, ducking down to kiss her.

The day was young, and Clara had baking to do. She should be doing laundry, but the mere thought of being up to her elbows in cold water was appalling. And besides, how would the laundry possibly dry? Their bucket of drinking water had a thick layer of ice on it every morning.

William returned from his jaunt for wood far sooner than Clara expected. She opened the door for him, heart full of hope that he had found wood.

But something was wrong. His face was contorted in pain, and he walked slowly and deliberately.

"William!" Clara burst out as he sunk into one of the kitchen chairs. She pulled his gloves, hat, and scarf off. In spite of the cold reddening his cheeks, the rest of his face was pale.

"I am so stupid," William mumbled to himself.

"Wha—"

William rested his head on his hand. He sucked in a breath of cold air. "The timber was wet…frozen. I swung my axe at it, and it bounced off the tree like rubber, out of my hands, and into my foot."

Clara squatted down, pulling William's boots from under the table and propping them on the next chair. She pressed cold fingers to her lips, heart beating wildly.

"William, you're bleeding." She said it as coolly as she could manage.

"I know," he snapped, rubbing his forehead with his fingers. "How could I be so stupid?"

Instead of replying to his question, Clara's mind flew. He was bleeding. Badly. The snow caked around his boot was red, and more blood seeped from the four-inch gash in the leather. Clara didn't want to know what his foot looked like.

"Get your coat off," she ordered, standing up and bringing the water bucket over to the table. "And Archie, go get Mama some rags. Quick now."

Archie ran off. Clara began unlacing William's boots, pulling the undamaged one off first. Then she came to the injured one. Getting the boot off was easy—it loosened considerably once the laces were undone, and she was able to pull it off without causing him much pain.

Clara inspected the boot. She could fix it. Leather was repairable. The sock, too, could be mended. And the foot—Clara swallowed down her lunch.

Seating herself in another chair, she laid the bloody mess in her lap, took the rags from Archie, and began cleaning the wound. The gash itself was at least three inches long.

"I'm all right, Buddy."

William's words made Clara glance up. Archie stood near his father, eyes wide and mouth open. She cringed. She shouldn't have let him see it until she had cleaned the blood.

"Your Mama takes good care of me." William pulled Archie close to him and rested his cheek on the little boy's head.

Even as he held Archie against him, Clara could feel the tension in William's body despite the stoic, even look on his face. He was in horrid pain.

Gently wiping the blood away, Clara inspected the cut. It wasn't jagged, thank goodness, but long and deep. Her heart plummeted when she saw bone peeking out beneath the ever-pooling blood. Granted, the skin over the top of feet was thin.

Swallowing again, Clara laid a clean cloth over the long slice and squeezed it. What could she do? He needed a doctor at the very least.

Impossible.

There was at least three feet of snow on the ground. Getting to Spokane before dark without freezing would be impossible, not to mention entirely foolish. If an accident like this happened in Chicago, a doctor could have come inside of an hour.

But this wasn't Chicago.

"Hold it there," she instructed, bending William's knee and crossing the injured leg over the working one. William grasped the cloth and held it.

Clara dipped her hands in the water and dried them. Then, she pulled the bloody apron off, fetched her hat, mittens, and scarf, and put on William's heavy coat. It was still warm.

"Where are you going?" William asked.

"To Hazzard's for silk thread; I don't have any." Clara reached into the cupboard and pulled out a quarter and a dime. "Your foot needs to be sewn up."

William's eyes bugged. "And you're going to do it?"

"Unless you want to." Clara gave each of the boys a stern look. "Take care of your Father. I'll be back as soon as I can."

It wasn't snowing anymore, and the sun was high in the sky. Even so, a bitter wind attacked Clara and made her uncovered cheeks burn almost instantly. Cold seeped through her clothing, deep into her skin. How could it possibly be so cold when the sun was shining?

Katie's house was nearly two miles away, and Hazzard's was just over a mile. Though Clara desperately wanted her sister's support and assistance, William's cut needed to be sewn up fast. Thoughts of gangrene dominated Clara's thoughts.

"Good afternoon, Mrs. McDonald." Mr. Hazzard's powerful voice rang in Clara's ears after the silence of the frozen prairie. "How can I help you today?"

Clara took her mittens off and rubbed her cheeks. They were dangerously cold. "Thread," she chattered. "Silk thread. And a bottle of the most powerful brandy you have."

Brandy. Dousing the wound in alcohol, painful as it would be, would kill any infection that might be lurking.

Mr. Hazzard's eyebrows raised considerably, and he regarded Clara with a perplexed look. She turned her back and held her hands over the potbellied stove, gasping in the warm air. Would the burning in her lungs never go away?

"That will be thirty-two cents," Mr. Hazzard said. "What color of thread would you like?"

"Anything."

"Mrs. McDonald, is everything all right? I've never known your husband to be a drinker. Unless of course, you will be using the whisky to ward off coughs."

Clara walked to the counter, her numb fingers fumbling to retrieve the coins from her pocket. "William cut himself with an axe. I am trying to keep infection from setting in."

"Oh, dear! Will he be all right?"

"I hope so."

Clara slipped the thread into her pocket and tucked the whisky bottle inside William's coat. The coat itself was large enough that two of her could have fit comfortably. "Thank you, Mr. Hazzard."

Once back home, Clara set to work immediately. She made William a cup of tea from bitter herbs that would help dull the pain. Then, sending the boys upstairs and laying William's foot over a bucket, she peeled back the rag and opened the bottle of brandy

"This is going to hurt," she warned.

"I know."

Clara splashed some of the clear liquid over the still-bleeding wound. Bile rose in her throat at William's suppressed cry, and she dug her fingernails into her palm.

Oh, dear God, please take away his pain!

While the brandy continued to drip off his foot, Clara heated a sharp sewing needle over the fire, gathered scissors and thread, and set them on the table.

"Are you all right?" she asked, allowing her eyes upwards to William's face. It was bleached and his eyes were closed, jaw set firmly. He nodded.

Clara threaded the needle, drew William's foot into her lap, and held the needle over the foot. Her innards squirmed and the needle shook. How could she do this? She was no doctor. What if she did something horribly wrong?

Clenching her teeth, Clara pinched the needle tighter. She had to do it. If she didn't, William could lose a lot of blood, and perhaps even his entire leg if infection came.

Taking one more glance at his down turned face, Clara steeled her voice. "Here it comes."

Mercifully, William passed out after Clara had made two stitches, and she was able to make the other eight without his knowing it. He revived as Clara was spreading thick layer of salve over the wound.

"You're done?" He sounded almost surprised.

Clara nodded. "You just need a bandage now." She covered every inch of the long cut with sticky salve, then laid a rag over it. She used several more rags to pad the injury as well as apply compression.

William leaned against the table, his head resting in his hand. Clara snatched up the mug on the table and refilled it with hot water and the pain-numbing herbs. She coaxed William to drink it down, praying that it would dull the pain.

"Let's get you up to bed," Clara said, carefully lowering his feet from the chair onto the floor.

Clara slipped her arm around William's middle and helped him stand. "Don't put any weight on that leg, or the stitches will pop."

"That would be awful."

William carefully hopped on his good leg, leaning heavily on Clara. Going up the stairs wasn't easy, but the railing helped significantly. Clara lowered William onto the bed and helped him change from his dirty work clothes to warm flannel underclothes.

"Fa'ver better now?" Newton asked, climbing onto the bed.

"Getting there, little man." William pulled the toddler into his lap and cuddled him.

When William was as comfortable as Clara could get him, she returned to the kitchen to finish tidying up. Now that the ordeal was over, tears flooded Clara's eyes and her strong defensive walls began to crumble.

William was all right, praise God, but he was far from healed. That cut could still get infected. And wood—Clara hugged herself to ward off a chill. Even in the kitchen near the stove, it was miserably cold. But she could do nothing about the lack of wood on her own.

Sighing, she went to pick up the bucket William's foot had been sitting over, but gagged and backed away. Such a bloody mess it was. She had to clean—

Clara ran towards the door and leaned over the porch, retching what was left of her lunch. Darkness was falling, though it was only three o' clock. Another long, cold night stood ahead of them.

William slept peacefully all night long. The nasty-tasting herbs she had given him were doing their job.

It was dangerously cold in the bedroom, even under blankets. Clara lay as close to William as she could and pulled Newton's shivering body tightly against hers. Archie was on the other side of William— Clara could hear his open-mouthed breathing in the stillness of the night. What was she going to do about firewood?

Ivy Rose

Chapter 28

The scent of frying ham greeted Clara's nose. She blinked slowly and pushed a cluster of curls away from her eyes. Her head lay on William's chest and his arm was draped across her shoulders. The steady, in-and-out of his breathing told her that he was still asleep.

So who was frying ham? And where had the boys gone? Newton had spent most of the night pinned tightly against Clara for warmth.

She stretched her legs, her foggy brain struggling to make sense of the food cooking. Her toes no longer felt like icicles. Clara touched her cheek. Even it was warm.

A sudden burst of laughter met her ears. She recognized the two small voices as those of her sons, but there was a deeper, more grown-up sounding voice that accompanied them. Was Frank here? What time was it, anyway?

Clara lifted her head and sat up. The sun shone brightly through the curtain over the window. And the air in the bedroom could almost be considered warm— so different than the coldness of last night. What was going on?

Swinging her feet over the edge of the bed, Clara quickly dressed and re-braided her messy hair. She wanted to look at least presentable for their unexpected company, even if it was just Frank.

William sighed and groaned, shifting himself around on the bed. When he saw her, he smiled. "Morning, Darlin'."

"Good morning," she said, hurrying to secure her braid with a ribbon. "Don't get out of bed without me. I'll be right back."

It only got warmer as Clara drew closer to the kitchen. The door to the spare bedroom had been nailed up with boards. Who had done that? And why?

"Hi, Mama!" Archie hollered from the table where he sat, bright eyed and grinning. Newton sat near him, and they were both dressed. She didn't remember setting their clothes out.

"Mr. Dunn makin' bref'dist," Newton reported proudly.

Clara glanced up to the stove. Sure enough, there John Dunn stood, brandishing a wooden spoon.

"Good mornin', Missus McDonald," he greeted, nodding his head. "I didn't see any fiery glow in your house this mornin' like usual when I woke up, so I figured I'd come over and check on you all. Durn good thing I did, too. The fire was near out and it was mighty cold in here."

Mr. Dunn had let himself in the house? Clara wasn't the least bit afraid of him, but it was rather strange for someone to waltz into a neighbor's home uninvited.

"I brought some wood over from my house, seein' as you had none. The hearth fire was plumb cold, and this here fire in the stove was almost out. I got them both roarin' before them little fellas awoke."

"Mr. Dunn got our clothes and washed our faces and now he's cookin' breakfast!" Archie's eyes glowed.

Clara couldn't find the breath to speak. Her eyes searched those of her little sons' to those of the kindly—unusual—neighbor, who wore one of her aprons around his waist. "I—I don't know what to say," Clara laughed, tears stinging her eyes. "Thank you. Thank you so very much."

Mr. Dunn's face glowed. "Aww, twasn't nothin'. Just the neighborly thing to do."

Slumping in a chair, Clara inhaled sharply. "It's more than neighborly," she choked. "William went out to find timber yesterday, but since the tree was frozen, his axe jumped out of his hands and injured his foot badly."

"I'm sorry to hear that," Mr. Dunn said. "Will he be all right?"

Clara nodded. "I hope so. But we have no more wood, and I don't know exactly what to do."

Mr. Dunn crossed his arms over his chest and lowered his chin, the wooden spoon protruding out one side. "Don't you worry about that none, Missus McDonald. After these here little fellas and yourself have eaten your fill, I'll stuff rags in the winders and under doors to keep the heat in. I'll take care of the firewood. Don't ye fret none about that."

Clara nodded, wondering just exactly how he was going to 'take care of it.'

Mr. Dunn served the little boys nicely-cooked ham and hotcakes while Clara went back upstairs to help William.

She found him sitting on the edge of the bed, pulling on a pair of britches.

"William Joseph McDonald, what do you think you're doing?" Clara planted her fists on her hips and scowled at him.

The frightened look on William's face was almost comical. "What's going on down there? You didn't come back fast enough!"

"Well, I apologize." Clara took the pant legs of his trousers and pulled them off.

"Clara!"

"You are staying in bed today." She gave him a gentle push to prove her point.

"Who's downstairs?"

"John Dunn."

William's eyes fell to the floor and his lips shaped the words, John Dunn.

"You've met him at church," Clara prompted. "He lives on an adjoining homestead."

"What's he doing here?"

Clara lowered herself onto the bed beside William. "Cooking breakfast."

"Wha—?"

"Apparently, he didn't see the fire's glow coming through the window, so he came up to check on us." Clara paused and swallowed. "And thank goodness. He brought wood up from his place and lit the stove and the hearth."

"That's why it's so warm in here." William stared at his hands. "I have to thank him." He moved to stand.

"No." Clara held him down. "You can thank him later, or I can send him up here if you wish."

"Do that—send him up."

"Do you want some breakfast?"

A sly smile came to William's face. "Can he cook? Well?"

Clara chuckled and stretched to kiss William's cheek. "He can cook."

"Then I'd love some."

After situating William back in bed with his foot propped on blankets, Clara went back downstairs. The boys were finished eating, but Mr. Dunn had prepared two plates and had set them on the table. Clara looked around for the man, but he was nowhere.

"Where is Mr. Dunn?" she asked the boys.

"I don't know," Archie said, rubbing greasy hands on his britches. "He said that he'd be back in a few hours."

Drat! If only she had expressed her thanks a little more. "I wonder what he's doing?"

The sun was beginning to lower in the sky when Mr. Dunn arrived back. Clara ran to the porch to greet him, but her steps stalled when she saw an entire troop of friends and neighbors following behind his sleigh. The sleigh itself was stacked high with wood.

Clara's hands flew to her face. Was this really happening? Had their neighbors done this for real?

Familiar arms were wrapped around Clara as the ladies from church came up. Most of them carried something with them: jars of food or loaves of bread and even some meats.

"This should help your husband's wound heal faster." A lady Clara didn't know placed a small jar of brown substance in her hand.

Clara managed to mutter "thank you" as things were placed in her arms and well wishes from friends and neighbors were given. Her heart tripped when she saw two more sleighs, stacked high with wood, pulling up to the sides of the house. It was enough to last them the rest of the winter. Already, the men and boys were unloading the firewood and stacking it neatly beside the house.

"I—I can't believe this," Clara breathed. Mary Ann put her arm around Clara's shoulders and squeezed tightly.

"You're welcome."

"But why—?"

"Because this is what neighbors do." Mary Ann frowned a little. "Though I'm slightly upset that you didn't tell me you needed firewood before now."

Clara just laughed a breathless laugh, bidding the tears away. They had more friends on the prairie than she'd realized.

Within two weeks, William was back on his feet again. It was nothing short of a miracle that there had been no infection. Even Katie was flabbergasted.

At the end of the third week, Clara pulled out the stitches. Though the ordeal wasn't entirely pleasant for William, he decided that removing stitches was far more bearable than having them placed. Clara wholeheartedly agreed with him. Lord willing, she would never have to stitch up him, or anyone else, again.

"Clara, a letter from Chicago!" William came jogging through the door, bringing in a cold blast of early March air with him. Clara couldn't help but wonder if spring would ever come. Their one-year anniversary of being on the prairie would come in just a few short weeks, yet there were no signs of the wild roses or even blooms on trees that had been here when she first arrived.

"From whom?" Clara hastily brushed her hands along her apron, leaving the wooden spoon inside the pot of stew.

"Your father."

Clara reached for the letter, but William held it high above his head, his mouth twisted into a smirk. "Ask nicely, miss."

She stood on her toes and pressed her lips against his. "How's that?"

He smiled. "Good enough, I suppose."

She snatched the envelope and sat down at the table.

"Oh!" She turned back to William. "Would you please fetch more water?"

William nodded, and, grasping the bucket, headed back outside.

Clara's heart swelled to see her father's familiar handwriting. Oh, how she missed him. All of them, but her mother and father especially.

Before unfolding the paper, Clara pressed it to her nose and inhaled deeply. It still smelled of Chicago's home.

Dearest Clara,

I am beyond grieved to tell you that your mother has unexpectedly passed away. This will come as a shock, I'm sure.

None of us expected it. The doctor thinks she suffered heart ailment.

Clara stopped reading and suppressed a cry. Her heart pounded in her ears. Her mother was dead? How? When? She had been the image of health just last year!

Though every fiber in her wished to tear her eyes from the paper, she couldn't.

I wish I were there to tell you this news in person, but that is quite impossible. My prayers are with you always, but even more so in the days that follow this letter.

If it is any consolation, your mother did not suffer in the least. Her death was sudden and instant. We can praise God that no long illness was involved.

A tear splashed onto the paper, making Clara jump away from it and rub at her eyes. The ink would get smudged.

I'm having a difficult time coping with her death…

…Whether or not this letter will reach you in time, the funeral is set for March eleventh. I do not expect you to come back for it, but I thought you would like to know when it will be…

…Will you and William allow me to come and be near you in Washington? Would you tell me if you didn't want me to come? I trust you, Clara, above your sisters to tell me honestly what your wishes are.

*Pass the news of this letter along to Katie if you will. I
cannot bear to pen another like it.*

Grieving but living in the Lord,
Father

Clara vainly wiped at her tears and set the letter on
the table. Her mother was dead. Her dear, darling
mother who had been there for almost every moment
in her life was no longer living.

Memories flashed before Clara's eyes…good ones
and bad ones, happy and sad. The smiling face of her
mother was etched in her brain, but the tearful,
encouraging smile Clara remembered as she and the
boys left the Chicago station was more vivid.

Clara rested her face in her hands, willing the pain
to go away. How could this even happen? Her mother
was so young!

The door squeaked, and a firm, gentle hand settled
on her shoulder. A deep voice spoke, but it was
nothing more than gabbling to her numb ears. She
couldn't find the words to tell him what the letter said.

He carefully pried her hands away from her face
and, seeing the fear in his eyes, she managed to say,
"The letter."

Suddenly, Clara was lifted to her feet, then pulled
back down—onto William's lap. She curled into him
and attempted to slow her breathing, but it was futile.
Paper rustled as he picked up the letter, his other hand
holding her gently against him.

Her mother was gone. Dead. Deceased. Never to be seen in this world again. Clara wondered if she would ever again be the same. Her lungs burned and ached. Already there was puffiness in her eyes.

Paper crinkled again, and William's other hand pressed Clara's head tightly into his chest. He stroked her hair and began speaking, though Clara couldn't comprehend the words. She thought he was praying, but couldn't be sure. Why were her ears ringing so badly?

It was quite a long while before Clara exhausted herself and relaxed against William. Her skin felt hot, but no longer did she feel so hysterical.

"Do you want to go back for the funeral?" William asked softly, rubbing his thumb back and forth over Clara's forearm. "You could make it in time."

They had no money for such things; Clara knew that as well as he did. They barely had enough to purchase basic necessities, much less a train ticket to Chicago and back.

"No. The boys are too little for me to leave them."

William didn't argue. "Your father can certainly come here; there is no reason for him not to. We have enough room for him to stay with us, if he so wishes."

"He's so sensitive about intruding. I don't want him to be uncomfortable."

"Will you mind if he lives with us?" William asked.

"No, not at all. I would enjoy it."

"Then tell him that."

Clara nodded, sniffling. "I'll write him. Tonight."

Ivy Rose

Chapter 29

Telling Katie that their mother had died was one of the most difficult things Clara had ever done. And she couldn't even say everything before her voice failed, forcing William to finish for her.

The Newells couldn't afford for Katie to go back for the funeral, either. It was assuredly as hard for her as it was for Clara. Instead of fretting about it, Clara spent much time planning and preparing the guest room for their father, who would be arriving within a few weeks.

The little boys didn't remember their grandparents well, especially Newton, so their grandma's death was of less gravity than it would have been otherwise. They were, however, excited to learn that Grandpa Boutwell was coming to live with them.

Clara took the photo her parents had given her for Christmas so many years ago and set it on the mantle. Difficult as it was to see their faces smiling back at her, especially that of her mother's, she felt more at peace with a constant reminder to pray for her father as they grieved the terrible loss.

Frank was to meet Mr. Boutwell at the station the day he arrived. William wanted to go as well, but he had just been promoted to an engineer for the Buckeye Lumber Company, which was quite the step up from his night watchman job. He earned $2.50 a day, which was no small fortune. They couldn't afford for him to miss a day of work.

Leaving early the night before Mr. Boutwell's train was to arrive, Frank set off towards Spokane in Mr. Carter's hack. That wagon was used far more by neighbors than it was by the owners, but wagons terribly expensive and it was no wonder that so few people actually owned them.

Frank arrived back the following evening, just as darkness was falling. Clara ran outdoors as soon as she heard the wagon coming near, with William and the boys at her heels.

Her father had changed—that much was easy to see. He had grown thin and his face bore far more wrinkles than Clara remembered.

Clara walked towards him as he alighted from the wagon, and she threw her arms around his now-frail body. Her throat grew thick yet again and her eyes stung, but she fought the emotions back. She needed to be strong for her father.

"Welcome!" she managed after a time, pulling out of her father's embrace. "We're happy to have you. How was your journey?"

Mr. Boutwell hugged William. "Very long, I'm afraid, but uneventful."

Clara gestured for the little boys to come nearer. They did so, casting shy glances upwards at their grandfather.

"Father, you remember the boys—Archie and Newton."

Mr. Boutwell knelt down and managed a small smile for the little ones. "Indeed I do. You both have grown up much since I saw you last."

Archie grinned and puffed his chest out, while Newton offered a smile from behind Clara's skirt.

"Please, come in. Supper is ready."

Frank and William carried in her father's large trunk and set it in his bedroom. Then, Frank raised his hat, saying that he would bring the rest of his family to see Grandpa Boutwell in the morning.

During supper, Clara tried desperately to keep her eyes off her Father's face, but it was nearly impossible. How different he looked! The face of a man once so strong, yet now so broken. Could this truly be her tenacious, passionate father?

Tired from the long journey, Mr. Boutwell went to bed soon after the little boys, leaving William and Clara alone with their thoughts and a pile of dirty dishes.

"I hope this doesn't kill him," Clara muttered, pausing in her scrubbing and letting her eyes rest on a pattern of wood in the wall. Tears were stinging her eyes again, and her throat tightened. *Please God, I can't lose him, too.*

Footsteps sounded behind her, and strong arms crossed over her chest, a wet rag balled in one hand. Clara rested her achy head on William's shoulder and closed her eyes. He laid his cheek against hers and sighed.

"He'll be all right," William said. "His faith is unwavering; I can see that clearly. He won't leave us anytime soon."

Clara hoped William was right. What would she do without her parents? Already she was motherless. Being fatherless, too, would be insufferable.

"Our anniversary is coming up," William said softly. "What will this be—seven? Eight?"

"Seven." A smile twitched at Clara's lips. "Your thirty-second birthday is coming, too."

William let out a breathy chuckle. "No need to remind me."

"We should do something. For both."

"The birthday can be skipped." William pulled Clara tighter. "But the anniversary…yes."

"How about a cake? Everyone can enjoy that."

William nodded and placed a kiss on Clara's cheek. "Sounds perfect."

Even through the end of March, the warm spring weather refused to show itself, leaving the prairie covered in a pile of dirty, wet snow. Such an ugly sight it was, with dark ground showing through the snow in patches. A bitter wind whipped around the house and moaned through the trees. Clara thought it sounded just like her grieving heart.

Her mother's death was taking a toll on Clara far worse than she had imagined. Life felt empty without her dear mother available to read a long, heartfelt letter and return one of equal emotion. Daily duties had become drudgery. The pain in her chest seemed to reverberate throughout her entire body.

Her father was in better shape than Clara herself was, and he had quickly settled into a relaxed routine of prairie life. He found relief in the little boys that even Clara couldn't.

William was an ever-present shoulder to cry on, which Clara took advantage of many times. He comforted without judgment and wiped her tears away with a loving hand. Scripture seemed to evade Clara during those difficult moments, but William helped her along by quoting verses and praying with her. At times, it felt like only thing keeping her going was William and the Lord.

While the pain in Clara's heart didn't dull any, her body weakened. By the time she realized that something terrible, other than grief, was going on inside, it was too late.

It was a snowy morning when her strength gave out and she trembled all over with fever. Only then did Clara allow her father to take her up to bed. Once underneath warm blankets with hot rocks at her feet, she drifted in and out of a delusional sleep.

She awoke to a soft hand stroking her face and familiar voices all around. Opening her swollen, puffy eyes, she saw Katie, Addie Smith, and Mary Ann all crowded around her bed. There were a few other women that Clara recognized but couldn't name.

The blurry form that was Katie put her arm around Clara's shoulders while Addie put a mug in front of her mouth. Their words were jumbling together, but Clara took the hint that they wanted her to drink from the mug. She did, though it burned her throat all the way down.

Were the boys safe? What was all the clattering she heard downstairs? Clara tried to understand what was happening, but in vain. She soon felt herself sink into the mattress again. It was impossible to stop sleep from coming.

The next time Clara awoke, it was to William's rough hands pressing her forehead and squeezing her arms.

"William—" She wanted nothing more than to have this horrid pain taken away. Her chest burned and rattled, and she trembled with cold.

"Shhh, Darlin'." William stroked her hair and kissed her forehead. His lips were cold. "You're very sick and must stay calm. Do you need anything?"

Clara felt tears rising in her eyes, but she was too tired to cry. "No," she said, squeezing his hand tighter. "The boys—"

"They're with Katie."

Katie had the boys. A heavy weight slipped off Clara's shoulders, and she drifted back to sleep.

Clara remembered little of the next few days. The concerned voices of her neighbors and friends, William's strained tones, chilly hands touching her face, sticky salves over her chest—it all blended together in a muddy, smelly mess. If only her brain would stop spinning, Clara might be able to figure out what was going on. But no, her mind wouldn't stop and, consequently, made her vomit multiple times. Even in sleep, turbulent dreams allowed Clara little rest. Was this what dying felt like?

Someone was poking her. Again. Asking her to wake up.

Painfully, Clara raised her eyelids and tried to focus on the figure looming above her. Her eyes cleared and she could see that the figure was a man, and an elderly one at that.

"I'm going to sit you up and have you take a medicine."

Clara tried to acknowledge that she heard the man, but no sounds would come from her sandpaper mouth. He pulled her up to a sitting position and asked her to open her mouth. Who was he? She didn't recognize him as a neighbor.

"Clara."

Straining, Clara focused on another figure that came into her field of vision. It was William. He was holding her hand, rubbing his thumb back and forth across her knuckles.

"Open your mouth for Dr. Elderkin."

Doctor? Where had the doctor come from? Was she really so sick to need one?

Feeling William's finger tap her lips, Clara let her jaw fall open. Dr. Elderkin put in a spoonful of something that burned like fire. She swallowed it quickly, but it burned all the way down.

"One more." The doctor shoved another spoonful of the wretched liquid in Clara's mouth before she had time to protest.

A fleeting thought of hope that the medicine would stay down passed in front of her mind, but left just as quickly. Even if she vomited, it was unlikely that the doctor would stop forcing things down her throat.

Once laid on her back again, Clara heard the distinct mumbling of William, the old doctor, and Addie Smith. She couldn't comprehend what they were saying and didn't bother trying.

By the following morning, Clara awoke to find the burning in her chest greatly diminished, and she wasn't half as cold. Addie was seated at her side, her elbows on the bed and head in her hands. Dozing.

Clara shifted around to find a comfortable spot in the mattress. Addie straightened, rubbing sleep from her eyes.

"Can I have some water?" Her voice croaked pitifully.

Addie drew a cup of water from the pitcher at the side of the bed. She helped Clara sit up and drink it, then lowered her back onto the pillows.

It was still quite early; Clara could tell from the way the light came in the window. Gazing around, Clara saw that she and Addie were the only ones in the room.

"Where's William?"

There were tears in Addie's eyes. "He's resting. You've been sick for several days, and we finally got William to leave your side and sleep so that he wouldn't fall ill, too."

"What day is it?"

"April eighth. You've been down for five days."

Five days! Such a long time that was, yet Clara remembered little of it.

"We weren't sure if you would make it."

Clara's eyes sought Addie's tear-filled ones. She didn't know this woman very well. They had only talked a few times after church and at community gatherings, yet she had been willing to sit up all night with Clara.

"Are the boys all right?" Clara desperately hoped that her children had escaped the illness.

"They're just fine. Katie still has them."

Clara nodded and closed her eyes. The wretched trembling had stopped, and no longer did her head spin. Tiredness was setting in again, but no longer were her dreams disturbed by nightmares.

When she awoke again, it was William who sat in the chair near her bed. Her hand was clasped in his and he held it to his lips, watching her with scrutinizing eyes.

"How do you feel?" he asked, straightening up a bit and trying to smile.

"Better. Far better." She managed a weak grin.

"Can I get you anything?"

Clara shook her head. Her eyes closed again.

"Clara."

William's voice held urgency, and Clara dragged her gummy eyelids open once again. A drop of water splashed on her arm. Looking up, she saw that William's eyes were brimming.

"I thought I was going to lose you." The words came out slowly, brokenly, and another tear dripped onto her hand.

Clara wished she had the strength to pull herself into his lap and assure him that she was all right, that she wasn't going to die. But she couldn't. Just keeping her eyes open took an enormous effort.

Pulling William down closer, she laid her arms around his neck. Not a most comfortable position for him, but it was the best she could manage.

Clara's recovery was slow, long, and difficult. Typhoid fever, Dr. Elkerdin had called it. She daily praised God that no one else had caught it.

William told Clara that the first day she fell sick, he came home to a kitchen full of neighbor men lining the walls, and he had counted fifteen women in the bedroom alone. It shocked Clara to hear of the speedy response of their neighbors. Such dear friends they all were.

After the third day of the illness, William told, it became apparent that she needed a doctor. None of the men wanted to put their team out on the bad roads, but Dan Trolan, Mary Ann's husband, offered to do it. It was near nine o'clock at night, and his team had only just returned from Spokane. But he turned them around and headed back in to fetch the doctor.

The doctor that saved Clara's life.

A shudder passed through Clara as it dawned on her how near she had been to death. The thought of leaving her two darling little boys without a mother was almost too much to bear.

Chapter 30

Throughout the spring and summer, Clara enjoyed planting another large garden and tending it. Gardening had always been fun for her, but now that it served as more than a simple hobby, it was all the more enjoyable. With her hands in the dirt, Clara felt freed from the aching in her heart. True, the past months had helped to dull the pain of her mother's death, but it was a long process. And her illness made the emotional recovery take even longer.

Clara loved having her father live with them, though he continually hinted at the fact that he wanted to homestead his own plot of land. In honesty, Clara was worried about her father living by himself. He was getting up in years, and she wished him to be close by. Not that she ever told him so, but she and William had plenty of conversations about it.

A warm night in late August, Clara and William sat outside on the front porch, utilizing the waning twilight to read and work by. Both boys had been snuggled into bed long ago, and Mr. Boutwell had also retired. Though it was unusual for the couple to have time in the evenings entirely to themselves, not many words passed between them. Perhaps now would be a good time to tell him…

"Will?"

After a second, William folded the paper. "Hmm?"

Clara let Archie's trousers fall into her lap. "Do you still like the idea of having ten children?"

His brows furrowed. "Well, yeah. Of course."

Clara cleared her throat, watching the last shreds of sunlight reflect in William's clear eyes. "Do you think Newton will make a good big brother?" She went on before he could answer, a slight smile tugging at her lips. "Because I think he's going to get a chance."

William said nothing for a long moment. "Do you mean…?"

Nodding, Clara stood and accepted his open arms. They tightened around her firmly, and she smiled into his cotton shirt.

"When will it be?" he asked.

"Sometime in March, I think." The thought that was never far from her mind loomed closer. What if this baby died, like the last one had? She wasn't sure if she could handle another death. Especially that of her child.

William grew much more experienced at chopping wood, and, when winter dumped heaps of snow on them again, they were prepared. Even Mr. Boutwell insisted on helping chop wood. It frightened Clara to see her father swinging the heavy axe, especially since he was only just learning how to use one. Wood was purchased in Chicago, not chopped by homeowners. But despite her fears, he did beautifully and saved William a good bit of time.

Around Christmas, the McDonald's received two letters from Chicago—one from Esther and Lewis and the other from William's parents. Both bore good news. Esther had given birth to a darling baby girl in late October, and both mama and baby were doing well. Clara rejoiced with her sister, hoping that someday she would get a chance to meet her little niece.

The second letter, from William's parents, said that they were all in good health and prayerfully considering moving to Washington in order to be closer to their son, daughter-in-law, and grandchildren. Clara was excited about that idea; having them nearby would be such a blessing. William wrote back immediately and told them so.

Aside from her typical morning sickness early on, Clara's pregnancy went quite well. Back in Chicago, she had been able to rest a considerable amount during her pregnancies with Archie and Newton, but out on the prairie, she couldn't afford to rest. Her family needed her, and there was no one who could completely take over household duties. Mary Ann, Katie, and Addie each took their turn coming over to help with laundry and such as Clara got nearer to the little one's birth, but for the most part, Clara had to make do on her own

This baby was proving to be an active one. Clara would often awake in the night to its painful stretching and somersaults. Newton had been so calm and still before birth, as had the last little boy, but this one…this one was almost as active as Archie had been.

Do you really think I can handle another Archie, Lord? Clara smiled at the idea. Archie wasn't an easy child, but like her father had promised soon after he was born, she wouldn't have changed him for the world.

The one-year anniversary of her mother's death was soon upon them. Clara felt that she coped with it quite well, but her father had a far more difficult time. She often found him wandering aimlessly in the sea of yellow roses, sometimes bending down to pluck one out of the earth.

His wandering wasn't truly aimless, though; Clara could sometimes see his lips moving and would watch as he fell to his knees, hands clasped and head bowed. He was coping the only way he knew how—with Jesus.

The pains came on suddenly and with a vengeance. Clara woke up moaning, and it took several minutes before she realized what had awakened her.

She glanced toward the window; it was still dark. William slept soundly at her side, snoring quietly. She didn't want to wake him yet. It would likely be hours before the little one made his or her appearance.

Another contraction struck Clara and she covered her mouth to keep from moaning. It was difficult to remain still. The pain eased, and she was left breathing hard and sweating a little.

Fear flitted through Clara's mind. These pains were so much like the ones that had come with the last baby—fast and hard. Would this baby die, as the last one had?

Please Lord, let me keep this one. Clara chewed her lip and stared at the ceiling. It was useless to try and sleep, yet her body ached for rest. She hadn't been able to sleep soundly for the past few nights.

Another contraction seized her before she had time to relax. This time, Clara couldn't muffle her moans and she tossed and turned. This baby was coming fast, exactly as its older brother had. But this time, praise God, William was close by.

"What's the matter, Clara?" his gravelly, sleepy voice croaked.

Clara panted as the pain eased. "The baby's coming. Fast. Katie—"

"Shh, shh. It's all right." William clasped her hand and kissed her cheek. "You've done this before. I'll go fetch Katie." He slid off the bed.

"No! Will—" Clara reached for his hand and gripped it tightly. "Stay with me. It's coming too fast."

"I don't know what to do!" William cried.

Breathing deeply, Clara tried to focus her thoughts. "The book. It's on the shelf. Look at that."

Clara felt the bed move as William slid off, lit the lamp on the dresser, and fetched the *Family Doctor*. She hoped it would help him. There was no possible way she could wait for Katie or any other neighbor to get here, and talking him through it herself likely wouldn't go well.

Another pain came on and Clara moaned, gripping the sheets with all her strength. William returned to the bedside and stroked her arm, but Clara saw out of the corner of her eye that his were glued to the book.

"I'll be right back," he said once Clara's pain had momentarily ceased.

"Where are you going?" She *couldn't* deliver another baby herself.

"To get water heating. That's what it says."

The front door slammed as William ran out to the creek with the water bucket, and when he returned, she heard the stove squeak and crack as he stoked the fire.

He wasn't out of the room for more than ten minutes, but in that time Clara had several contractions. They were coming closer together now.

"William!" she yelled, not even caring if her cry awoke the little boys. Her father was here. He could take them on a midnight jaunt across the prairie, if need be.

Within seconds William was at her side, kissing her face and smoothing back sweaty curls. There was a stack of towels and blankets at the foot of the bed and a basin of warm water on the dresser.

Clara's tight throat eased just to have someone with her. If this little one had died, or would die, she didn't want to be the first to know. She couldn't bear that pain again.

It wasn't long before William handed Clara a squalling, angry baby wrapped loosely in a towel.

Thank You, Jesus! Clara laid the little one on her chest and didn't stop the tears that fell from her eyes.

The baby was all right; its gusty screams said that much. The Lord was letting her keep this one.

"What is it?" Clara asked, suddenly realizing that William hadn't told her the gender of the baby.

"I didn't look." His voice strained in concentration.

Clara unwrapped the baby slightly and rolled its body to the side. "A girl," she breathed, a smile coming to her face along with more tears. Her first daughter.

"Sweet little girl. Mama loves you so much." Clara kissed her head, which was coated in dark, still-wet hair. She had stopped screaming now and lay contentedly over Clara, dark little eyes surveying the world.

While William finished tidying up the bed, Clara nursed her little daughter. The baby was vigorous and strong, kicking, grunting, and squirming about just like a newborn should. Clara was just happy that she was alive.

William brought Clara a cool cup of water. He sat on the edge of the bed and took her hand in his, bending down to kiss her. Clara noticed that he looked a bit pale.

"How are you doing?" he asked.

Clara smiled up at him, her heart tingling. "I feel wonderful. You did excellent."

William ran a hand over his face. "I hope I didn't do anything wrong."

"There isn't much you can do wrong." Clara chuckled. "Babies practically birth themselves."

William kept the *Family Doctor* book at his side while he bathed the baby and dressed her. Clara sipped at the water he had brought and watched him caring for their daughter, a smile in her heart.

When baby was bathed, dressed, and wrapped snugly, William settled her into the crook of Clara's arm.

"What should we name her?" he asked as Clara sank deeper into the pillows, closing her eyes.

"Name?" Clara's eyes opened again. She'd almost forgotten that the baby needed a name. "I've always liked the name Vera. And Marguerite, for your mother."

"Vera Marguerite, then? I like that."

Clara looked at the scrunched-up, sleeping baby next to her. "Little Vera."

A firm knock was heard on the door, and, after a questioning glance at each other, William rose to answer it.

"Is everything all right?"

William opened the door wider. "She's fine. Would you like to meet your new granddaughter?"

Clara smiled, not bothering to sit up any higher. Her father, clad in a long dressing gown, walked with slow steps, though his face told that he had been awake for awhile. Her commotion must have roused him.

She thought she saw tears sparkling in his eyes as he sat down in the chair near the bed and brushed his finger along the baby's cheek.

"What—" he cleared his throat. "Does she have a name?"

"Vera Marguerite."

Her father sat and stared at the baby for a long time before kissing Clara and rising to leave the room. "If she turns out to be the slightest bit like her mother or aunts, I will be one proud Grandpa."

Clara smiled at her father's wink. He shut the door partway as he exited, letting a cool draft in. It was the end of February, after all, and the hearth fire needed to be built.

"The boys will be waking up soon," William said, looking towards the door as if he expected the little boys to come barging in at any moment. "I'll keep them out of here for a while so you can rest."

Clara nodded, letting her arm tighten about little Vera. *Thank You, Jesus, for letting me keep her!*

Katie came over to see her little niece as soon as she heard the news. She applauded William for a job well done and mooned over the baby.

Archie and Newton were quite excited about their new little sister. Newton, who had just turned four the past November, was quite possessive of her and wanted to hold her at every chance. Clara let him, so long as he remained sitting down. She had seen the careful way he handled animals and had no doubt that his little sister would be treated with equal caution.

Archie, on the other hand, was far too busy to sit still for long. He held the baby once or twice, but only for a few moments each time before he was up and running around like the prairie wind. Clara didn't doubt his love for his sister—he just showed it differently than Newton did.

Within two weeks of Vera's birth, Clara was back on her feet and going full power once again. Vera was fussier and needier than Newton had been, but with her father, Newton, and Archie around to do little things for the baby, Clara's days were much easier than they had been when she was on her own.

Chapter 31

William brought another letter home. The address on the envelope was written in a hand that Clara didn't recognize, but it said it was from the Kopp's, so Clara eagerly tore into it.

She had only read a paragraph before she ran outdoors and let her stomach empty itself.

Emma was dead.

Her quite, reserved, sweet spirited sister was dead, leaving a heartbroken husband and two little girls behind. Clara couldn't believe it. First her baby, then her mother, and now Emma. Who was next?

William's footsteps shook the porch beneath her, and he handed her a rag. Clara cleaned herself and turned to him, burying her face in his chest. She didn't even want to read the rest of the letter.

William led her inside and to one of the kitchen chairs. In her blurred vision, she saw her father standing on the opposite side of the table. Keeping his arm securely about her shoulders, William cleared his throat and read Wesley's letter.

Dear Father Boutwell, Clara, William, Katie, Frank, and children,

I am heartbroken to tell you all that Emma has died. A diphtheria epidemic swept through the city. Mercifully, the girls and I were spared, though I wish that I had been the one to die instead of Emma. Life without her is almost unbearable. The girls are the only reason I want to live.

I have given preaching over to Mr. Green, the head elder, for a time. The congregation has been amazingly supportive during this trial.

Thank God, the girls are well. I am considering returning to the East—to my parents—so that the girls can be raised properly with a mother figure.

Much love,

Wesley, Maud, and Hazel

Clara didn't stop her tears from falling and focused on taking deep breaths. William set the letter on the table, pulling her close and kissing her hair. She opened her eyes briefly to see that her father no longer stood across from them. The kitchen door slammed. He was going back to roaming the fields, cold as it might be.

Emma's death was a shock to them all, but Clara felt that she coped with it far better that she had with her mother's death. Perhaps it was because she had a new baby demanding every last scrap of her attention, as well as two men and two boys to care for. Or maybe, it was because she was gaining a deeper understanding that how no matter how difficult life got, no matter how hopeless it appeared, God always had a reason bigger than anything she could imagine.

When spring finally came upon them, Clara began to worry about the garden. She had failed to plant enough last year and, consequently, they had been short on vegetables toward the end of winter. On the prairie, the growing season was so short and hot that it was difficult to grow anything. Squash, pumpkins, and melons couldn't be grown at all.

She had heard from many other homesteaders that the weather was far more mild and the summers longer on the Spokane River, which flowed not even fifteen miles southwest of the prairie. There was also a lot of untouched land there, just waiting for homesteaders. Part of Clara wondered if it would be worthwhile to move to the river, where they could claim a large plot of nutrient-rich land—where she could escape from the memories of the three deaths that had happened while on the prairie. But another part of her wanted to stay close to Katie and the other friends they had made on Wild Rose.

William helped Clara till up more ground so she could expand the garden and make do with the growing season they had. Clara soon ran into a problem, though; Vera was too little to be indoors by herself and, yet, when Clara put her in a laundry basket near where she would be working, she cried. The baby was only content when being held, which was impossible when Clara had her hands in the dirt.

Mary Ann happened to stop by one day to find Vera screaming in her basket while Clara hurried to finish planting a row of carrots. Mary Ann scooped up the baby and comforted her while Clara finished and cleaned her hands.

"I don't know what I'm going to do," Clara moaned, taking the baby into her arms and ushering Mary Ann to follow her indoors. "She isn't happy unless someone is holding her. I can't get anything done!"

Clara slumped into a kitchen chair unbuttoned her blouse. Perhaps Vera was just hungry. If she would eat and fall asleep for a few hours, Clara could finish the planting.

Mary Ann poured herself and Clara a cup of water.

"I had the same problem with Danny when we first came here. He wanted to be held all the time, but I couldn't do it because I was helping Dan build our cabin."

"What did you do?"

Mary Ann chuckled. "Some locals heard Danny's squalls and came to see what the problem was. You can imagine my fright as two Indian women walked into our yard and over to my baby."

Clara's lips parted. "Indians?"

"Yes, Indians. They didn't appear hostile, as I had expected, and asked with gestures if they could pick Danny up. As soon as he was comfortably in the woman's arms, he stopped squalling. The two women jabbered for a while, then one reached into the small bag she carried and pulled out a long piece of colorful cloth. She began wrapping the material around me—"

"And you let them?" Clara was shocked that her fiery friend would let strangers hold her baby and wrap a cloth around her.

"I did. Once they got it situated, the woman holding Danny put him on my back, tied into the fabric. At first, I was afraid that he would fall out, but after jumping up and down and bending over a few times, I was convinced that he wouldn't. I carried him like that until he was more than a year old. He was perfectly happy in there. I won't need the cloth unless another baby comes along. Let me run back home and fetch it."

"Are you sure?" Clara's tone carried more desperation than she had hoped.

"Positive. I'll be back in a while."

Sure enough, Vera was completely content to be tied on her mother's back. Her constant whimpering stopped, and she rarely cried. Clara was able to work in the garden without interruption and housework became substantially easier, as well. If only she had known about such a thing when Newton and Archie were babies!

Sundays were a time of rest and relaxation; Clara looked forward to them all week long. The inviting June sun sent splashes of light through the church's windows, along with some welcome warmth.

Emma always sat as near to the church's big window as she could when they were children.

Emma.

Clara's throat tightened. Though ever prim and proper, with her hands neatly folded in her lap, Clara remembered how her sister's eyes would stray through the window and to the clouds beyond. She always said she could hear the sermon better if she could see part of Jesus's beauty. And Emma never failed to see his beauty in the clouds.

As the pastor droned on, Clara swallowed down the thickness in her throat. In spite of herself, a smile grew on her face as she bounced Vera in her arms. Such a cute baby she was. Would she be as tough and adventurous as her brothers when she grew older?

Archie fidgeted in his seat beside Clara. Without looking, she gave the boy a warning nudge and went back to focusing on the sermon.

Minutes later, Clara heard a rather loud *"ribbit!"* come from the seat beside her, and she felt the bench jostle as the boys giggled.

She stole a glance in their direction. The sight she saw made her heart leap into her throat. Hastily shoving the baby into William's arms, Clara stood and grasped both boys firmly by their upper arms.

The trio clattered out of the church, Clara's face burning. Archie and Newton said nothing, but Clara felt the resistance in their movements.

Once outdoors, away from the eyes and ears of fellow church-goers, Clara turned the boys to face her. Archie cradled a rather large frog in his palm. Where he had gotten such a large frog this time of year, Clara had no idea. Their sheepish, guilty looks softened Clara's heart a bit, and she took a deep breath before speaking.

"Why did you bring that frog to church?" she asked evenly, looking her first born in the eyes.

"I wanted to show him to George." Archie's eyes showed no defiance, just matter-of-fact impishness. A blast of prairie wind whipped his ruddy hair around his head.

"Ain't he big, Mama?" Newton asked, his eyes glittering as he stroked the frog with a careful finger.

Clara bit back a laugh, trying to keep her face emotionless. "Archie, you know it's naughty to bring animals to church. When we are at church, we need to be listening to the pastor so we can understand Jesus more. Do you think it makes Jesus happy when you are being sneaky and playing with things when we're supposed to be listening?"

The impishness melted, and he dropped his head to his chest. "No, prob'ly not."

"Would you like to let the frog go, or go put him underneath that bucket over there and show George after church?"

Archie's eyes lit. "The bucket!"

Clara nodded. "Do it quickly and wipe your hands in the grass."

Archie did as she instructed, and soon the three were replaced on their bench. Archie sat with his hands folded in his lap, face downcast. Newton stole a few glances up at his older brother and copied his position. Clara tried to still her shaking shoulders. They looked comical, so grown-up like.

When the sermon was over, and everyone tumbled outdoors, Clara nudged William as a man came up behind them. William spun about.

"Morning!" The man extended his hand to William first, then Clara. "My name is Barney Kolker. I was told that you might be looking for a place to live along the mighty Spokane river."

William shifted his weight on his feet. "That's right. The growing season here is a little too short for our liking and we're exploring some other options."

Mr. Kolker nodded. "Sure thing. Are you thinking seriously about moving?"

"We've talked about it a bit. We're thinking that it would suit our needs better."

"'Course; sure thing. Well, I heard a rumor that my neighbor is selling his relinquishment homestead. One-hundred and eight acres, he wants to git rid of. I'll let him know that you folks might be interested."

"Thank you, Mr. Kolker." William grinned. "We appreciate it."

Mr. Kolker shook their hands again and smiled at Vera, then was off.

Clara couldn't stop her squeal of excitement. They *had* talked about moving to the river. Quite seriously, actually. The more she heard from people like Mr. Kolker, the more excited she was about possibly living there.

"Calm down." William put a gentle hand over her shoulders and chuckled. "We aren't moving yet."

Maybe not yet, but soon, Clara was sure.

Sure enough, the next week after church, another stranger approached. He introduced himself as Freize.

"I heard from Barney thet ye might be iner'ested in some river land."

"We are."

Freize shoved his hands in his pockets. "Well, you might say that I bit off a tad more than I could chew, and I'm lookin' to sell my homestead on the river. It's one-hundred and eight acres. Iffen you folks was interested, yer more than welcome to come take a look at the land. I'd sell it to ya for a fair price."

Hope soared in Clara's heart. One hundred eight acres? On the river? It was almost too good to be true. She squeezed William's arm.

"We'd love to see it," William said. "Would next Saturday work?"

"'Course, course."

Freize went on to give them directions to his homestead. It really was directly on the banks of the river. Clara couldn't keep the grin off her face.

The week couldn't go by fast enough. William had arranged to borrow Mr. Carter's hack and horse, and Mr. Boutwell offered to watch the boys.

They drove out of the yard just as the sun was rising over Mt. Spokane. It was a warm July morning, and Clara wore only a light shawl over her shoulders to ward off the chill. Vera slept soundly in her lap, bundled in a blanket. Clara leaned down and kissed her little daughter's chubby face.

The rather long ride gave Clara and William ample time to talk. They talked of the children, his parents who wanted to come west as soon as possible, and how they would afford this new land if it met their needs.

"We should get ourselves a wagon and team," Clara said. "If we live on the river, you will have to drive to work."

William agreed with her logic, but finding the funds might prove a challenge. It all depended on how much Freize would sell his land for.

Freize had said that going down Kolker Hill and taking the river road was the fastest way to get to his property. The river road, appropriately named for its two-mile stretch that wound along the banks of the river, seemed to be the fastest way to get anywhere. It was the route that was frequently used when going to Spokane, unless one was carrying a tall or fragile wagon load. In that case, the long, flat trail across the prairies was used.

Kolker Hill was terribly steep, Clara already knew. She had to lean back in the seat and stand on the footboard just to keep from sliding off.

William kept the horse moving slowly down the slope. Everything was going wonderfully until a sharp, sickening crack pierced Clara's ears and the horse bolted away from the wagon, taking William with him. She let out a scream as the wagon, now disconnected from the horse, picked up speed and veered off towards the edge of the road.

Lord, help us!

In a second, Clara dropped Vera into her lap and pulled her skirts around the baby. Hopefully it would pad her if—when—they were thrown.

Sure enough, the wagon struck a log on the side of the road, tossing Clara and Vera out like they were no more than a bushel of wheat. Clara gasped for air as she landed squarely on her back. A cutting pain reverberated through her spine and set stars before her eyes.

The world went black.

Ivy Rose

Chapter 32

Clara's eyes opened again and she panted to catch her breath, which had momentarily been taken away from her. Her chest pounded both from hurried breathing and a rapid heart rate. Glancing to the side, she saw Vera, lying in a heap next to her, cooing and waving her arms. A long breath escaped her. The baby was all right.

"Clara!" William's terror-filled voice met her ears. "Clara! Where are you!"

"I'm here," Clara yelled back. She tried to push herself up, but the pain in her back was so sharp she cried out and fell back to the ground.

William appeared at her side, falling to his knees. His face was pale and drawn, and he pressed her arms, legs, and ribs. Clara saw his eyes flit to the happy, oblivious baby lying near.

"What happened?" Clara fought to keep herself from blacking out again. The pain was crushing.

"The horse's breeching broke loose from the wagon," William said tautly, prodding the back of her neck.

"I can't get up," Clara breathed, squeezing her eyes shut to seal in the tears.

"What hurts?"

"My back."

William slid his hand underneath Clara and pressed on her spine in a few places.

"Please, stop," she moaned, pushing his hand back. Would the pain ever ease?

William sat back on his heels and stared at the sun, as if contemplating what to do.

"Did you get the horse?" Clara asked.

"Yeah, he's over there."

"Who lives around here?"

William sighed, biting his lower lip. "Kolkers have to be somewhere since the hill was named after them, but he said he owned about two-hundred acres, so..."

Two hundred acres? Finding a house on that much land was hardly better than looking for a needle in a haystack.

With sudden revelation, William snapped his eyes o Clara. "Will you be all right with Vera if I walk on a and see if I can find anyone to help? I'd be able to ve faster if I left her here."

The mere thought of being left in the forest, ble to move, with an infant was enough to terrify a, but what other option did she have? She couldn't even sit up, much less walk. And though the very last thing she wanted was for William to leave, she nodded.

William stood and went to the wagon, which lay on its side. One edge of the box was mere splinters, as was the right front wheel. He pulled the loaded shotgun from its mount under the seat and laid it beside Clara without a word. She wasn't sure if she could use it should the need arise, but just having it nearby eased her mind.

He bent down and kissed her. "I'll be as quick as I can."

Clara could hear William's retreating footsteps for a long while. Other than Vera's playful chatter, it was peaceful. Birds sung, bugs chirped, and occasionally she would hear the screech of an eagle. She might have enjoyed the stillness had her back not hurt so badly. *How will I make it home?* The question flashed before her.

Vera began to fuss after playing with herself for awhile, so Clara carefully pulled the baby closer to her and kissed her again and again. Praise God she wasn't hurt. What would she have done if Vera had been injured or killed in the wreck? That would be far worse than being injured herself.

It seemed like hours before Clara heard the rattling of a wagon approaching and saw William's tall form. He was soon at her side along with a strange man whom he introduced as Lew Stone. Clara's cheeks burned that he should see her in this undignified position, but the kindness and pity in Mr. Stone's eyes was unmistakable.

Just lying still had worked wonders for the pain, but when William helped her to her feet, Clara couldn't hold back a cry. It felt as if her spine were shattered into a million pieces.

To Clara's surprise, the wagon was no more than a frame and wheels. The box was gone. How was this contraption, with running boards nailed across the frame, supposed to get them home safely?

William helped Clara lie flat on the hard running boards—an excruciatingly painful process—then fetched the shotgun and other items that had been tossed out of the wagon in the crash.

Where had Vera gone? Clara was focusing more on staying conscious than to where her baby was. Glancing to the side, she saw Mr. Stone, standing near the wagon, holding Vera in one hand while keeping his other hand on the reins. He must be a father himself to be able to carry a baby so young with such ease.

William tied the Carter's horse to the back of Mr. Stone's wagon, took his daughter in his arms, and sat on the running boards at Clara's head. He folded his cotton overshirt and situated it as a pillow for her.

"Thank you," Clara breathed through clenched teeth.

He flashed a concerned smile and squeezed her hand.

Mr. Stone clucked to the horse and they started back up the hill.

"Can't we see the land?" Clara asked, glancing up at William.

"I saw part of it from Lew's house. It's beautiful."

"But Mr. Freize will be expecting us."

"He was at the river bank when Lew and I came back. I told him what happened and he gave his apologies, saying that we could talk next time he is in church."

Tears stung Clara's eyes. She was so close to seeing the beautiful river land Freize had talked about, yet now they were heading back home. Three more long hours of a bumpy wagon ride. It was terribly unfair.

Lew Stone had been hauling wood, he told them, which was the reason his wagon had no box. Despite his efforts to avoid ruts and bumps, it did little to help. Clara clenched her teeth so hard to keep from yelling, she feared they would fall out.

Once back home, William handed Vera to Archie and helped Clara inside and up to bed. He thanked Lew Stone profusely on his way inside, and Lew waved back, saying that he and his family would be praying for Clara's recovery.

As always, Mr. Boutwell was very concerned for Clara. He kept the hungry baby mildly content while William helped Clara out of her dirty clothes and into a nightgown. It took every ounce of will Clara had left to keep from screaming at each little movement. Something was terribly wrong with her back. A nagging in the back of her mind that said she would be in bed for a good long while.

It was too hot for Clara to bear having blankets over her. William opened the window and brought in Vera so she could be fed. Clara asked for some of the pain-relieving tea that was in the cupboard downstairs, and William ran to make it.

Though lying flat helped considerably with the discomfort, burning tingles shot up and down her back each time she drew a breath. Clara prayed that God would heal whatever was broken inside her. It frightened her terribly not to know.

Six long, terrible weeks went by. Clara was finally able to get out of bed without screaming by week four, but it wasn't until the sixth week that she could resume her normal household duties, and even then she required a considerable amount of help.

She never did fully understand what had happened to her back, but she praised God that she could move again, relatively pain free. William suspected that she had broken her spine. Katie agreed, and also guessed that she had jostled a few ribs out of place. Either way, Clara was more than grateful to be out of bed.

William purchased the land from Freize the next time he came to church. Though he had only seen the land from a distance—and only a small segment of it at that, it was enough, and he convinced Clara that she would love it, too. Much to her relief, Freize was more than fair on the price.

Mr. Boutwell had found a small, one-cabin homestead not far from the Hazzard store. He purchased the small bit of land, saying that he was ready to be on his own and wanted to try farming for himself. Clara worried about him, but there was nothing she could do to change his mind, and she let the matter go.

A letter from William's parents said that they were interested in buying the prairie homestead from their son and daughter-in-law. Clara wasn't exactly sure how William's high-class parents would adjust to prairie life, but it wasn't her problem to worry about. They were to be arriving shortly after the first of October, not long after Clara and William would move to the river.

During the month of September, Clara canned what she could, thinking of the massive harvest she would reap next year living so close to the water. It was an exciting prospect. She *was* slightly worried about the condition of the small cabin Freize had on the property. He hadn't struck her as a tidy kind of fellow. But no matter; if it needed to made bigger, there was plenty of time before winter set in.

Moving their belongings down to the river land was a joint affair. William had purchased a wagon and team, which was loaded with foodstuffs and furniture. Mr. Smith, Addie's husband, followed behind with another wagon loaded with furniture and chickens. He also carried the passengers—Clara and the children.

Their trip down to the river was uneventful, though it took a bit longer than it typically would have because the horses had such heavy loads to carry. Clara found herself clutching the wagon seat as they descended Kolker Hill. No part of her wished to repeat the sequence of her last experience.

When they had reached the bottom and drove a mile or two downstream on the beautiful river road, Clara gasped and a wide, unstoppable smile rushed over her face.

The river valley was breathtakingly magnificent. There were so many trees flanking the water's edge that she couldn't see very far down or upriver. On one side of the water loomed a rather large mountain and, on the same side, further downstream at the river's bend, was another towering mountain that appeared to have a scoop taken out of it.

William continued to lead the two-wagon caravan further and further down along the bank until they came upon a rather nice-sized log cabin and swath of flat land.

"This is it!" he announced, turning the horses toward the structure and stopping in front of it.

The cabin proved to be in better shape than Clara had expected. It was smaller and less fancy than their house on the prairie, but that didn't bother her in the least. The size was more than adequate for her, William, and the three children.

At one end of the cabin, there was a fireplace. The stones were smooth, taken from the river, no doubt.

There was a door that branched off into a large lean-to that contained a small cot. Clara smiled. That would be replaced with her and William's bed in a few days, once she re-stuffed their mattress. For tonight, they would all be sleeping on the floor.

Opposite the fireplace, a lovely black stove stood. There were counters and cupboards, a water bucket, and stool. Glass windows were on all sides of the house. Clara couldn't help but smile. The cabin truly was beautiful and far more luxurious than many other cabins she had been in.

With Mr. Smith's help, the McDonald's belongings were soon brought inside. He helped William assemble the beds before congratulating them on their new home and mounting the Carter's wagon.

Even though things were hardly put to order, Clara couldn't resist running out to the river's edge. The overcast sky made the water sheen a stunning grey. It sparkled like crystal as the slight breeze made ripples on the surface. The same breeze blew about Clara, rustling her skirts and tossing her curls about her face.

"What'cha doin, Mama?" Archie asked, skipping up behind her.

Clara looked down at him, a smile twisting her face. "I'm looking at the water. Isn't it pretty?"

Archie's eyes sought the rippling sheen. He gazed at it for a long moment, squinting his little eyes, then shrugged. "I guess so." He turned back to her. "What's for supper?"

Their first supper in the new home was plain. Clara didn't want to dig out all of her cooking utensils, so they ate bread she had baked earlier in the week and some dried venison. That, along with the fresh river water, made a filling meal.

Clara did as much unpacking as she could before darkness fell. William helped the boys get the chickens to safety in the coop that Frieze had built just for them. When it became too dark to see, they came inside and readied for sleep.

The wooden floor was quite hard, even with the padding of multiple blankets and quilts, but Clara didn't care. Vera lay at her side, snuggled into her mother's warmth. She dropped a kiss on her little daughter's head as her eyes closed and she drifted off.

Chapter 33

Clara was working on scrubbing the outside of the cabin when an unfamiliar man's voice spoke behind her. Her heart leapt out of her chest and she pushed herself against the log wall.

It wasn't one man, but two.

They both had long, black hair that was neatly braided down their backs. Bushy eyebrows knit together into one on the taller man's brow, and his deep, golden-brown skin glowed in the sunlight. Though they both wore trousers and shirts not unlike William's, the delicately beaded moccasins on their feet and animal-tooth necklaces told what they were.

Indians.

Clara had heard stories of the terrible things Indians did to unprotected woman and children. She had also heard plenty of stories of them helping settlers and becoming great friends. Lew Stone had even said that the local Indians were entirely harmless. But those good stories scattered at the tall man's terrifying scowl. His steely eyes bored into Clara, sizing her up and down.

Her eyes darted from side to side, looking for an escape. Nothing. The wheelbarrow was in the way to her right and the chimney to her left. But even if she could have run, her feet were stuck to the dirt.

Clara pressed herself against the cabin until Vera, secured to her back, began to squirm in discomfort. Why hadn't she been paying closer attention? If she had seen, or heard, them coming, she could have gotten into the house. Even if they were friendly, she would feel far more secure within arm's reach of a shotgun. Her eyes flitted to where she had last seen Archie and Newton playing. They were gone.

"Freize siwash here?" the tall Indian asked, squinting at Clara. His voice wasn't at all the gruff, gravely tone she expected—it was smooth and deep.

Clara released a little of her pent up breath. The men certainly weren't acting hostile. "No," she said, swallowing to moisten her dry mouth. "No, he doesn't live here anymore."

The tall man turned to the shorter and they gabbled in a language Clara couldn't understand. Lew had told them that most of the local Indians spoke Salish, and almost all spoke Chinook Jargon, the trade language of the Pacific Northwest. Clara knew neither, though now she desperately wished she did.

"You cheechako?" the tall man asked, turning to face her again.

Cheechako? What did that mean? She bit her lip. "I…I don't understand."

"Where you siwash?"

Couldn't they speak more English than just here, you, and where? Clara's head spun for an idea of how to answer them. They were obviously looking for something, or someone. But who, or what? And what were they planning to do?

Then, it clicked. Lew had jokingly called Freize a wordy siwash; a talkative man. They were asking where her husband was.

"Ah…" Should she tell them that William was gone? It didn't seem like a good idea, yet what else could she say? "My husband is working."

Clara brushed her hands against her apron. Lew had said that giving the Indians goods often made them leave. "Would you like some food?"

The tall man cocked his head and gave her a questioning look. His eyes had softened considerably during their discussion.

"Food," Clara repeated. "Sugar?"

His face brightened, and he nodded. Clara willed her feet to move towards the house, but she kept a close eye on both men as they rounded the corner. She hadn't expected them to follow her indoors, but unfortunately, they did. The tall man held the shorter one by the arm as they walked.

Clara hurried to wrap up a loaf of bread and a tiny bit of sugar. Lew had told her that the Indians loved sugar and coffee. Surely that would get them to leave.

When she turned to the men, she noticed that the shorter one kept his gaze fixed straight ahead. She could see now that his eyes were cloudy. *Blind.* The taller man, however, was taking in everything. He was captivated by William's cavalry sabre, which hung above the fireplace.

"Big knife," he said, and she nodded in agreement.

He took the items from Clara's hand and nodded curtly, then took his companion by the arm and stepped out. Clara heaved a sigh as they walked down the riverbank. Her heart still pounded and she pressed her hand against her forehead. *Thank you, God!*

The door to the chicken coop creaked. Archie and Newton peeked their heads out—then, the rest of their bodies followed. "Who were they, Mama? What did they want? Did they hurt you? Are they going to come back?"

The questions flowed in a typical stream from Archie's mouth, his eyes on the Indians. Clara shuddered. "I hope they don't."

Lew Stone came to check on the McDonald's on Wednesday, and Clara poured out her Indian story to him.

"I was so terribly frightened," she told him. "I could hardly understand what they were saying but it didn't sound good. They called me a cheen-cheka, or something like that."

Clara thought she saw Lew's shoulders shake.

"Being called a cheechako isn't bad, Mrs. McDonald." Lew's calm, even voice held more than a hint of a smile. "'Cheechako' is Chinook Jargon for 'newcomer.'"

"Newcomer?" Clara thought back to her conversation with the tall Indian. "So, they were asking if we were newcomers?"

Lew nodded. "Probably. They like to keep track of who lives around here. I assure you, Mrs. McDonald, the tribe is entirely peaceful and have been for years. They wouldn't think of hurting anyone." Lew smiled at her and played with his coffee cup. "Though, I can imagine it would be frightening to have them visit when you are here alone with the children."

Clara nodded miserably.

"Though I wish I could say otherwise, they will be back. They fish downriver, just around the bend. They're here every spring and fall, spearing salmon. You can expect to see lots more of them. Though they can be annoying at times, they aren't out to hurt anyone."

The mere thought of having an entire tribe of Indians living so close by was more than frightening, but it wasn't as though she could do anything about it. Lew said that they wouldn't hurt her. She trusted him, but still didn't welcome the idea of Indians visiting.

"What did the two who visited look like?"

Clara searched her brain. "They were big." That much she could remember clearly. "One was quite tall

389

and wore a beaded necklace. His hair was long, but well kept. And the other—he was shorter. I think he might have been blind."

Lew nodded and took another long gulp of coffee. "That was Chief Enock and Old Blind Alec. They're harmless, as are the rest of the tribe." He grinned at his coffee cup. "You should feel blessed. Not many people get a visit from the chief."

Clara shot him a dagger-like glare.

"Pardon me, Mrs. McDonald."

His voice sounded awful high for remorse.

On Friday, another set of visitors came. Only these visitors had red hair, freckles, and green eyes.

"Patrick Gannon," the man introduced himself. "But all me friends call me Pat."

Erma was his wife, and they had three children: Johnny, Josephine, and Martha. Clara couldn't help but notice how big their smiles were. They acted as if meeting her was the best thing in the world.

"Please, come in!" Clara gestured towards the cabin, a smile creeping to her own face. "My husband isn't here at the moment, but we can enjoy coffee, even without him."

The children were respectfully quiet as they sat on the table benches. Clara brought out a jar of ginger cookies she had recently made. Since they didn't yet have a cow, there was no milk for the children. She paused in her bustling. What could she give them to drink?

"If ye doont mind, they ken have coffee."

Clara turned at the sound of Erma's soft, sweet voice.

"Of course I don't mind!" She hurried to get more mugs.

"'Ave ye been long in these parts?" Pat asked, munching on a cookie.

Clara pulled the coffee pot from the stove and began pouring it. "We haven't been here a week yet. Before this house, we lived on Wild Rose."

"Pretty land, thet is there."

Padding feet outside told Clara that the boys were coming. Archie darted through the open door. "Mama! Look what we—oh!"

He stopped suddenly when he saw their visitors, and Newton, hardly two steps behind, barreled into his brother. His mouth opened for a sharp rebuke, but snapped shut again. Both of their eyes grew to the size of saucers.

Clara bit back a laugh. "Boys, these are our neighbors, the Gannons."

Archie managed a short nod, and Clara turned to their company.

"My boys: Archie and Newton."

Pat smiled over his coffee at the board-stiff boys. "Och, fine lads ye have, Mrs. MocDoonauld."

Clara grinned at her little sons. Newton still looked as if he wanted to melt, but Archie had set eyes on the coffee and cookies. She ushered them to the washbasin, then seated herself.

"Where do ye come from—afore Wild Roose?" Erma's soft musical tone danced in Clara's ears.

"We were in Chicago."

Pat straightened, his eyes dancing. "Och! City folk, are ye? How do ye like country life?"

"We enjoy it far better than the city." Clara grinned. "Though, it wasn't easy to adapt when we first arrived."

The children polished off their cookies and coffee long before the adults did, and Archie, seeming to have completely forgotten his rather boisterous introduction to the neighbors, begged to take the Gannon children outdoors to play. Clara and the Gannon parents consented and, within moments, the five children had flown out the door.

Clara absently brushed Archie's crumbs off the table while Pat spoke about how he and Erma came to live in Washington. They came to America from Ireland as newlyweds, twenty years previous. Pat said that he liked wide-open spaces, and pursuing that had pushed them further and further west until they arrived at the Spokane River a few years ago.

Erma was far quieter than her husband. She was delicate and sweet and obviously delighted to have a female neighbor. Clara felt the same way. So many men lived along the river, but few women. And the Gannons lived only four miles upstream.

As they talked, Vera, secured in the Indian cloth on Clara's back, awoke from her nap and began to fuss. Clara pulled her from the little pouch and sat her upright on her lap. Vera's deep eyes sleepily surveyed the people before her before breaking into a large smile.

"Darling lassie!" Erma cried, reaching forward and brushing Vera's chubby cheeks. "Och, I miss the days when me own young ones were small."

Sundays were blissful times. William had to leave for work soon after lunch, but the mornings were quiet and peaceful. There was no nearby church, and it made little sense for them to travel all the way back to the prairie—a three-hour trip. Instead, William led his little family in a worship service at the cabin.

They were all sitting quietly, listening to William read the Bible when suddenly the door was tossed open and a poorly dressed Indian let himself in. Archie and Newton scurried under the bed, and Clara stood, clutching Vera to her. This Indian was different than the ones she had met earlier in the week. He was much more savage looking.

"'E see big knife," he demanded, pointing to William's sabre hanging on the mantle.

Calmly and slowly, William laid the Bible on the table and stood. He pulled the sabre off its hooks, unsheathed it, and went through a short cavalry drill before offering it to the Indian.

393

To Clara's surprise, a grin grew on the Indian's weathered face as he carefully waved the sword around the same way William had. After weighing it in his hands, he passed it back to William.

"You got good knife."

William nodded, and the Indian left as abruptly as he had come. Hoof beats were heard on the rocky riverbank as he retreated towards the rest of the tribe around the bend of the river.

"Was he one of the ones that—"

Clara shook her head, squeezing Vera so tightly that the baby squawked.

"I wonder how he knew I had a big knife?" William stared down at the sword in his hands for a moment, then chuckled, re-sheathed it, and hung it back on the hooks.

How was William *not* frightened? Clara was sure that everyone within ten miles could hear the frantic beating of her own heart. William didn't seem scared in the least.

"I'd like to understand their language better." He glanced up at Clara with a smile. "Perhaps they could teach us something about fishing and living off the land."

It was an idea. Not a bad one, either; the Indians knew, likely better than anyone, how to utilize the river.

Despite her pounding heart, a grin stole over Clara's face. Ten years ago, she had been a middle-class Chicago city girl, desperately wanting to go west but never thinking that it would actually happen. Now, she lived twenty miles from the nearest post office, but hardly one mile from a real Indian tribe. And they had only been in the west for two years.

What could possibly be next?

Afterword

Nearly all of the events that take place in this book actually happened. Though it was necessary at times to use a storyteller's license, I strove to keep William and Clara's story as close to the real events as possible. Clara McDonald's memoirs, written by her in 1938 at the age of 70, was the main document I drew from to write the events of this book.

Acknowledgements

I'd like to thank, first of all, my grandparents, Don and Pam McDonald, for everything that they have done and continue to do in my life. If you hadn't let me dig around in boxes of old photos, I might never have gotten the inspiration to write this book.

Thank you so much, Mom and Dad, for letting me escape to my "cave of writerdom" as I needed to. But more than anything, thank you for believing in me. I love you!

And to my siblings, for listening when I needed to whine. And for bringing me chocolate.

Thanks to my amazing team of beta-readers, this book is far more polished than it would be otherwise. Abigayle E., Hope A., Jesseca D., Deborah C., Victoria M., Sarah H., Hannah L., Pam M., Olivia R., and Jada M. You guys are so awesome! Thanks for putting up with me!

Thank you, Aunt Linda and Benita Mason, for letting me pick your brain and look through old photos.

And thank you Jesus, for making me crazy enough to write a book.

About the Author

Ivy Rose is an 18 year old history lover and literary enthusiast. Aside from writing, she enjoys being outdoors, chocolate, travelling, reading, and ATVing (preferably if there is mud involved). She resides with her family of 9 on the banks of the Long Lake in eastern Washington.

To learn more about Ivy, visit
www.LakesidePublications.com

33908504R00239

Made in the USA
Middletown, DE
01 August 2016